FOR THE DEEPEST LOVE

A PRIDE & PREJUDICE VARIATION

MARY ANNE MUSHATT

Quills & Quartos
PUBLISHING

ISBN 978-1-951033-81-1 (ebook) and 978-1-951033-82-8 (paperback)

Edited by V. Lewis and Mary McLaughlin

Cover Design by Holly Perret

For my boys
—David, John and Jacob—
for all you are.
And for Amy and Vickie for all you do.

CONTENTS

CHAPTER ONE

London, March 1812

It was with no little curiosity that Fitzwilliam Darcy would attend the Sackville dinner. The Gardiners and their much talked-of niece were expected, and he wished to gain an introduction to, if not share a conversation with, the lady who had caused such a stir amongst those of the highest circles. *It is amazing how this country lass has, within a season, established herself in the most fashionable circles and beyond. She was beguiling at the Phelps' salon, and I have even heard of her at the chess club. Beauty, intelligence, wit—and those eyes!* He prepared to exit his coach. *Passion, surely, buried perhaps, but the fire in her eyes promises great things.*

Giving his coat to the footman, Darcy overheard two other guests gossiping. "Rumour has it that Blainard will offer for the bewitching Miss Bennet."

His ears pricked up at that, but he continued towards

his hosts. Was he too late already? *I must find a way to meet her,* he thought while bowing to Lord Sackville. Extending his hand to take Lady Sackville's, he saw her. She was sitting along the wall with two other ladies. She wore a sage green gown, delicate beadwork glinting on the silk bodice. Jade pieces encircled her neck, with a triangular pendant resting on her bosom. Their eyes met as she looked up and smiled at him. Heart pounding like a schoolboy's, he nodded in return, until Lady Sackville reclaimed his attention with a knowing smirk.

They were seated at opposite ends of the table, much to his disappointment. *This is torture. She is beyond my reach, and while she entices with bon mots of wit and intelligence, I must endure the tittering drivel of Miss Bradshaw.*

When the men re-joined the ladies after dinner, he headed in her direction. *Damn a proper introduction!* Yet as he approached, Miss Bennet's companion snapped her fan and leaned in to speak.

"I cannot believe he came."

He diverted his steps, making it seem he had been walking towards the window nearest them.

"I beg your pardon?" Miss Bennet replied, even as her eyes darted towards him.

"Have you not heard of the infamous Darcys? It is delicious. His young sister nearly eloped—with the son of their steward."

Taking a deep breath, Miss Bennet asked, "How old was she?"

"Oh, she was but fifteen, I believe." The young lady sounded as though she had been unprepared for the question.

Miss Bennet sighed before replying. "That is my

sister Lydia's age. A difficult time in any young lady's life."

Darcy's eyes widened at the sincerity in her voice. *It has been a long time—a very long time—since any kindness was attached to my name or Georgiana's.*

"But that is not the most scandalous part, Elizabeth. It was his response that was most shocking."

Ah, here it comes, thought Darcy. *My character flayed at the stake of propriety.*

"Mr Darcy allowed the poor girl's infamy to be broadcast throughout society! *He* let it be known how that rake, Mr Wickham, attempted to elope with her."

Darcy bit his cheek, waiting for Miss Bennet's reaction.

"I believe," she began, "it took a great deal of courage for Mr and Miss Darcy to allow this to be known by all."

"Elizabeth!"—Darcy cringed at the scold in the young woman's voice—"Courage indeed! She is ruined amongst society, by his hand."

Miss Bennet laughed. "I should hope people will soon forgive the indiscretion of a fifteen-year-old child. However, many unsuspecting families are now fore-warned of this Mr Wickham's character, and for that, I am grateful. If more people spoke honestly, then women would be better protected. Do you not agree?"

Darcy recoiled at her companion's dubious response.

"Put that way, there is sense in what you say. Oh look, there is Mr Ambrose. Come, let us make haste."

The women moved away, leaving Darcy stunned. *Never has there been such an unqualified defence or understanding of my actions.* A wave of sorrow shook him, and he reached out to steady himself against the nearby pillar. *Nor of what this has cost my sister. Not only does she feel betrayed by that bounder, but Lady Catherine continues to harangue her at every opportunity.*

His gaze sought Miss Bennet. *And yet, she understands, can see the sacrifice and courage of my little sister. Thank you, Miss Elizabeth Bennet, for replenishing my faith in the decency of the human heart.*

SEVERAL EVENINGS LATER, RETURNING HOME AFTER A dissatisfying night of insipid conversation with the 'acceptable' females of high society, Darcy pondered his growing unease. *Is it so wrong to desire someone who ignites my heart, mind, and passion as a companion I must endure for the rest of my life? Is it wrong to hold to these ideals rather than prattle on at the simpletons parading before me at every opportunity? I think not.*

Shaking his head, he pressed his lips together with determination. *Till I meet that paragon of womanly perfection, I shall remain as I am. Oh, I know what is being said about me, but I do not care.* The image of Elizabeth as she looked one evening at the opera came to him. *Beautiful! That gown—I was jealous of the fabric wrapped around her body. That ivory neck of hers teased from behind those curls, enticing my eyes to the neckline of her gown. And when she laughed!* He sighed. *And her eyes. Even from across the foyer, they sparkled. She is a jewel worth pursuing.*

It cannot be true what they say about her and Blainard, he thought, dismissing his man, who had come to help him undress. *But then, why was she in his box?* He had nearly laughed aloud when she rolled her eyes after that wastrel whispered in her ear. He might have doubted her reputation as a brilliant young woman had he not seen that. *But she is such a woman, not a girl. And I, if nothing else, am a man.*

Rinsing his face, he grabbed a towel. *There is something about her. She is beautiful, but many women are. Antoinette is beautiful, and yet, here I stand, captured by this wisp of a woman.*

DARCY WAS DISAPPOINTED AGAIN THE NEXT NIGHT AFTER another unsuccessful attempt to meet Mr Gardiner's niece. His frustration flourished as she was continuously surrounded by men, including Blainard. He found the situation intolerable as, standing on the outskirts of her admirers, her witty observations revealed her understanding of the world was greater than the majority of women—or men—of his acquaintance. He banged his hand on the armrest of his chair.

"This yearning to hear her mind, her heart—could this be...? Not since Penelope has the notion of love entered my mind. But I learned my lesson *then* and shall not repeat it. No. My father's body was barely cold in the grave before I was hounded by matrimony-minded matrons." He paced about the library. "And Penny was the worst of the lot. I thank God above I found out before she and her long-time lover made an even greater fool of me." He leaned both hands on the marble mantel. "Father was right. 'Do not trifle with a woman's heart, Fitzwilliam. It will only lead to sorrow.'" He shook his head.

"But I burn for her."

HIS THOUGHTS HAD NOT PROGRESSED MUCH FURTHER BY the time he attended his next engagement at Titledom House, two nights later. The approach of Charles Bingley and his sister Caroline jarred Darcy from his silent musings. His slight smile of greeting soured at her smirk, and her shrewd eyes latching onto his person deflated his hopes for the evening. *If not for the knowledge that Miss Bennet is attending, I should return home. Or visit Antoinette.*

"Mr Darcy, what a surprise to find you at one of the most auspicious events of the London Season," Miss Bingley simpered. Her betrothed, Mr Oswald, trailed behind her.

"Charles, Miss Bingley, Oswald. Good to see you," Darcy greeted them. A burst of anticipation shot through his chest, and he turned. Glimmering in a golden dress, *she* was looking at him with a longing he understood. Then, in a heartbeat, she was gone. The thrill of feeling her attention focused on him, even for that moment, split the world open into vibrant splendour, only to plunge it further into darkness. He sighed and asked Miss Bingley to dance.

"EMMA, WHO IS THAT MAN OVER THERE?" ELIZABETH asked her friend, Miss Dalton.

"Who? There?" she replied, nodding in the direction of a blond gentleman with curls cascading along his collar.

"No, not him. The man next to him, the very tall, handsome one."

"Oh, him." Miss Dalton frowned. "That *gentleman* is

Mr Darcy. He is handsome enough, Lizzy, but he is not for you. You surely have heard the rumours about town?"

Elizabeth gave her friend a gently censuring frown. "I did not think you so hard. Why should his sister's mistake make the man a pariah?"

"It is not that, Lizzy—not only that, in any case. He is notorious really, and a bit of a rake, so I am told. He does not converse with decent women and has yet to form a *serious* alliance with a woman of good standing. And..." Miss Dalton leaned closer, and as she whispered, Elizabeth's eyes widened.

"Oh indeed? Well, that is a shame." Giving Mr Darcy one last look, Elizabeth turned as Lord Blainard claimed her for a dance. Her many admirers enabled her to avoid Mr Darcy and his piercing stares for the rest of the evening.

DARCY LOOKED OUT FROM HIS CARRIAGE WINDOW INTO the London night. Watching the passing traffic, he pushed away the thoughts racing across his mind. Unable to quell his restlessness, he rapped on the roof. When they were stopped, he stepped out and addressed his driver. "Go home, Barton. I shall find my way back."

"Aye, sir," Barton nodded.

Darcy walked down the street, Miss Bennet still plaguing his mind. Night and day, she intruded into his thoughts, leading them from her enticing laugh and flashing eyes to the carnal desires fuelling his dreams.

Antoinette welcomed him into her home. *"Cherie,"* she purred, but Darcy drew back at the perceived seduc-

tion in her eyes. Looking about her parlour, he cata-
logued the strategically placed candelabra, and how her
smile seemed calculated to entice. He turned to look at
her with growing concern.

"*Vin?*" she asked with a touch of uncertainty.

Darcy nodded. She poured a glass for each of them,
which he took but did not drink. Draining her own,
Antoinette reclaimed his glass, putting them both on a
side table. His hands remained at his sides; his eyes
boring into her. She stepped back, and Darcy turned his
head away.

"*Cherie*, what is it?"

He looked anywhere but at her.

"Have we not always shared our concerns?"

"I am sorry, Antoinette."

"Darcy?" She stepped forward but stopped as he
recoiled. "William?"

"Antoinette. We are family and have known each
other for most of our lives. As you know, Darcys take
care of our own." He gave her a slender smile. "But I
fear you misinterpret my affection. We are cousins.
Nothing more." He paused. "I believe it best that, for
now, we maintain a distance."

She gasped.

"Fear not, I shall always see you cared for, and shall
always be your friend. If you need anything, tell Celeste,
and I shall see to it."

"But—"

He shook his head.

"I understand," she choked out.

Darcy looked about the room. "Well then." He

headed to the door. "I am sorry, I cannot… I should not have come." Darcy clasped his hands.

"Will you return?"

He closed the door quietly behind himself as his only reply.

CHAPTER TWO

Something is wrong, I just know it. But what? Elizabeth paused her pacing. *And why will they not trust me to help? I know they are entitled to their own counsel, but after all they have done for me, for my sisters. To think we would not offer to help! If nothing else, we may provide a willing ear to hear their troubles.*

Elizabeth stopped, looking around her chamber in the Gardiner household. Deciding her course of action, she took up a glass from her dressing table and poured the excess liquid into the wash basin. Opening her chamber door, she searched the empty hall. Creeping to the Gardiners' bedchamber, she took another surreptitious glance, then placed the glass against the wall, and her ear to the glass.

"Surely it cannot be that bad," her aunt pleaded.

"It is, my dear. He took nearly all the company's cash reserves. My vendors have not been paid in six months."

"Dear Lord!"

"I am negotiating with the banks. However, it is not promising."

"Oh, Edward." Her aunt's voice trembled.

"Let us not give up hope yet. Finch's bank has not refused me. Not yet anyway."

Elizabeth's eyes widened as she heard her aunt sob. She pulled away from the door, blinking back her own tears, and returned to her chamber in a daze. *What are we to do? Who had access to my uncle's accounts? I cannot believe any of the clerks capable of such villainy.*

Preoccupied, she dressed for bed, but it was hours before she was able to quiet her mind enough to sleep. She dreamed of walking into a grand ballroom as a gossamer web embraced her like a shawl. Beads of pearl formed at the ends of the filaments, latching to her gown. It was a familiar dream that had begun when she met Lord Blainard, but this night, the filaments thickened, stretching across and crushing her chest. Fear pierced her sleep, and she woke gasping for breath as panic filled her heart. She gulped the air, grounding herself in the grey light of early morning, and shivered, even though the maid had already stoked the fire in her room.

"COME ON NOW, UP YOU GO." DARCY AIDED HIS companion into his carriage. An old friend from Cambridge, Finch had overindulged in excellent wine and required assistance in getting home.

"Bloody good of you, Darcy, lending me your carriage," Finch mumbled as he staggered to his seat.

"Too true," Darcy replied. *Why am I the one always cleaning up after other people's indulgences?*

The carriage took off in silence until a rut jarred them. Finch returned to consciousness with a snort. "So, what did you think of her, Darcy?"

"Who do you mean?" he hedged.

"Miss Bennet, of course," Finch replied with a drunken smile. "You remember, the woman you stared at the *entire* evening? Gardiner's niece? Brown curls dangling about her neck, delightful——"

"Yes, yes, I know who you mean," Darcy snapped.

"Do not get your nose bent. I noticed you tracked her every move." Finch sat back, smiling like a cat in an aviary. "Damn shame about her uncle, though."

"How so?"

"He applied to our bank for a sizeable loan." Finch leant forward to emphasise his point. "Seems like he needs it in quite a hurry, too."

"Will he get it?"

"Cannot say."

Darcy looked askance at his friend.

"Oh, no, it is not that I do not trust your discretion, Darcy. I know you keep your secrets until the grave. No, it is odd, but after processing the paperwork, which was all in order mind you, the file was taken out of my hands."

Darcy's brow furrowed. "Is that customary?"

"Without a scintilla of explanation? Not at all." Finch shook his head. "It went straight to Mr Merriweather himself—one of our habitually silent partners. And with Merriweather it yet remains, as if it no longer exists. Most unusual, as Gardiner is known not only for the success of his businesses but also for his honour."

"Very strange," Darcy remarked, and the subject was left at that.

Once he delivered his friend home, Darcy set off for his own house. Upon arriving, he retired directly to his study. He needed no thought for the transaction he proposed and set about the business with industry. With a snifter of brandy beside him, he wrote a note to a very resourceful, very discreet business acquaintance. After sanding and sealing it, he sat back in his armchair and smiled, raising his glass in tribute. "Perhaps we can be of service to each other, Miss Bennet. To what, I am sure, will be our mutual pleasure and delight."

Before he drank, he gloried in the thought, *She will be mine.* A log in the fire popped and crackled before bursting into flame.

ELIZABETH SPENT THE AFTERNOON WANDERING THROUGH St James's Park with the Gardiner children, who played, along with their nanny, by the lake. The girls fed a gaggle of ducks while the boys sailed a boat fashioned by their father. Seeing them well situated, Elizabeth migrated to the perimeter of the green, lost in recollections of the previous night and reflections on how she might assist her uncle. *There is our little filly, Roan, but then, she is promised to Lord Wellington. None of the other horses are ready to sell. And even so, surely if my uncle thought we might be able to help, he would have asked, would he not? Could the amount be that great? How much did this embezzler take? And who is he?*

"Good morning, Miss Bennet."

Turning, Elizabeth looked into the piercing brown eyes of a tall, well-formed gentleman. *Mr Darcy.* Her friend's warning of fallen women whirled in her head. She executed a wary curtsey. "Mr Darcy, is it?"

Surprise and a glint of pleasure warmed his aspect. Elizabeth reassessed the handsome man, noting the appeal of his eyes upon her own. She turned her gaze back to the pond and her cousins. *What can he mean, seeking me out so—in public?*

"May I join you?"

"As you wish."

Closing the short distance between them, Mr Darcy smiled, his eyes softening into a palpable caress, sweeping over her person. She frowned and began a leisurely stroll, acutely aware of his proximity.

"We do not know one another, sir. Do you often introduce yourself to young ladies in the park?"

"Not at all. Only when I see such captivating beauty before me."

"I have heard you are a country gentleman, sir."

"I am, madam."

"Then by captivating beauty, I must assume you mean the *flora*...do you not? As such, you must realise March is too early for any to be at their prime."

He chuckled. "Perhaps I speak of another *type* of bloom."

Elizabeth stopped immediately, searching his eyes. She was not of a mind to be preyed upon by a rake. "If you will excuse me, sir—"

He interrupted before she could leave. "Miss Bennet, is all well with the Gardiners?"

She drew back. "I beg your pardon?"

"I hear they are in some straitened circumstances."

"Sir, it is hardly proper to bandy about the business concerns of those unknown to you."

"Little do I care about propriety, Miss Bennet. You must know this of me."

"I have heard tales of you."

"Then your shock is misplaced. Or were you hoping I would be as disingenuous as Lord Blainard? An empty façade, hiding a corrupt soul?"

"Lord Blainard?" she challenged him. "What has he done?"

"What Blainard has done is not pertinent to this conversation. I have sought you out this afternoon with a proposal for your consideration."

Elizabeth's stomach tightened, and pulling away, she rubbed her right temple as her head spun. "A proposal? What can you mean?"

He did not clarify his meaning. She looked up at his face, unprepared for the warmth in his eyes. *He is not cold or judgmental. His eyes…they are unfathomable…and strong. So strong.*

"Will you at least hear me?" Mr Darcy asked.

Though unnerved, she watched his thoughts play across his face and animate his eyes. The pragmatist in her nodded.

"Thank you." He offered her his arm, and after a slight hesitation and a glance to ensure her cousins were still well attended, she took it, and they continued to walk. "I have heard that Gardiner and Whitecastle is in need of a great deal of funds, which for reasons yet unknown, they are unable to secure."

"I would think that you would refuse to listen to

rumours, especially of a family and enterprise so wholly unconnected to you."

"As I was saying, one of my acquaintances mentioned that, due to the actions of Mr Whitecastle—"

"Mr Whitecastle!" The missing piece of her uncle's puzzle slipped into place. Elizabeth's stomach lurched. *Of course! How could I not see this before? He has not been seen —not since before I came to town.*

Mr Darcy continued his tale, pulling her from her thoughts. "Yes. He has left the country, apparently, and it appears, taken not only the profits but the working capital of your uncle's business with him, leaving Mr Gardiner responsible for accounts that are long past due. Without an influx of funds, which he has been unable to secure through his customary lines of credit, his establishment will enter foreclosure, and all that he has worked for his entire life will be lost."

Elizabeth gasped and pulled her arm from his. Immediately she turned, wanting to hide the tears that had sprung to her eyes. She had taken only two steps away before Mr Darcy followed her.

"I am willing to provide the funds necessary to salvage your uncle's business, and in such a manner that no one would ever know of his close brush with failure or bankruptcy. He, and his family, will avoid the taint of ruination."

Elizabeth turned quickly to regard him, surprised and suspicious. "You would do that? For a man you do not—*Do* you even know my uncle?"

Mr Darcy shook his head. "I do not."

"Then why?"

He gave her a smile that sent shivers to the pit of her

stomach. Taking her hand, he placed it back on his arm, and led them onward. "I want something for my generosity. In exchange for saving him."

Elizabeth stopped, his smile unnerving to her. She pulled back her hand and crossed her arms over her chest. "What do you want?"

"Your hand."

"My hand? As in marriage?"

"That is the usual meaning, Miss Bennet."

"I do not understand. Why? Why would you wish to marry me? We do not even know one another."

"I would think that would be obvious."

She quirked her brow, waiting for an explanation. When none emerged, she added, "I am sorry sir, but it is not obvious to me at all."

"As a prospective member of your family, I would be privy to its internal workings. Your uncle need not know of our arrangement. As my wife, you would have access to my funds, and it would be the most natural thing for you to offer him aid."

"Yes, but that would necessitate an immediate union."

His smile widened, while his eyes narrowed. "It would, indeed. With a licence, we could be married within the week."

"The week!" Elizabeth sputtered. "You ask me to make this momentous decision—this *life-altering* decision —in less than a week?"

"If you wish to save your uncle the scandal of being dragged through the courts for funds he no longer possesses, yes. It is not my timetable, Miss Bennet, nor is this regrettable situation my doing."

"Your logic is flawless, save for your reasons for wishing to marry *me*." She paced, rubbing her hands together. "While I understand why I should want to marry you, what compels you to marry me?"

"I have my reasons."

"Am I not to know them?"

Folding his arms across his chest, he looked down at her. "Suffice it to say, I harbour no nefarious reasons to take you as my wife. You are a woman of many talents. You are spoken well of by people I esteem for their judgment. But, more importantly—" He steadied himself with a long, slow inhalation. "You are the first, nay, the only person who has ever defended or understood either my sister or myself in relation to our misadventures with George Wickham. No one else has ever seen that the blame is on him and not my sister. As for myself..." He shrugged.

She studied his face, saw the pain in his eyes, pain that many believed he had brought on himself for his refusal to cower and hide, or deny its existence. "You overheard me? I do not recall where—"

"Lord and Lady Sackville's dinner. You wore a green gown. You said...you said that—"

"I said I admired your courage in unmasking that cur. And I still do. Really, if more people would sacrifice reputation for truth, it would be a far less dangerous world for unsuspecting young ladies. But for this you are willing to not only marry me, a stranger to you, but to also put forth the funds to salvage my uncle's business?" She watched him, her curiosity reaching unforeseen intensity.

"You intrigue me." Mr Darcy clasped his hands

behind his back. "And one thing I have learned through these last years is that character, a good, honourable character, is worth more than just about anything." He returned her quizzical glare till it transformed into a half-roguish, half-boyish smile. "And I believe we would be a good match."

Elizabeth's spine shivered, and her heart raced. *Oh, he is compelling.* She perused his face, noting the aquiline nose, full, sensual lips, and his impressive physique—a broad chest, flat stomach, and strong thighs. *And though his proposition is remarkable and most unexpected, something tells me to consider this. I have trusted my instinct throughout my life; it has never led me astray. It tells me to keep an open mind.*

"You have given me much to consider, Mr Darcy. May I at least have the day to reflect upon your proposal?"

He nodded. "Shall we meet tomorrow?" Taking her hand, he bowed and placed a kiss upon it.

"Until tomorrow, Mr Darcy."

"Without fail, Miss Bennet."

CHAPTER THREE

E lizabeth paced the confines of her room, pondering her future, long after the household was abed. *How can I even contemplate accepting this proposal? But then, how can I not save my family from ruin? I can only imagine how much this entails, if my uncle is unwilling to even discuss it with me.* Though her questions were legion, answers were nonexistent.

I have always promised Jane I would marry for love. And here I am, considering marriage to a complete stranger—and one whose reputation does not bode well for my domestic felicity. She took another lap around her chamber.

What do I know of him, beyond his sister's near elopement when she was but fifteen? My friends were certainly set against him. Elizabeth slid her hands up and down her arms. *They say he might keep a mistress, though many men of his station do. But can I live with it? To know, before even entering the marital state, that this value, which I consider fundamental to a felicitous marriage, is not shared between us?*

She sent a plaintive gaze to her chamber door. *If only I could confide in Aunt Gardiner. She would know how to advise me. And Uncle—he is always there for me, listening, urging me to see the bright side when I tend to dwell on the worst. He was there to help purchase Longbourn outright from that fool, Mr Collins, after Father's death.*

She flopped onto the window bench. *Regardless of Mr Darcy's character, how can I leave my aunt and uncle to suffer for the misdeeds of Mr Whitecastle when I have the opportunity to save them? I love them too much.*

She sat bolt upright as realisation dawned. *That is it! I shall marry for a love of the deepest kind.*

As Elizabeth entered the park, Mr Darcy rose from the bench. Seeing him sitting there, a wave of nerves crashed over her. His unnerving presence almost buckled her knees, and she nibbled her lower lip as she regained her composure. *He is overbearingly tall, those broad shoulders… He must be incredibly strong. And that face…those eyes…*

Forcing herself to steady her step, she continued to approach, focusing on an errant, dark curl falling across his forehead. *What it must feel like to run one's fingers through that jolly curl, to brush it away and kiss his cheek.* Heat flared on her cheeks. *Oh my, this will not do at all. Elizabeth, you must keep your wits about you or you shall be undone.*

"Good morning, Miss Bennet." He bowed.

"Good morning, Mr Darcy."

"Would you care to sit or continue walking?"

"For now, I should prefer to sit." She did so, leaving ample space for him. He returned to the bench, and she fancied that she felt his eyes rake over her. She blushed and turned her head, her racing heart warming her skin.

"Have you come to a decision?" His voice was so soft she had to lean towards him.

"Yes, I have. But first, let me explain that many years ago, my sister Jane and I promised each other to marry only for the deepest love. Indeed, I have refused an offer or two in order to keep my promise." She looked him directly in the eye. "As I have in the past, I intend to continue."

"You do not mean to refuse me?"

She laughed lightly. "Pray, is the great Fitzwilliam Darcy unaccustomed to being refused? You will find, sir, I am no ordinary country lass."

"That is an understatement if ever I heard one."

Elizabeth rubbed her gloved hands along her knees. "After thinking long and hard throughout the night, I have come to the conclusion that, although it may not be the *kind* of love my sister and I once had in mind, marrying you *would* be for a love of the deepest kind."

His eyes sprang wide open.

Feeling mischievous, she said, "After all, I do love—"

"Your uncle!" he blurted out.

"Exactly." She gave him a wide smile. "I cannot let him come to harm, not if it is within my power to prevent his humiliation."

He smiled, revealing two dimples, then took her hand and kissed it. "Excellent, Miss Bennet, well done. I respect your loyalty. Once we speak with your uncle, I shall obtain the licence. Do you have a preference as to in which church we should wed?"

"Mr Darcy, before we proceed with the details of the

ceremony, I must ask you something." Elizabeth gathered her courage. "What I mean to say is…how do you envision this marriage?"

"I assume you will have your say in this?"

"It would be best, Mr Darcy, for I am known to possess a temper when crossed."

"As am I."

She looked at him with an arched brow. The mirth in his eyes reassured her, and her fear dissipated. "I believe that honesty saves time and trouble. Shall I be first to lay out my thoughts and state that I expect them to hold for the both of us?"

Visibly taken aback, he replied, "Pray, continue."

"My parents were not blessed with marital felicity, due to the dichotomy in their understanding. We, that is to say, you and I, are practically strangers, are we not?"

He nodded.

"I should like for us to attempt a friendship first, before proceeding to the more…intimate particulars of marriage."

"For how long?"

"As long as required," she shot back immediately.

"I do not think I can…um…"

She levelled a steely gaze upon him. "You would take me against my will?"

He looked at her, then away, then back again, a flush appearing on his cheeks.

"Surely *you*, of all men, realise the advantages of a woman who is *willing* to enter the marital bed, no, Mr Darcy?"

He chuckled, which lightened the mood, and shook his head. "You are absolutely right, Miss Bennet. I should never want any woman in my bed who was unwilling to be there." His eyes darkened, and he took her hand to his lips, kissing it slowly. He kept hold of it, drawing circles on its back with his thumb. "As I mentioned previously, people I esteem are greatly impressed with your wit, your intelligence, and your character. You caught me in your web before my hungry eyes ever laid hold of you. I shall wait until you call me to your bed."

"Thank you," she said. Then, drawing a breath against the distractions of his lips on her gloved hand, she asked, "And your notions of fidelity?"

"Of course, I expect fidelity," he said with a grin.

"For both of us?"

He stopped his ministrations to her hand, looked hard into her eyes, and spoke with utter confidence. "Yes. For both of us."

As the park began to fill with nursemaids and their charges, Mr Darcy and Elizabeth's conversation turned to the more practical matter of arranging a wedding in less than a week. When they had sketched a rough outline of events, he stood, offering his arm.

"Shall we go and speak to your uncle?"

THEY PROCEEDED TO MR GARDINER'S STUDY, WHERE they found him reviewing his accounts. "Uncle?" Elizabeth said as they entered his sanctum. "Are we disturbing you?"

"No, my dear, never." Mr Gardiner eyed the unknown gentleman.

"May I present Mr Fitzwilliam Darcy? Mr Darcy, my uncle, Mr Edward Gardiner."

"Mr Darcy." Mr Gardiner dipped his head, looking to Elizabeth questioningly.

"Uncle, I…we…that is, Mr Darcy and I have something of importance to discuss with you."

"Please, both of you, take a seat." He turned his chair to face them. "Now, how may I help you?"

Elizabeth looked at Mr Darcy, who was looking at her. She nodded in her uncle's direction.

"Mr Gardiner," Mr Darcy began. "I have asked Miss Bennet to marry me, and she has graciously accepted." He swallowed hard. "Therefore, I now ask you for your consent."

Mr Gardiner stared, appearing shocked. "In marriage?" Though he remained still, his eyes alternated between the couple. "Forgive me, I was unaware you were acquainted."

"It is of short duration, but yes, sir, we are acquainted," Elizabeth replied.

Mr Gardiner sat back, elbows resting on the arms of his chair, fingers steepled in front of him. Mr Darcy and Elizabeth waited for him to speak.

"And you, Lizzy, are in agreement with this?" Mr Gardiner watched her closely after he asked.

Elizabeth held his gaze, hoping she appeared confident. "Yes, Uncle, I am."

Turning to Mr Darcy, Mr Gardiner asked, "You are aware of Elizabeth's circumstances, are you not?"

Mr Darcy shook his head.

"She is the second of five daughters, of my late sister and her husband, Mr Thomas Bennet of Longbourn. It is a small estate in Hertfordshire. Her dowry is only five—"

"Sir, while I appreciate these details, they do not concern me. Without too much exaggeration, money is not my primary concern."

"Understood. I simply wish to present the facts."

"I appreciate your candour."

Both men nodded.

Mr Gardiner began again. "Mr Darcy, a moment's indulgence, if you please. Elizabeth and her sisters were left, almost six years ago, as orphans, when their parents perished in a carriage accident. Elizabeth—"

"Along with Jane," Elizabeth added.

Her uncle chuckled. "Along with Jane, convinced me to approach a distant cousin, a Mr Collins, on whom Longbourn was entailed."

"I see," Mr Darcy said.

"We—I purchased Longbourn outright for them. Then, under Elizabeth's stewardship—along with Jane —" Mr Gardiner smiled at his niece who was about to interrupt him. "They have repaid my initial investment, plus interest, to own the property outright. And, for the last year or so, have turned a modest profit from their endeavours. I believe it extremely unwise to underestimate my niece, Mr Darcy. She has an excellent mind, matched by an excellent heart." He quirked a brow. "And you, sir, what may be said on your behalf?"

Mr Darcy appeared to be at a loss for words, and Elizabeth leapt into the fray. "Uncle, Mr Darcy has demonstrated great courage in the face of daunting odds. He stands firm in what he believes and is brave enough to take me on as his wife."

Both gentlemen smiled, and Mr Gardiner retreated. "Very well, Lizzy. When will the happy event occur?"

"If I may?" Mr Darcy intruded. "Our wish is to marry expediently."

"Expediently?" Mr Gardiner's eyes narrowed. "*How* soon is soon?"

"Within the week," Elizabeth murmured.

"The *week*?" Mr Gardiner's geniality was lost, and he turned a hard eye on the younger man. "Is there reason for such haste?"

Mr Darcy coughed. "No, sir, we are just impatient. I have business that demands my return to Pemberley— my estate in Derbyshire. And I fear a delay would diminish my intended's affection."

"I seriously doubt that, Mr Darcy. One thing I have learned about Elizabeth—which *you* must learn as well— is that once her mind is made up, it is set as if in stone." Mr Gardiner kept him under scrutiny. Elizabeth blushed.

"Be that as it may, I wish to marry as soon as possible. Once we have gained your blessing, I shall obtain the licence. I wish my sister to attend the ceremony. She has been in Derbyshire at the home of my aunt and uncle. They return on the morrow."

"I also would like my sister Jane to attend." Elizabeth looked to Mr Darcy.

"How long would it take for her to arrive?"

"She remains at Longbourn, a few hours' journey. While it is unfortunate that my younger sisters remain at school up north, as long as Jane is with me, I shall be well."

"Then by all means. Will you send an express?"

Elizabeth nodded.

"Well then," said Mr Gardiner. "I suggest we go and tell your aunt, so you may be on your way, Mr Darcy. It seems we all have a bit of work ahead of us."

"Mr Gardiner, if I may have a moment more of your time?" Mr Darcy asked, and her uncle nodded. Elizabeth waited by the door. "I have taken the liberty of contacting my solicitor, who assures me the articles will be ready this afternoon. May I call again later today?"

Mr Gardiner replied, "I have pressing business this afternoon. Perhaps you could join us for dinner?"

A smile spread over Mr Darcy's face. "Thank you, I would enjoy that."

"Until this evening then."

When they came into the parlour, they found Lord Blainard waiting, holding a bouquet of roses.

"Ah, Lord Blainard, Mrs Gardiner, children, gather round." Mr Gardiner stood with Elizabeth and Darcy. "Lizzy and Mr Darcy have an announcement."

Mrs Gardiner and Lord Blainard waited expectantly as Darcy smiled, and said, "Yes, well...just this morning, Miss Bennet agreed to be my wife."

Reactions around the room varied. The children chattered noisily and excitedly about fairy princesses and handsome, dark knights. Mrs Gardiner looked between him and Elizabeth, dumbfounded. Lord Blainard stiffened and then glared, his eyes locked onto Elizabeth until she blushed, at which point he turned an icy glare to Darcy, which he held. Blainard was the one to ultimately turn away.

Darcy watched Blainard watch Elizabeth. *There is something odd there. A ferocity I had not expected, least of all from him. He bears watching.*

Mrs Gardiner embraced him. "Welcome to the family, Mr Darcy. Congratulations." She repeated the gesture with her niece, whispering something Darcy could not hear.

Lord Blainard stood immobile, though his bouquet fell to the ground. The young girls gathered the scattered stems, and Mrs Gardiner sent them to the pantry for a vase.

"Let me be among the first to wish you joy, Miss Bennet, Darcy," Blainard finally said. "Have you set a date?"

"Within the week," Darcy declared.

Mrs Gardiner gasped. "Impossible! Lizzy, are you out of your senses? Think of the preparations. How are we to complete everything in one week?" She looked between her niece and future nephew.

"Elizabeth's sister—Jane?" Darcy looked to Elizabeth, who nodded. "I shall send my carriage for her. My own sister returns to town tomorrow. The breakfast can be held at Darcy House, if that is amenable. And now, I am off to procure a licence. As for any expenses the ceremony may incur, I shall arrange an account to be opened for my future wife at the shops on Bond Street."

"That is very generous of you, Mr Darcy, but hardly necessary," Mr Gardiner pronounced.

"But it will be, once the week is past, sir." Darcy smiled. "Have no fear, I shall ask no questions regarding her gown. I know brides enjoy their secrets."

"As do grooms," hissed Blainard. Darcy shot a glare at the earl.

"Miss Bennet, Mr Gardiner, a word, if I may?" Blainard indicated the study. Mr Gardiner and Elizabeth looked at each other, then at Darcy who was as bewildered as they, but more suspicious.

"Yes, of course," Elizabeth replied.

ELIZABETH FOLLOWED HER UNCLE AND LORD BLAINARD into the study. Mr Gardiner shut the door before taking his seat behind his desk. Elizabeth sat on one of the armchairs in front of it. The earl paced the length of the room. She waited while he gathered his thoughts.

At last, he turned to them both. "Miss Bennet, I beg you to reconsider. Please, on all that you consider holy, do not do this."

Shocked, Elizabeth stared at him, but he was not done. "Mr Gardiner, you are a man of sense. Please, consider the character of this man. He is a reprobate. His sister—"

"Was fifteen when she was nearly seduced by a thirty-year-old man. Both she and Mr Darcy had the courage to reveal this to the world so that silly girls—" Elizabeth's eyes cut to her uncle— "would be safe from such reprehensible behaviour."

Lord Blainard looked between the two, deflated for the moment.

"Have you anything else against him, my lord?" she challenged. "Other than the dreadful habit of refusing to disguise the truth?"

"Yes, I have." Lord Blainard came to her, capturing

her hands in his. "It pains me to be the one to tell you this. Had I known Mr Darcy was a rival, I should have found a way to reveal this in a less brusque manner."

Elizabeth watched him warily.

"It is well known, among our set, that Darcy keeps a mistress. As did his father."

Hearing this aloud in front of her uncle crushed her. She had suspected it, but to hear it said so plainly, was distressing. Lowering her head, she fought to remain calm. After a prolonged silence, she looked at her uncle, then walked to the door. "Thank you, Lord Blainard, for this information."

Leaving the study, Elizabeth made her way to the parlour. "Aunt, may I have a moment with Mr Darcy?"

Mrs Gardiner acquiesced. "I shall take the children upstairs."

"Mr Darcy, shall we sit?" Elizabeth indicated two seats by the window, and they settled into them.

"What did Blainard say to cause such distress?" Darcy asked, almost as soon as he was seated.

"He began with an attack on your character regarding your dealings with your sister, which I deflected, I believe quite successfully." She took in a deep breath, letting out a remorseful sigh. "As I had heard this before, I was not surprised. Mortified, but not surprised. As was my uncle, when his lordship announced that, at present, you keep a mistress, sir, and it is a family…trait. He also claims this is apparently well known among his set."

Elizabeth watched as Mr Darcy lowered his eyes and exhaled. "I… Yes, Miss Bennet, there *is* a woman whose name is…*connected* with mine. Mademoiselle Antoinette du Marché. She is a refugee and is charming, talented, witty—"

She held up her palm. "I hardly wish to know the details, though I reserve the right to enquire into *that* in the future. At this moment, I believe I can only tolerate a yes or no response."

"Of course. But please, I beg the chance to explain at a later date."

She nodded then made to leave. "Good day, Mr Darcy."

He came to her, so close she could feel his breath on her hair. In a low, intimate tone, he said, "You must tell me if our bargain still holds."

She looked up at him. "Yes, sir. Love for my family overrides my disgust for you."

Mr Darcy grabbed her hands. "It is not what you think. I *long* for those illusive qualities—companionship, honesty, *faithfulness*—on both sides, as well as beauty and passion." Pulling her to his chest, he kissed her breath away.

Taken aback by his brashness, his words penetrated her reserve. *Faithfulness*. Without further thought, she returned his kiss with an unexpected need rising in her. Her hands slid up his chest, stroking his neck through the cloth of his cravat until they combed through his hair, pulling his head closer to her own. When their lungs insisted, their lips parted and, gasping for breath, they rested their foreheads together.

"I cannot explain what I feel for you," she whispered, searching his eyes for the understanding that she was not alone in this unfamiliar depth of emotion.

"Elizabeth?" Mr Gardiner's warning rang through

FOR THE DEEPEST LOVE

the room. Slowly, Mr Darcy relinquished his hold on her waist but retained control of her hand.

"We had just finished discussing the information Lord Blainard revealed," Elizabeth told her uncle.

"Am I to assume the matter is resolved?" Mr Gardiner looked to Mr Darcy with a hard glare.

"Yes, sir, quite satisfactorily," Elizabeth responded with a smile upon seeing Lord Blainard's scowl behind her uncle.

"Well then, I must return to my work," said her uncle. "Mr Darcy, until this evening. Lord Blainard, I shall see you out."

"Yes, sir." Lord Blainard glared at Darcy before nodding to Mr Gardiner. He went to Elizabeth and took her hand. "Miss Bennet, I sincerely wish I could express my joy for you. However, I feel you will regret your decision."

"I understand, my lord. Good day," she replied.

"Until we meet again." He bowed, then said with pain in his eyes, "If only you had waited for me."

CHAPTER FOUR

The carriage rumbled away from Bond Street, where the women had spent the morning selecting Elizabeth's trousseau. A slight rain fell, heightening the intimacy within. As the women gazed at the droplets washing away the debris of London's street, Lady Matlock spoke. "There is something I must address."

Elizabeth and her aunt exchanged a wary glance. "By all means, Lady Matlock," Mrs Gardiner replied.

Her ladyship nodded. "As you may surmise, you are not wholly unknown to me, Mrs Gardiner. Indeed, as we support a number of the same charities, I am surprised we have not met before. I know some judge those who aid women fallen on...*difficult times* as unfashionable, but our work serves a great need. Especially as we are at war, for many are now widows. You have a reputation as a woman of quality, and a great supporter of London's culture as well."

Mrs Gardiner smiled, while Elizabeth beamed at her aunt.

"The same may be said for yourself, madam," Mrs Gardiner replied. "You are known as a kind woman of superior intellect, and a cornerstone of society."

"I thank you." Her ladyship smiled graciously. "You are, I am sure, aware of the tragedy that has befallen my niece, Georgiana?" Her smile turned to a frown.

"Only what I have heard from—"

"No doubt the gossipmongers still spread their bile about my family."

Elizabeth blushed. "Mr Darcy has not told me his side of the story, yet madam."

"And your thoughts on what you have heard, Miss Bennet?"

"That a scurrilous"—Elizabeth struggled for the right word—"unmentionable beast wished to impose himself on Miss Darcy but was foiled by her brother. Society faults Mr Darcy for making the villain known."

Lady Matlock smiled and appeared to relax against the squabs.

Elizabeth continued with a steady gaze. "I have three younger sisters to protect. Thanks to Mr Darcy's courage, there is one less threat to their virtue and equanimity. This Mr Wickham has been unmasked and for that I am grateful, not condemning."

"Even if his sister's reputation was damaged?" Lady Matlock prodded.

Elizabeth looked out of the carriage window. "I had not really thought about Miss Darcy. I admit, I thought more of my own sisters. Not knowing her, I can hardly comment." She took a deep breath before continuing. "I believe she was but fifteen?"

Lady Matlock nodded.

"Then her youth must excuse her. That a man approaching thirty would importune an innocent is beyond belief." Elizabeth's temper flared.

Both older ladies chuckled at Elizabeth's vehemence.

"Miss Bennet." Lady Matlock patted the young woman's arm and took a deep breath. "Darcy did not want to reveal Georgiana's error. He well understood what that would mean for her. However, Mr Wickham became insufferable. Frustrated at losing her thirty-thousand-pound dowry, he attempted to blackmail Darcy for his silence."

Elizabeth and her aunt looked to each other with unease.

"Darcy was gathering the funds when Wickham, a little too far in his cups and too long at the tables, bartered the information to settle a gambling debt to a Mr Merriweather. This man had a particular grievance against our family, as my sister-in-law, Lady Catherine de Bourgh, refused his offer of marriage for her daughter, Anne, in a very public manner. The fact that Mr Merriweather and Anne actually cared for each other, which believe me was a miracle in and of itself, meant nothing to Catherine."

"So, Mr Merriweather exposed Miss Darcy? As vengeance for a thwarted romance?" Mrs Gardiner gasped.

Lady Matlock nodded. "Yes. You see, Lady Catherine has always claimed and believed that Anne and Darcy were destined to marry. Some nonsense about

Darcy's mother wishing it on her deathbed. Utter nonsense, as Catherine did not visit my sister once when she took ill."

"Mr Darcy did not try to unmask this Wickham?" Elizabeth asked, with a tinge of disappointment.

"No, he did not. However, he did not deny the truth once it was out. Darcy has been Georgiana's guardian for five years now, as well as managing Pemberley and all its responsibilities for even longer. Georgiana is all he has left of his immediate family. He would never have sacrificed her to bring down a worthless bit of trash such as George Wickham. However, once the news was out, he spoke with Georgiana, and together the two of them stood against Wickham and then society. They have done nothing to quell the rumours, believing that with the information out, it is best to go on."

"What of this Merriweather? Has he faced any repercussions for revealing Miss Darcy's misery?" Mrs Gardiner asked.

Lady Matlock shook her head. "He achieved his aim. The Darcy family was brought low for not protecting Georgiana's reputation. If Darcy had acquiesced, and paid Wickham in time, nothing would have happened, and Georgiana would still be pristine enough for the first circle. But he did not, and both have suffered. Georgiana is distraught. Her confidence decimated, and my nephew? His standing in society has been tarnished."

The countess gave them a rueful smile. "One blessing is that Lady Catherine has reluctantly declared Darcy unsuitable for Anne, and he is free from all but the most desperate of fortune hunters."

Elizabeth and her aunt gasped.

"Oh, please, I did not mean—Darcy has assured me this is his choice, Miss Bennet, and that he had to convince you. I must say I am relieved you accepted him. As his aunt, I am grateful that someone of your quality has accepted the challenge."

Elizabeth blushed.

"Has Darcy told you anything about Georgiana?"

"No, he has not," Elizabeth replied. "I admit to a great curiosity in meeting her."

A dark look crossed the countess's face. "My niece was always a timid creature, secluded for the most part in Derbyshire, especially after the loss of her parents. Wickham was raised at Pemberley and was considered a family friend." She looked away, appearing to be struggling with her emotions. "She was ripe for his treachery. Now her faith is all but destroyed. She hardly speaks to anyone, even her brother. She eats little, never smiles, never laughs."

Elizabeth reached for her ladyship's hand, and Mrs Gardiner gave a sympathetic smile. No one spoke till they reached Darcy House on Grosvenor Square, where they were to have tea. As the carriage drew up, Lady Matlock composed herself, sending a look of gratitude to Elizabeth and her aunt.

Mr Darcy awaited them at the door, smiling as the three emerged from the carriage. A man in regimentals joined him at the threshold.

"Lady Matlock, Mrs Gardiner, Elizabeth, welcome to my home." Mr Darcy bowed to the older women, then took Elizabeth's hand to his lips before wrapping it around his arm. He gallantly offered his other arm to

Mrs Gardiner as the military man stepped up to escort Lady Matlock.

Elizabeth and her aunt smiled at the stately elegance of the architecture and furnishings within. The servants, courteous and efficient, snuck glances at the woman soon to be their mistress.

"How kind of you to come in this dreadful weather." Mr Darcy squeezed Elizabeth's hand, still resting on his arm.

As they entered the parlour, an older gentleman smiled. Next to him sat a young woman of no more than seventeen. She was fashionably dressed but listless. Her eyes were vacant, and her hands lay idle in her lap, her quietude an indication of the trauma she still endured.

"Miss Bennet, Mrs Gardiner, may I present to you my family? You know my aunt of course." He turned to the jovial, older man to his left. "My uncle, Lord Matlock. My cousin, Colonel Richard Fitzwilliam, and my sister, Miss Georgiana Darcy."

The girl barely raised her head, but she nodded.

Pleasantries were exchanged, and when it was disclosed that Elizabeth hailed from Hertfordshire, Colonel Fitzwilliam asked, "That is the seat of Noah's Promise is it not?"

Elizabeth blushed while her aunt chuckled. "It is. Noah's Promise is Elizabeth's pet project, as it were," Mrs Gardiner explained.

"Remarkable," the earl said.

"How is it you began such an unusual enterprise?" Mr Darcy asked, recovering from the revelation.

"Lizzy began her equine experimentation about… ten years ago, was it?" Mrs Gardiner asked her niece.

."Why, you must have been just a slip of a thing," Lady Matlock interjected.

"But forever in my brother's library reading all the latest scientific papers," Mrs Gardiner added. "She begged Thomas, her father, to purchase two horses, which she specifically selected after spending hours researching their bloodlines. Of course, one was male, the other female."

"Following Noah's charge to gather the animals, two by two," Elizabeth said with a modest smile.

"Astounding." Lord Matlock shook his head. "And will you continue the stables once you are married, Miss Bennet?"

With a quick glance at Mr Darcy, Elizabeth replied unreservedly, "Yes."

"Capital!" Lord Matlock clapped his hands. "It will be spectacular to have an inside connexion to the most well-bred horses in the land."

"Word is that Wellington is interested in one of your stallions," the colonel remarked.

"Indeed he is, sir. We shall present him with one of our best to thank him for his service to our country," Elizabeth replied. "Although our gift is a mare."

"Will he come himself to collect?" asked Mr Darcy.

"We are as yet uncertain, but we are hopeful. Our correspondence has been with General Waring."

"Excellent." The colonel smiled at both Elizabeth and his cousin. "What a pleasant surprise. Noah's Promise has produced the most coveted horses in England for years. I dare say even Darcy was surprised at the connexion, eh Darcy?"

While the women had gathered after tea, Georgiana remained by the window, gazing at the still falling drizzle. Elizabeth went to her. It seemed the girl barely heard her approach, so she lightly touched her arm.

Georgiana then looked at her. "Sister," she whispered. Elizabeth gave her as much compassion as could be communicated without words, and the girl held her gaze for a little while before something in her seemed to snap. Trembling with emotion, Georgiana's eyes moistened. With tears cascading down her cheeks, she ran from the room. Elizabeth looked after her, then to Mr Darcy, who focused on the door through which his sister had escaped.

Lady Matlock sighed, heading to Elizabeth. Putting her hands on the young woman's arms, she abruptly hugged her. "You must not let Georgiana's moods distress you. She is not the same since..."

Elizabeth nodded and returned the embrace. Leading Elizabeth back to her aunt, Lady Matlock hastened to follow her own niece.

Sipping from her now cold cup, Elizabeth looked to Mr Darcy, finding trepidation in his eyes. She smiled and his shoulders and eyes relaxed.

Finally, a small smile came to his lips and he crossed the room to speak to her. "I am pleased you sought her out."

"Of course."

"While I wished, hoped, she would not, I am not surprised Georgiana ran off as she did."

"The poor lamb was overwhelmed," Elizabeth replied. "But she was here, and we have met."

"All in all, an auspicious beginning," he concluded.

JANE BENNET LEFT HERTFORDSHIRE AT SUNRISE, alarmed by Elizabeth's intent to marry in such haste. *I am sure Longbourn will be fine for a week or two. Long enough for me to talk sense into that silly head of hers.* She leaned back as the carriage entered London proper. *Lizzy has never been this impetuous before, at least not about love, and certainly not regarding marriage. Was it not just before she left that we discussed her disappointment over Mr Simmons, and how she must try her heart again?* She sat up at the sudden thought. *She would not have... No, Lizzy would never marry just to prove a point. My aunt would never allow that.*

Jane focused on the familiar landmarks of Gracechurch Street. As the carriage stopped, she was relieved that Elizabeth, looking well and content, waited at the door. If there were any scandal in this, her sister would have shown it in her eyes.

The sisters embraced on the steps. Without a word, they walked into the parlour, where Mrs Gardiner was pouring tea. Once the maid had quitted the room, Jane began her interrogation.

"What are you about, Lizzy? When one travels, it is customary to return with a trinket or new shawl as a souvenir. You," she pushed her index finger into Elizabeth's shoulder, "you will return with a husband." They laughed, but Jane continued in a tone that demanded the unvarnished truth. "Why have we not heard of this Mr Darcy before receiving a letter announcing your betrothal?" She watched as Elizabeth looked to her aunt, twisting her fingers.

Perhaps sensing their need for privacy, Mrs Gardiner spoke. "I shall go and see if the children are up from their nap. They will be happy to see you, Jane." She kissed Jane's cheek, whispering, "I am so glad you are here." She then placed her hand on Elizabeth's shoulder, squeezing it before leaving the room.

Once the door had shut, Jane returned her attention to her sister. "Lizzy?"

Elizabeth walked to the window. "How to explain all that has happened?"

"What became of Lord Blainard?" She joined Elizabeth at the window. "I heard from both you and Aunt Gardiner that he was paying you a great deal of attention. Had his ardour cooled?"

"Oh, Jane! So much has happened these last few weeks, I barely know where to begin. Perhaps we could walk out?"

About to chastise her for avoiding her queries, Jane caught the serious expression in Elizabeth's eyes. Fear shimmered down her spine. *There is more to this than I imagined.* "Yes, I feel the need to stretch my legs after this morning's travel."

FOR THE FIRST FIVE MINUTES, THE TWO SISTERS WALKED in silence, taking in their surroundings. The spring air was cool, fresh, and full of hope.

"Now, explain yourself, and leave off nothing if you wish me to accept this," Jane began.

"Lord Blainard was—*did* pay his attentions to me, Jane, but, well, he is not the man for me."

"And this Mr Darcy is?"

Elizabeth gave Jane a half-smile. "Perhaps."

"Lizzy." Jane scowled.

Elizabeth grabbed her hand. "There is so much more to consider in this."

"Explain it to me. For I am this close to insisting uncle stop this—"

"No! You must not. You must trust me. Mr Darcy is a good man. Perhaps the best of men."

"But is he the best man for you?"

Elizabeth took a step away, gathering her courage, then turned to face her sister. "A number of weeks ago, I noticed things were not well with my uncle." She wrung her hands, pacing in front of her sister, who listened intently. "You may scold me, but I found myself burning with curiosity to know what was wrong."

"You did not!" Jane gaped. "Lizzy, you are a grown woman. *Beyond* too old to engage in such childish practices."

Feeling a tad guilty, Elizabeth looked to the grass. "I did, but it was for the best. I had to know what caused the daily anguish of both my aunt and uncle. It was awful, the sobs, the sighs, the strain in their eyes. It was as if all joy had left the house."

"Aunt seems subdued, but I thought it was due to your betrothal."

"It may be, in part." Elizabeth took Jane's arm in hand. "But you must believe me, Jane, this torment existed long before Mr Darcy made his offer."

"And what, exactly is that offer? You vowed you would marry only for the deepest love."

"And I shall."

"How can you claim to love Mr Darcy, a man you barely know?"

Again, Elizabeth twisted one hand around the other. "While Mr Darcy daily improves in my estimation, I admit, I do not love him—yet. However," Elizabeth looked at Jane, whose eyes locked onto her. "I *do* deeply love my aunt and uncle."

"My uncle would never force you to marry anyone."

"No. Nothing of the kind." Elizabeth began pacing. "Mr Whitecastle—"

"Who is Mr Whitecastle, Elizabeth? How many men are involved in this sordid tale of yours?"

"It is not sordid. Please believe me!" Elizabeth cried. "Mr Whitecastle is my uncle's partner. 'Gardiner and Whitecastle'?"

"Oh yes."

"He left the country, taking the majority of the company's profits and operating funds. The vendors have not been paid for months."

Jane gasped. "My poor uncle. And Aunt Gardiner! Oh, Lizzy!"

"Mr Darcy learned of my uncle's distress. As his wife, I shall have access to funds to fulfil uncle's obligations. Mr Darcy has even expressed the desire to join in partnership with him. My uncle will suffer no disgrace, and I...I shall have a most unusual husband."

Jane peered at Elizabeth searchingly. "Could we not give him the funds?"

Elizabeth shook her head. "It is beyond our ability. And to borrow the sum would take too long."

"And you have made your peace with this?"

"Yes, Jane, I have. Mr Darcy is a bit unconventional,

45

and we have much to settle between us. Yet, on the whole, I feel I shall have no cause to regret my decision. It could have been much worse. If my uncle had not helped us when mother and father died, you or I would be Mrs Collins by now."

Despite the weight of their discussion, they giggled.

"Come, let us return. Mr Darcy has promised to come to tea. He is eager to meet you."

They returned arm in arm, surprised there were two visitors instead of one awaiting them in their aunt's parlour.

"Miss Elizabeth," Mr Darcy began. "May I introduce my dear friend, Mr Bingley? When he heard our good news, he insisted on making your acquaintance as soon as possible. He will do me the honour of standing up with me at our wedding, and I thought it prudent to introduce him to you. And your sister, if she is to perform the same office for you."

"Mr Bingley, it is a pleasure to meet you. I hope you gentlemen were not kept waiting long?" Elizabeth smiled at both men. "Mr Darcy, Mr Bingley, may I present my sister, Miss Jane Bennet?" Jane curtseyed, and the gentlemen bowed. Elizabeth noticed that Mr Bingley immediately returned his gaze to her lovely, flaxen-haired sister.

"Miss Bennet," Mr Bingley said, "May I be one of the first to welcome you to London?"

"Thank you, Mr Bingley."

"I trust your journey was pleasant, Miss Bennet?" Mr Darcy asked.

"Oh yes, sir, most pleasant. I was anxious to arrive before you and my sister exchanged your vows."

FOR THE DEEPEST LOVE

Mrs Gardiner arrived, followed by a maid with a refreshed tea service. The group enjoyed a pleasant conversation, leading to an invitation to the theatre the next evening and dinner at Darcy House before the wedding.

"Then we shall see you tomorrow evening." Mr Darcy kept his eyes on her.

"I look forward to it, sir." Elizabeth walked with him to the hall where the housekeeper had laid his overcoat. Taking it from her, Elizabeth smiled mischievously as she prepared to assist Mr Darcy herself.

He smirked. "Shall I inform my valet his services will no longer be necessary?"

Blushing, she took up his gloves. "Oh, I claim no knowledge of what duties that esteemed gentleman must offer."

"No?" He took his hat from her.

"I suppose a man must have some mystery about him."

"Because Lord knows a woman has more than her share."

"Mr Darcy!" Elizabeth shook her head, catching sight, as she did, of her sister's blush as *she* leaned closer to hear Mr Bingley. "Well, I suppose we do."

Mr Darcy followed her gaze and sighed.

"Mr Darcy? Do you wish to share that thought?"

He looked up from studying his boot. "It is just... Bingley is all that is amiable, Elizabeth. Truly, one of the best men I know. However..."

"However?" Elizabeth quirked her brow.

"He has a tendency to...appreciate a beautiful woman."

"Appreciate?" she scowled.

"No, not like that. He is no rake. But he gives his heart too easily and is therefore easily disappointed."

"Oh." Her ire deflated. "I see, in a way. But you do not have to worry about Jane." She looked to the lady. "I have never seen her so interested in a man, and there have been many who sought her affection."

"I can only imagine." He took one of her hands to his lips. "Shall we leave it to them?"

Elizabeth smiled.

He kissed her hand again.

CHAPTER FIVE

Lord Blainard was loquacious in his vitriol over you foiling his plans for Miss Bennet. In the presence of three gentlemen, he elaborated his efforts to both lead White-castle to gamble to excess and then embezzle his partner, all to coerce Miss Bennet to accept his carte blanche. I shall spare you the details, but I know marriage was never his objective.

Darcy rubbed his chest, which suddenly ached with a pulsing pain. His left hand clenched into a fist while his right crunched the edges of his man's missive, then he continued reading.

Blainard crowed over his success in blocking Gardiner's attempts to secure credit. There was something unsettling in his eyes at this point, and he grew cagey until another bottle of brandy was opened. He claims there is an alliance burgeoning on our shores, a brotherhood of sorts, that he utilised in foiling Gardiner's efforts to redeem his business.

Sir, I must congratulate you on your timely action. Blainard is a vile creature, willing to bring down not only a highly respectable man of business but endanger twenty or more men working for him, all to force Miss Bennet into his protection.

Darcy's blood pounded in his ears, his vision grew dark, and his breathing shallowed into laboured pants. Images of Elizabeth beholden to Blainard ran through his mind, each one more degrading than the last. He had heard rumours of Blainard's preferences, but to think that Elizabeth was nearly in his grasp! Elbows bent on the desk, he bowed his head to rest on his clasped hands. "Thank you, merciful God, for saving her from that fate. I vow to protect her, honour and love her as the brilliant gift she is." Allowing his heart to ease, Darcy lifted his head and picked up his private detective's dispatch and continued reading.

I have investigated Blainard's claim of influence with the banks, and found, in accordance with Mr Finch's account, that indeed pressure was put to bear on the case. But not from Blainard. As close as I could get without raising too much suspicion, someone in the Exchequer's office intervened. I heard the name 'Vickers' mentioned. That said, I advise you sir, not to underestimate Blainard. While I concur with your assessment of his character, it appears he does have highly and widely placed connexions. Through this network, he becomes a more substantial adversary.

Darcy came to his feet and paced until his anger had ebbed to a smouldering ember. After Wickham's debauchery, he thought he had seen the worst of man's behaviour, but he was wrong. So very, very wrong.

"He would have taken her. She would have been crushed, but what choice would she have had?" He hung his head as a discomfiting realisation struck him. "Am I any better? I did not lead Whitecastle to ruin to ensnare her, but I set a hefty price in exchange for my aid." Darcy lowered his face into his hands. "How have I sunk this low?"

Images of those lonely years of anguish and overbearing duty filled his mind. Once he had mastered the responsibilities of Pemberley and coping with his grief, he formally re-entered the circus of parties and balls full of empty heads and proud demeanours. Vacuous, heartless, and meaningless. Recoiling from the mercenary ne'er-do-wells passing themselves off as England's best, the younger Darcy had turned away, indulging his intellectual curiosity, revisiting the philosophical and literary societies his father had introduced him to as a youth.

Only when forced by Lady Matlock would I attend two or three functions each Season. Antoinette would enjoy my tales of the follies of the ladies and dandies cavorting about in their self-importance. Now those evenings are gone, as are the musical concerts Georgiana and I used to attend—when she would still brave public gatherings. Those were the only moments even approaching happiness I have known. And now? Antoinette's comfort is tainted, as she desires more than I can offer or feel for her. Even Georgiana, in her own way, has left me. And yet I regret nothing.

His mind's eye wandered to Elizabeth. *That mischievous smile, those eyes, sparkling with wit, intelligence, and compassion. She is all that is wonderful. And though our beginnings were inauspicious, there is something between us. Something good and wonderful.*

Darcy closed his eyes and smiled. *I am hers, and she will be mine.*

DARCY'S CARRIAGE COLLECTED THE GARDINER PARTY FOR Covent Garden's production of *Love's Labour's Lost*, and he noted a nervousness in the Gardiners' demeanour. He searched Elizabeth's face for a clue, but she avoided his gaze, turning to the darkening sky. *I must trust she will tell me what troubles her, and I shall find a way to help.*

The gentlemen disembarked, turning to assist their female companions in doing likewise. As Darcy took Elizabeth's hand, he was relieved there was nothing tentative in her grasp as he guided her descent. Yet she relied on her own strength to land. Walking to the entrance, her brilliant smile sent a rush of warmth and unexpected joy through his heart. *I have never experienced anything similar before.* They walked through the crowd, and Darcy noticed many who turned to look at them. *No doubt they are amazed that not one, but the three ladies in my party are respectable, beautiful women.* He listened to their whispers as he walked.

"Darcy always had an eye for beauty."

"I hear he stole Miss Bennet from right under Blainard's nose."

"Jolly good. I think Miss Bennet a cut above Blainard's due. Would not wish him upon my worst enemy's sister."

"Darcy will take prodigious care of her, I dare say."

There were many such murmurings as the striking

couples made their way through the antechamber. Miss Bingley and Mr Oswald stood at the side along with Mr and Mrs Hurst. Darcy heard Caroline call out to her brother. "Charles? Charles, come over here!"

Bingley winced. Turning his head to the group, he said, "My sisters, Caroline and Louisa. May I introduce you?"

Jane agreed. Bingley looked to Darcy, but he shook his head, their longstanding code that Darcy's box was not receiving visitors. Bingley led Jane away from the others, and Darcy watched them go, knowing the warning bell would soon rescue them.

Settled in their seats, Darcy huffed. *Those goats acknowledge me now because Elizabeth is on my arm. Of this, there is no doubt. How could they not? That gown is very becoming, and the rosebuds emphasise her alluring neckline. How I long to pluck them.*

Elizabeth glowed while she watched the players on the stage. He watched her being diverted by the acts, although more often than not, his mind created its own drama—that of the day she might at last permit him into her bed. A faint groan escaped him, and Elizabeth turned, her eyes posing a silent question. He blushed and shook his head, refocusing on the stage. However, her intoxicating presence, and the memory of his imaginings, pulled his gaze back to her. She was in profile, eyes smiling, as were her lips. The air in the box grew warm and Darcy's cravat grew tight.

At length, perhaps sensing his agitation even if she did not understand the cause of it, Elizabeth leant over and took his hand. She squeezed it, and he placed both hands on his leg. Elizabeth lowered her eyelids, and he felt her breath upon his cheek before she pulled back. Her scent mingled with his, and he felt his breath grow ragged in his chest even while he wondered if she knew what she was about.

Suddenly, applause roared around them, catching them unaware. Turning to face him, she blushed, and he felt himself grow even warmer in reply. He was mortified at the things he had been thinking and feeling, until her brow arched, and she smiled at him. He smiled back and relaxed his hold upon her hand so they could join in praising the performance.

THAT EVENING, THE GARDINERS HOSTED THE GENTLEMEN for a light, late-night supper. Darcy and Elizabeth were uncharacteristically reticent in sharing their thoughts of the performance. While Jane was concerned, her aunt smirked to her husband. "Judging by the fire in their eyes, I would place money I am correct in my suppositions. They will be very happy when they wed."

Before the gentlemen took their leave, Elizabeth handed Darcy his hat and gloves, her eyes begging for a moment.

"Bingley, I shall meet you in the carriage."

"No hurry, man. I am very happy where I stand," replied Bingley, looking at Jane, who returned his smile.

Elizabeth led Darcy to the more secluded end of the hall. "Is there any way you could speak with my uncle tomorrow?"

"Of course, but why?"

"There has been no word from the bank, which means any hope of credit they may extend will not arrive in time to satisfy his creditors. Things have come to a head rather prematurely but, so it is." Her eyes grew anxious, and she twisted her fingers.

Taking her hands, Darcy kissed each finger. "I shall speak to him first thing tomorrow. I have already prepared the sum for the day after our wedding. Two days early makes no difference, especially if it will bring you peace, my dearest Elizabeth." He lifted one hand to cup her cheek, marvelling at how just one touch from her could command him so. "I am amazed how quickly you have taken hold of me. I only pray you never let me go."

She gasped. "How did this begin?" she asked. "How can it be so strong?"

"I do not know," he said, leaning down to take her lips with his own.

ELIZABETH GAPED AT HER IMAGE IN THE MIRROR. Having taken Georgiana's suggestion to trust Madame Lestrat, proprietor of the most celebrated modiste on Bond Street, La Celeste, she marvelled at her transformation. Her eyes misted at the beauty of the silk organza encasing her body, its crystal-beaded bodice sparkling in the sunlight. It was softness and elegance combined.

Jane shed bittersweet tears. "Oh, Lizzy, if Papa could see you now. He would be so proud of you. If it were not for you, I do not know what would have become of us."

Elizabeth went to her sister, and they embraced, while their aunt stood by wiping away tears of her own. "'Tis true, Elizabeth. You are the glue that holds us all together. Mr Darcy will be breathless when he sees you at the altar."

Madame Lestrat bustled into the dressing room fluffing her crowning glory—an organza veil adorned with gardenia blossoms—but stopped without interrupting her emotional clients. "*Mon Dieu!* Monsieur Darcy weds? Can this be? But why the tears?" Taking a deep breath, she stepped forward. "Ladies, this will not do. Clarice!"

A young girl entered and was introduced as Madame Lestrat's niece before being sent to fetch tea for them all. The ladies calmed themselves, while admiring the beautiful gown Madame Lestrat had fashioned. Profuse thanks were given and well received.

WHILE ELIZABETH CHANGED BACK INTO HER MORNING gown, Jane wandered to the front of the shop. Running her fingers over the luxurious fabrics, she envisioned the gowns she might order when she joined Elizabeth in town next Season. She was soon lost in thoughts of dancing with the charming Mr Bingley until Mr Darcy bustled through the shop and a clerk rushed off towards the back rooms. Puzzled by his apparent distress, she stepped backwards, out of sight, and waited.

"Mr Darcy," Madame Lestrat hastened towards him.

"Madame?"

"Your bride is lovely, Monsieur," she said with pursed lips.

Mr Darcy bristled.

"Oh," she waved her hand. "I understand, it was

never to be. I only wish a word." She looked to the dressing rooms.

"I was not informed that my sister recommended your talents to my intended."

"This is sudden."

He nodded.

"Very well, I shall speak to Antoinette. Worry not."

"Thank you, Celeste," he said with relief. "How is she?"

Madame sighed. "She is…disappointed, but we knew she would be. I am sorry, Darcy. I tried to tell her."

"No, no, do not blame yourself. We both know how she is."

Madame Lestrat patted his arm. "You deserve happiness, *mon amie*. And it seems Miss Bennet will give that to you."

He smiled.

"I shall let them know you are here."

"Thank you, Celeste. For taking such good care of Antoinette."

Jane froze, one hand suspended above a bolt of intricate lace until Elizabeth greeted Mr Darcy and Mrs Gardiner came to collect her.

"Jane, what is it dear?" Mrs Gardiner asked with great concern. She took Jane's hand. "Are you well?"

"Of course," Jane replied, but Elizabeth was not fooled.

"Jane, in truth you look quite ill. What happened?" From her sister's stern demeanour, it was clear Elizabeth would brook no opposition.

Noting Darcy's agitation, she replied, "The room

became overheated, that is all. All shall be well once I take in some fresh air."

Elizabeth squeezed her sister's hand. "We shall speak of this at the Gardiners'."

Jane nodded and they headed to the Darcy carriage.

CHAPTER SIX

D arcy knocked on the door.

"Enter!" Mr Gardiner looked up from scattered papers and ledger books as Darcy entered. "Ah, Mr Darcy, what can I do for you this fine morning?" His jovial smile failed to mask his deep concern.

"Sir, it is what I can do for you." Darcy took a chair near his future uncle. "It has come to my attention that Mr Whitecastle may have left your establishment at a disadvantage. I hope you will allow my investment. As a way of pleasing Elizabeth." Darcy pulled a bank cheque from his coat pocket, handing it to the man.

Mr Gardiner, who had stiffened when Darcy spoke the name Whitecastle, stared at the note, seeming lost in thought as the seconds collected into minutes. He steepled his hands in front of his mouth then said, "Mr Darcy, Elizabeth is not, and has never been, for sale."

Darcy blinked, shocked. "I never——"

"How long have you known of my misfortune? And how does it factor in your hasty proposal to my niece, sir?" Mr Gardiner flew out of his chair towards the startled Darcy. "Take your money and leave my house, and do not return." He flung the bank note back at him. Storming to the door he opened it, and with a sweep of his arm, he indicated the direction for Darcy to exit.

"Elizabeth has pledged herself to me of her own free will."

"Believe that if it gives you pleasure, but I know Elizabeth, her kind heart. If she knew of our troubles, she would leave no stone unturned to aid us. She does not love you, Mr Darcy, and I will not subjugate her to that kind of future, simply to placate—"

"Mr Gardiner!" Darcy's booming shout reverberated throughout the chamber. "Elizabeth has agreed to marry me and marry me she will. There is nothing you can do to change that. Now you have the opportunity to save yourself, and your family's reputation—or not. I pray that you will, as I respect your integrity and hope to do business with you in the future. However, should you decide to oppose me, I shall not stop to think of the consequences to achieve my objective, which is to wed Elizabeth. Am I understood?"

"I beseech you, do not do this. It will only bring misery to you both."

"No, sir, it will not." Darcy paused to inhale deeply and lower his voice. "Elizabeth and I are suited for each other, made for each other if you will. As her guardian, her uncle, I implore you, do not oppose this union."

The two men engaged in a silent battle of wills until Darcy spoke again. "Perhaps our courtship has been irregular. However, I believe Elizabeth cares for me, and I, sir, care for her. More than I have ever imagined possible. All will be well, Mr Gardiner. On that you have my word."

The lively exchange of the women discharging their pelisses and purchases as they arrived home filtered through the thick walls. Soon, children's voices joined them. Mr Gardiner took Darcy's measure and relented. "Very well, Mr Darcy. I concede."

"It is not a matter of winners or losers, sir. We shall both have our desire—that of Elizabeth's happiness."

"I certainly hope you are right."

Darcy nodded. The cheque, lying on the floor, caught his eye, and he retrieved it, handing it to Mr Gardiner. "For Elizabeth's sake, I beg you to take this. It would break her heart to see you brought low by another's perfidy. Do not crush her with your pride. No one need ever know of this."

Mr Gardiner looked at the bank draft still in Darcy's hands. "I do not know how I can accept this offer," he said. The sound of his children's laughter pervaded the room, and he said then, "But how can I not?"

AFTER MR DARCY DEPARTED, ELIZABETH AND JANE WENT for a stroll. "Elizabeth, do you mean to tell me you know about this Mademoiselle du Marché?"

"Yes."

"And still you will marry him?" Jane asked, her eyes wide.

"Yes, I shall. Lord Blainard made me aware of how

things stood when Mr Darcy and I first became betrothed."

"Surely you would not marry him, knowing he keeps a woman?"

"I told him I expected his fidelity, and he promised I should have it. The particulars of his relationship with Mademoiselle du Marché I know not, though I have reserved the right to ask in the future."

"Forgive me, Lizzy, but can you trust him to honour his word?"

Elizabeth searched her heart for the answer. "I hope so, because I do believe him. I must." Jane was about to interrupt, but Elizabeth continued. "I do not know how to explain this feeling that has come over me."

"Mr Darcy is very handsome."

Elizabeth blushed. "Oh, there is that to be sure. But that is not all there is. When I am with him, I feel safe. I feel he will not harm me, and I have made my stance on Mademoiselle and her ilk abundantly clear!"

Jane laughed. "Thank you, I feel better knowing you have, as is your nature, addressed this directly."

The two smiled and continued around the pond. Leaving the park, Jane asked, "Lizzy, why would Miss Bingley wish to spread such gossip?"

"I do not know."

"It pains me to think there are people in this world who would willingly harm another, especially you. There must be some grave disappointment fuelling her ire."

"You have met her intended, Mr Oswald?"

"More likely kin to Mr Collins I have never met," Jane replied. The ladies giggled as they returned to the house.

ELIZABETH SAT AT THE DRESSING TABLE IN THE CHAMBER she shared with Jane. Darcy had sent over a beautiful emerald necklace that matched her gown. A pair of jewelled combs set with the dark stones sparkled in her hair, pinned atop her head. *I feel a bit like a princess.* She tilted her head. *And rather less like Lizzy of Longbourn.*

Her smile faltered, and she gazed at her reflection in the mirror, grateful that Jane was with her aunt. For the first time since her sister's arrival, she had a moment to herself to face what the future would bring.

Tomorrow, I leave all this behind, all that I have ever known, to join my life with a man I barely know. Fear welled in her heart, and she paced about the chamber. "What am I to do? I do not think I can marry him. We barely know each other. A week ago, I had no idea what this man was about. And now? What do I truly know? Oh, dear God, please help me. Give me a sign. What is right?"

Elizabeth sank onto the chair of her dressing table. *I want Jane to come and relieve my doubt. But that cannot happen, no matter how I wish it could.* She wanted to sob, but her tears would not come.

Her thoughts whirled between her family's distress, Darcy's aid, his character, and his preference for the company of Antoinette du Marché. *But he is marrying me, not taking me as his mistress.* "I do not understand. Why is he marrying me? He shared some of his reasons, but what if there is more? How can I trust him? And that he has…had a…a *mistress*!"

She returned to striding about the room. "What if he decides to leave me? Jamie said he loved me, and then he left me." Her pace increased as her agitation grew. "I cannot. I must! But I cannot. How can I trust him, when I do not know what kind of man he truly is?"

"So, this is what is in your heart." Jane walked into the bedchamber.

Elizabeth rushed to her. They embraced, and Elizabeth unleashed her fear, as her tears and her cries rushed from her heart to Jane's ear.

"Oh, Lizzy, dearest. Have faith, my darling sister. All will be well, I promise you."

"No, no, I must marry tomorrow."

"Hush. We shall speak with Uncle. He will make things right. I promise."

"Oh, Jane! What am I to do?"

"I am sure Mr Darcy will understand. One week is too much to expect when you two barely know each other." Jane squeezed Elizabeth's shoulders. "We have been through so much, and yet I cannot think ill of Mr Darcy. The way he looks at you, Lizzy, I fear not for your happiness anymore."

Elizabeth pulled back, swiping away her tears. "No?"

"But if you are this frightened, it does not bode well for you—for either of you, really."

Mrs Gardiner knocked on the door, appearing concerned when she saw the state of her two nieces. "Lizzy, child, what is it?"

"Aunt, I just do not know if I can do this."

"Jane, go and speak to your uncle. You and he must go and make our excuses. I shall stay with Lizzy. Do make haste."

Jane left, and within minutes, the heavier step of

their uncle was heard ascending the stairs. "Madelyn, Lizzy—is all well?"

"Take Jane to Darcy House and make our apologies," Mrs Gardiner instructed. "I shall try and calm Lizzy."

Mr Gardiner nodded and disappeared down the stairs, while Mrs Gardiner pulled Elizabeth tighter into her embrace. After almost twenty minutes of being rocked as though she were one of her aunt's children, Elizabeth pulled back, wiped her eyes, then struggled to unhook the emerald necklace.

"Allow me. Beautiful, is it not?"

Elizabeth nodded, as Mrs Gardiner removed the jewels from her neck.

"From the case, I should think this has been in his family quite a while."

Elizabeth looked at the worn velvet case as if for the first time, her fingers skimming the stones, cool to her touch. Even resting in their box, they caught and bounced the candle's light around the room in prisms of colour. In the centre of each stone, an ember of fire glowed.

"Mr Darcy must care a great deal for you to give you his family's jewels."

Elizabeth looked at her.

"Men do not give pieces worn by their mothers and grandmothers to just any pretty face," her aunt said with a smile. "For them, they purchase new pieces." Mrs Gardiner looked at Elizabeth in the mirror. "It is this that troubles you, is it not? That Mr Darcy has been with other women?"

"That Mr Darcy *kept* other women, Aunt. How can I

give my heart to a man who…how can I trust him? What if he takes another?"

Mrs Gardiner sat next to Elizabeth and took her hand. "Elizabeth, I do not condone the choices Mr Darcy made, not at all. However, this was before you came into his life."

"But what if—"

"Let us stick with the facts. What has Mr Darcy told you of this prior association of his?"

"Lord Blainard said—"

"Lord Blainard had his own objective in telling you of Mr Darcy's indiscretion."

"Indiscretion? Aunt, he kept a mistress! I have tried to work my way through this, truly, I have. I just do not know if it is possible."

A commotion was heard below stairs, followed by the rush of boots upon the stairs. A knock startled both women as Mr Darcy flung wide the door. His eyes looked wild with emotion as he took in the scene of the two ladies.

"Forgive me, Mr Gardiner explained… Mrs Gardiner, I implore you to give me a moment alone with Elizabeth?"

She looked to her niece and squeezed her hand, then left the chamber. Elizabeth tried to remove the tears from her cheeks.

"Why do you cry, Elizabeth? I cannot bear that it is because of me."

Elizabeth faced him but remained seated. "Mr Darcy, I cannot keep my promise to you. It is too soon. I have difficulty trusting people in general, and to marry when such doubt fills my heart… I must release you from our engagement."

"No, I cannot allow that. I cannot. I will not." His voice, which she believed would be angry, sounded sorrowful. "I do not think I could stand the pain of that."

Darcy took the seat vacated by Mrs Gardiner. "Elizabeth, you know my history. I have been alone too long, in a crowded world where no one understood my heart. No one cared to notice one still beats within my breast, until you entered my world. Do you remember the ball at Titledom House?"

She nodded.

"I saw you there, and for a brief moment, you looked at me. At *me*, not the master of Pemberley, not the scourge of London, but *me*. It was as if the sun shone upon me when the world was shrouded in grey. Hope woke in my heart after so many long years dormant. When you looked away, called away by Blainard, I was alone. Again. Only it was worse, because I knew then there was someone in this world who enlivened my heart simply by being. And that someone is you. I know I rushed you to be my wife and pushed you to accept me. My passion for you is strong, Elizabeth, very strong, but that is not my primary reason."

He looked away, and Elizabeth reached her hand to his, sliding hers into his grasp. He looked at their clasped hands, then took them to his lips. "I am ashamed to admit, I forced your hand because…" He paused. "I was afraid it was the only way you would accept me."

She was about to argue, but he continued, looking

directly into her eyes. "Not because of my family's reputation. I overheard you defending both myself and Georgiana to your friend on that score." He took a deep breath. "But I feared what you had heard of my relationship with Mademoiselle du Marché would turn you from me. That a woman of your character would be mortified and disappointed. I have acted abominably in forcing you to my will without explaining my history with her." He retreated to the window where he stared down onto the street. "I do release you, Elizabeth, from your pledge. You are free now, to go your own way." He turned towards her before she could speak. "I have paid your uncle." His smile was brief and sad. "After more effort than I thought possible, I convinced him to save his family."

She did not return his smile, and he returned his gaze to the window. His eyes lingered on the velvet box holding his mother's emeralds, and Elizabeth saw his shoulders slump. She crossed the room to stand behind him. "Your words have soothed me but please, answer me honestly. Is Mademoiselle du Marché now in your past?"

"No."

"No?" Elizabeth recoiled, feeling the syllable like a punch to her gut.

Darcy turned, reaching for her, but she stepped out of his reach. "Elizabeth, everyone believes that Antoinette and I are—were—lovers. That is not, I mean to say, she and her cousin are refugees from the Terror."

Elizabeth stared in surprise. "What?"

"When they arrived in England, they had only my father's name scribbled on a piece of paper. They are family, although distant. Our grandfathers were friends." He looked into her eyes. "When she was young, very young, she was violated by a French nobleman. By my father's account, the attack… It took her years to recover, though I believe the experience broke her spirit. She was with child, and my father established a safe haven for them both on one of our lesser estates until the child was born. They eventually settled here in London. Her cousin has raised the child into a wonderful young woman, but Antoinette… She remains uncomfortable with people. My father set them up in a business, but he and her cousin, Celeste—"

Elizabeth gasped as understanding dawned in her mind.

"They agreed it best to keep her from society." Darcy took Elizabeth's hands, which she allowed. "With time, she recovered much of her spirit, and we did appear at the occasional museum or some such. When the rumours arose regarding the nature of our relationship, it set her back, and she withdrew again." He hung his head. "Antoinette has reverted to be even more uncomfortable with strangers than I."

"Madame Lestrat is Antoinette's cousin? And the girl in the shop—Clarice—is her daughter?"

He nodded. "It was thought advantageous by all to raise Clarice without that knowledge. Antoinette was not able to take responsibility for anyone for a number of years. Celeste and my mother believed it best to remove Clarice from her care, telling the child that her mother had died. It was the only way Antoinette was able to accept the child, to think her an orphan that Madame has taken in. Antoinette's mind would not comprehend any other reality. To this day I do not think she suspects Clarice is hers."

"Dear Lord."

He nodded. "My mother helped them as much as possible, but when she died…"

"Celeste began her shop," Elizabeth added.

"While Celeste is talented in her own right, it is Antoinette's designs that earned La Celeste's reputation." He sighed. "And it was my father who maintained the connexion after my mother's death."

"It was interpreted as something illicit?"

He nodded.

"And you continued to support them after *his* death, and…?"

"And everyone believed I kept her as my mistress."

"But why?" Elizabeth cried out.

Darcy reached for her hand. "They left France to escape the blackguard who assaulted her. He made two further attempts to retake her here in England—that we know of. Once before my father's death, once after. She retreated, hiding from everyone, for her physical and emotional protection. When I became master of Pemberley, the rumours surfaced of our supposed liaison, and I admit it was beneath me, but it kept away many of the young women wishing to…"

"Become Mrs Darcy?"

"Yes. I am so sorry, Elizabeth, that I did not clear my reputation, and hers, sooner. But Antoinette was never going to join society. It was just not possible. She could not stand the strain. And it helped me, made room for me to breathe in those dark years after my father's death." Pain burned in his eyes, and he hung his head.

"Does Georgiana know of the connexion?"

"No. She was not born when they arrived. And by the time she could have understood, there were rumours…"

"Wickham."

He nodded.

"And now?"

"As we all grew, Antoinette and I drew closer. *As friends*," he emphasised. "Every now and then she fancies that I am her suitor. There has never been anything to it, as I am more than aware of her fragility in that area. But since the evening at Titledom House, I have not visited her. She had begun again to think…well, I thought it prudent to stop that line of thought, as my own heart was waking to another." Darcy smiled at her.

"And she was well with this?"

Darcy shrugged. "I have not heard of any problems from Celeste. And after the other morning, learning of our coming wedding, she would send word if Antoinette was overly troubled."

"I see."

"Do you?" He took hold of her hands. "Elizabeth, but say the word and I shall cease all communication with Antoinette."

"No, no, that is not necessary." She looked into his eyes. "She has lost so much, suffered so much. To deprive her of your *friendship*," she emphasised, "would be cruel." He kissed her hands with a smile, and she felt a great burden lifted from her heart. "And there have been no others?"

"No, and there never will be. You are the mistress of my heart, my body, and my soul." Hesitating but a moment, Darcy kissed her, and she returned it with a kiss of her own. He crushed her to his chest, and she held on to him with a strength that surprised her. Releasing her lips, his smile filled his eyes. "I want to cry out in joy that we have somehow got through this and hope for joy in our future."

"Then, Mr Darcy, perhaps you would help me with my jewels. We have a party to attend."

CHAPTER SEVEN

St George's Church

Darcy waited at the altar, Colonel Fitzwilliam and Charles Bingley alongside him. He was glad to have the support of both. His gasp filled the nave as Elizabeth appeared on the arm of Mr Gardiner. Her transparent veil atop her curls could not hide her beauty as she walked toward him, and he was enchanted. *After all I have endured in this life, she is pledging her trust and perhaps her love to me. If not today, I shall have the rest of my life to earn it.*

"Who giveth this woman this day?" the parson asked.

Mr Gardiner sounded emotional as he replied, "I do," placing Elizabeth's hand in Darcy's.

Linking their hands, they pledged their troth to one another, the whole of the business taking much less time than Darcy ever should have imagined.

Leaving Jane in London with the Gardiners, the Darcys headed to Longbourn for a brief wedding journey. As the carriage left the confines of London, its occupants fell into an almost uncomfortable silence. Darcy was preoccupied with thoughts of his wedding night. *I have promised to abstain until Elizabeth wishes for me, but it is a battle—my control against her loveliness. And her gown only heightens her allure. It is a mighty struggle, but earning her love, her trust, is worth so much more. My—nay, our future rides on my success.*

Elizabeth twisted the band on her left hand. The embedded rubies glimmered against the gold. Her brow furrowed, and her husband grew anxious.

"What causes such trepidation?" he asked, shifting in his seat.

"I am just wondering how you will go about making me Mrs Darcy."

Ah, the moment of truth. "Elizabeth, um… I am not a novice to…to—"

"Neither am I, Mr Darcy." She grinned as his eyes widened and his mouth fell open.

"I see," he said. "And you thought now, after our wedding, was the time to inform me of your past?"

"Perhaps, if we had had an extended engagement of oh, say two or three weeks, perhaps there would have been time to discuss our experiences and compare notes. I am not yet one-and-twenty, and yet I have experience of the world. More so than most women of my age."

His eyes narrowed and he leaned forward in his seat. "Exactly what do you mean?"

"Jamie—Mr James Simmons, grew up alongside us in Meryton. His family owns Beyford, a fair-sized estate

less than ten miles away. When my parents died, after…
when we…when Longbourn was truly ours, our neighbours offered help. Advice, mostly. Jamie would call to
keep an eye on us. He and I spent most of our time
outside with the horses. He was always around, like a big
brother to me—until one day, about three years ago,
when he…he kissed me and told me he loved me."

Darcy's jaw tightened, and he looked away.

"We were not always proper, but, well…"

"How far did it go?" he demanded, his voice rough
with emotion.

"Darcy!" she countered, sounding stunned by his
response.

"Elizabeth, I must know how far it went."

"Not so far as to damage my value on the bridal
block, sir." Her voice lowered the temperature in the
carriage.

"The thought of you with another took hold and—I
apologise. Forgive me, please. But why did you not tell
me of this before?"

"Would it have made a difference? Would you have
rescinded your offer over a few stolen kisses three years
ago? Would my heart be abandoned twice over Jamie
Simmons?"

Darcy's breath left him. He did his best to reassert
control of himself. "No." Gathering his courage, he
continued, "Did he ask you to marry him?"

"He did." She turned to look out of the window.

*She refused him! A young girl, alone in the world, did not run
to the first offer, even though she cared for him.* "Then why?
What happened?"

"He moved to America." Elizabeth clasped her

hands in her lap. "He wanted me to leave Longbourn and my family to go to America with him. I could not." Tears gathered in the corners of her eyes. "He begged for days. His mother pled his cause. When I did not capitulate, they—*she*—spread all sorts of vile accusations against me. That I led him on, broke his heart." She turned, looking him directly in the eye. "I could not! How could I leave Jane? Noah's Promise is what allowed us to stay together. How could I abandon them to run after Jamie's dream?" When she spoke next, her words were barely audible. "I suppose I did not love him enough."

"Or perhaps he did not love you enough." At her surprised look, Darcy continued, "If he could not see, could not honour your love, your bond to your sisters, what kind of love is that, Elizabeth?"

She tilted her head, weighing his words. "I do not know."

He opened his arms, and she crossed the carriage to his embrace. He caressed her back. "Thank you for telling me, Elizabeth. You continue to amaze me, in your courage, your loyalty, and your ability to humble me."

"Humble you?"

He nodded. "Yes. When this discussion first began, I assumed you had given more than your heart to this man. It enraged me, even though you are aware of my reputation." He felt her stiffen, and he held more firmly to her. "You forgave my perceived transgressions, even before knowing the truth, because I was even less forthcoming." He gently pulled back to look directly in her eyes. "My heart was never engaged. Elizabeth, I am truly sorry."

"Now, we are as open books, more or less," she quipped, the sparkle returning to her eyes.

"More or less."

She returned to his embrace, snuggling in his arms. He thought about what he must now say. "Elizabeth. What of Blainard?"

"Lord Blainard?"

"Yes, him."

Her unexpected laugh relaxed him. "Surely you know I would never marry one such as he."

"Perhaps not if left to your own wishes."

"Then to whose wishes would he appeal?"

"Those of your family, and your love for them."

"Like with a certain someone I know?" Her teasing words sounded barbed.

"Yes, but I offered my hand in *marriage*."

There was silence as she took in his unspoken meaning. "That is a heavy accusation even for Lord Blainard."

"I do not make it lightly, particularly not after his performance the day we announced our engagement. I felt there was more behind his reaction than that of a rejected suitor. There was no understanding between you?"

"Not at all."

He took her hand, running his finger over hers. "I had a man keep an eye on him. One evening, he was able—that is to say, he persuaded Blainard to confess his intentions. And it transpires that he not only encouraged Whitecastle's gaming habit but introduced the idea of leaving the country to avoid his insurmountable debts, taking your uncle's funds with him."

"No!" Elizabeth gasped.

"He intended to inform you of the impending scandal, offering to advance the funds to avoid it and your uncle's financial ruin in exchange for you accepting—"

"His hand?"

Darcy shifted in his seat. "Not exactly."

Elizabeth paled and pushed away, focusing on her fingers, clasped tightly together. "His mistress," she said flatly.

"Blainard has an understanding with his cousin," Darcy added. "He never had any intention of marrying you."

"How do you know this?"

"My man is very thorough. A bottle or two of brandy at his preferred hellhole loosened his tongue. It seems our betrothal destroyed his plan."

Elizabeth sat, immobile, save for the occasional swipe of errant tears.

"Elizabeth." Darcy gently turned her head up toward his. "Hush, my love. We are together, and no one will tear us apart. No one has touched my heart or my life as you have. I truly believe that you, Mrs Elizabeth Darcy, were born for me. Just as I, Mr Fitzwilliam Darcy, was born for you. There is no need to fear anymore."

Before the words were out of his mouth, Elizabeth placed a quick kiss on his lips. Returning to his embrace, she cried out, "Oh Fitzwilliam!"

I am eternally grateful, good Lord, for Finch's gossip, Darcy thought. *That I found her and took the risk.* He held her until they both fell into an exhausted sleep. He woke when Elizabeth began to straighten herself and her clothing. He saw unfamiliar terrain outside the carriage window.

"What is Longbourn like? And Hertfordshire? I confess it is unknown to me."

He was graced by a beautiful, grateful smile as Elizabeth regaled him with the lore of her home village. She held his hand as she recounted the history of local landmarks. "Do you walk, sir? I mean, as a habit. There is so much to you of which I am unaware."

"I enjoy walking, though I prefer to ride. Are there any horses in your stable we could employ for an afternoon or two?"

"I am sure we could find something suitable to your tastes."

She gave him an innocent, arch smile that sent a rush through him, and he tugged his cravat. *Control yourself, man. She is a gentlewoman, and you gave your word you would wait till she invites you to her bed.* Glancing at her increasing excitement gave him pause. *I have focused on my desire for her. But not on her. I do not think she will settle for a marriage of convention. And neither shall I.*

"Fitzwilliam?" Elizabeth turned her full attention to him. "What is it?"

Pulling back, he leaned against the squabs. "Elizabeth, I have thought of our marriage almost constantly but have not, not truly, considered how we shall continue on."

She took his hand, stroking it. "We shall continue on as we have been. We shall learn from each other. Neither of us are constrained by the limits of our sex or our place in society. Therefore, I hope we shall turn to each other to find our own way. The one that fits us." She smiled, but her eyes held uncertainty.

"And so we shall." He took her hand to his lips, then pulled her to his side.

They spoke of the horses of Noah's Promise, past and present, as well as those animals she hoped to obtain, and had a lively disagreement on the best method to introduce a young colt to the saddle. Their debate moved seamlessly from horses to equine references in Shakespeare, and then on to literature, poetry, before settling on politics just as the carriage entered the environs of Meryton. Elizabeth ceased her argument mid-thought, reaching eagerly for his hand, jolting them both. Their eyes met, finding certainty in the sudden need to touch.

"There is so much I wish to show you!" she exclaimed.

Darcy's smile deepened to his heart. *There is hope, old man, as I live and breathe, there is hope.*

THEY WERE GREETED AT LONGBOURN BY MRS HILL, THE housekeeper, who had a lovely meal of local delicacies and fresh bread prepared. Elizabeth relaxed and graced Darcy with frequent smiles. After a brief tour of the house, complete with family stories, she led him to the stables. There, in the most ordinary of stalls, were some of the most beautiful and well-maintained horses Darcy had ever seen. "They are outstanding, Elizabeth. I have not seen their equal."

"Thank you." She embraced her horse. Darcy watched as Elizabeth indulged him with sweet endearments and kisses. The horse whinnied and nuzzled his human. "This is my darling Xerxes. He is such a good boy. Shall we ride?" she asked eagerly.

Looking at her, full of hope and anticipation, he readily agreed. "Which mount would suit?"

Leaving Xerxes's side, Elizabeth walked along the stalls. Darcy followed. His question, asked innocently, turned into fire. He wanted to touch her and kiss her, and he maintained an inner monologue to control his craving for her. The thought of riding in his current state dampened his desires, and soon they were amiably discussing the horse flesh beautifully arrayed around them. He listened to her stories of the traits of each horse and from whence they came, gleaning a glimpse into her methodology and objectives for each horse and its progeny.

He made his selection and quicker than either of them thought possible, they were riding together across the open fields. Elizabeth expertly led Darcy on a merry chase, jumping fences and ditches as she identified the crops grown for feed and those that fed her family. Darcy was enchanted and intrigued as she enlightened him on the care and maintenance of her extraordinary animals. The information was new, her approach both novel and effective. He was eager to learn her method of training, for although an unknown mount, he and his horse responded well to each other's idiosyncrasies. Over the pounding of the hooves beneath him, he could hear Elizabeth's melodic laughter.

Nothing could quell his joy in riding out on a wonderous spring day with the beautiful woman he desired above all others, a woman who now belonged with him. He spurred his horse to catch her, and they cantered easily together. Her full smile lit her face, adding even more lustre to her sparkling eyes. His heart opened, and he knew he would do anything for her, to keep her by his side. *I no longer doubt these feelings so strong, so quick to develop. I just know what I feel, and these emotions coursing through my heart are so glorious I never want them to cease.*

"We're heading to the right, at the end of that field over there." Elizabeth pointed to a path at the far side of the clearing, three fields away. Bestowing a brilliant smile of his own, he kicked his horse firmly in the sides, and he was off. She spurred Xerxes into the race and soon they were riding at a breakneck speed, blood rushing in the thrill of competition.

As their horses drank from a stream, Elizabeth reached into her saddle bag, bringing forth two handkerchiefs, which she dipped in the refreshing water. Offering his hand, Darcy helped her from her knees. He closed his eyes as she placed the cool cloth against his skin and washed away the grit. Before she could pull her hand away, he took it, pressing her flesh to his cheek, and looked into her eyes. Their gazes locked, and he lifted her hand and kissed the inside of her palm. Her breath grew irregular, and she tilted her head, waiting.

"Elizabeth, I know this may be too early for you to hear, but I love—" he faltered. "I love you."

She smiled up at him. "How can this be so strong between us? I feel alive when I am with you, in ways I never thought to experience again."

"Again?" Darcy stepped back as though slapped. "You have felt this before?"

She saw his hope fall, but she was unwilling to create a falsehood. "Not to the degree I feel with you—not nearly—but the awakening of it, yes." Seeing his distress, she turned her head, taking a step away.

Darcy was unassuaged and in shock. Elizabeth stepped back. "I *felt* I loved Jamie. I am sorry if my saying so gives you pain, but it was before he went away to America. I was just a girl."

"Would you have gone with him if things had been different?"

She shook her head. "It does not serve to think upon it. It was long ago, almost three years. To think of how it could have or should have been creates too much misery."

Darcy lowered his head, staring unhappily at the ground.

She continued. "If Jamie and I had wed, then I never would have gone to London for the Season, and I would not have met you. And for that, I should be eternally sorry." This last sentence was whispered, her voice raw and pure and full of emotions over which she had no control.

He pulled her into his arms. "I shall blot him from your mind, Elizabeth, so all you see is me, all you feel is my love for you." Wrapping his strong arms around her, he pressed their bodies together.

Closing her eyes, she gave her heart permission to lead, and she relaxed against him. His eyes dropped to her parted lips, then he brought their lips together. Desire shot through her, and she felt hunger for him.

Her desire lifted her consciousness, twirling it around till she lost her bearings. Passion ignited quickly, and their lips met until Darcy pulled back, meeting Elizabeth's smile. "Elizabeth, you are the love I feared I should never find."

His words opened a part of her that had been closed for too long. She understood his fear, for it echoed her own. "I understand, because I, too, carried that fear, until you found me. You are my heart's hope. I love you."

Celebrating their confessions with abundant kisses, their ardour grew until Elizabeth drew a ragged breath. "While I am tempted to beg you to ravage me here and now," she said, "I think I should prefer the privacy of our chamber."

Darcy blinked, taking a moment. Then, offering his hand to his bride, he placed a quick kiss to her knuckles before linking arms with her and calling to their grazing horses. After helping each other appear presentable, they rode, with smiles on their faces, back to Longbourn.

CHAPTER EIGHT

The next morning, Darcy woke with a weight on his shoulder and waves of fragrant curls strewn across his face. Startled until he recognised the woman lying across his chest, he sighed, running his fingers up her spine, delving beneath the wayward strands. He combed his hand down her hair and along her back until she stirred, and his breath caught in his chest.

After dinner the night before, they had shared stories of their youth, and the breadth of their education. She had showed him her father's library, pulling down favourite tomes, explaining the scratch marks on the shelves where she had climbed as a child to reach those books deemed unsuitable for curious children.

Darcy marvelled at the memory of how easily he had laughed, how his heart had warmed whenever he made her smile reach her eyes. After dinner, they had retired to the parlour and pianoforte.

"Would you play for me?" he had asked.

She had smiled and moved to the instrument. "Any requests, sir?"

"Do you know any of Beethoven's work?"

"*Moonlight Sonata,* of course, and I am familiar with *Für Elise.*"

Darcy had stepped back to watch, riveted as she played from memory, leaning into the keys.

Having confirmed their love throughout the night and into the morning, the Darcys left their chamber after noon. They were eager to ride and headed into Meryton. Darcy was amazed his wife knew the entire town, and how everyone was more than pleasant, albeit surprised, when she introduced him as her new husband. They were more impressed with this than his grand estate. Being regarded as a gentleman, but without the weight of his history or wealth unnerved him at first, but with Elizabeth as his guide, it became a welcome diversion.

Riding home, Elizabeth urged Xerxes onward, her laughter catching on the wind. Darcy dug his heels into his mount and gave chase. She had gone into a wooded glen, and Darcy, unfamiliar with the land, was soon lost among the trees.

ELIZABETH TUGGED ON XERXES'S REINS, LOOKING about the glen for her husband. She waited for him to re-join her, but he did not. Beginning to worry, she turned, cutting between the trees in search of her beloved. A handsome rider on a familiar beast trotted towards her.

"Elizabeth!" he called, sounding relieved, as though he had been searching for a while.

"Jamie?" Elizabeth pulled back in her saddle. "You came back!"

"Indeed!" He laughed at her outright. "If this is what has become of your infamous wit in my absence, it bodes well I have returned."

He stopped alongside Xerxes and leaned forward. "I returned for you."

"For me?" she asked.

He paused, apparently unsettled by her reaction. "You are surprised?"

"Of course I am. It has been three years. How else would I be?"

"Relieved? Happy?"

"I am." Elizabeth focused on reining in her impatient beast, who had begun to snort and stomp. To herself she added, *And so much more.*

"Shall we adjourn to Longbourn?" he asked.

Elizabeth looked for her husband, hearing the sound of another horse. "I am not alone, Jamie. I am—"

"Elizabeth!" Darcy rode into the clearing.

"Fitzwilliam! Forgive me for losing you. I began to fear you were swallowed by the forest."

Elizabeth watched as the two men eyed one another.

"Who is this, Elizabeth?" Jamie demanded.

"Yes, *Elizabeth.*" Darcy drawled out her name. "Who is this gentleman I find you with?"

Elizabeth looked between them both, her heart thudding as her past collided with the present. "I... Fitzwilliam, this is Mr Simmons. I believe I mentioned him to you. Jamie—Mr Simmons, this is Mr Darcy. My husband." Elizabeth looked down, patting Xerxes's neck to avoid witnessing Jamie's reaction.

"Husband? Since when?"

"Since yesterday," Darcy said in a challenging tone.

"Yesterday? No banns were published. Why is it no one in Meryton knows of this marriage?" Jamie asked, sounding equally challenging.

"Our marriage was consecrated in London, sir," Elizabeth explained. "We are here on our honeymoon. You will forgive us if we only announced our news to those closest to us."

The old lovers looked at each other. Though still on her horse in the open air, Elizabeth felt constricted. "Come. We are going to Longbourn." She looked at Jamie and found hostility, then to Darcy and found vulnerability. She smiled at her husband, relieving one of them of his frown.

BACK AT LONGBOURN, DARCY DISMOUNTED, THEN HELPED Elizabeth onto solid ground. She slid willingly into his arms, and her eyes never left his, as though she searched for something in him. He bent down and kissed her. To his relief, she brought her hands up to his cheeks and caressed them.

Simmons rode by, catching the intimate moment. "Lizzy," he said, "I must not tarry. You will call upon us before you leave Longbourn? Or do you intend to settle here?"

"We leave within the week," Darcy answered, without releasing Elizabeth from his embrace.

"To London?"

"Yes," Elizabeth responded, her arms resting on Darcy's forearms.

"Then to Derbyshire." Darcy tightened his hold on her.

Simmons's eyes narrowed at their embrace. "Mr Darcy, Mrs Darcy. I shall tell my mother to expect your call. Perhaps tomorrow?"

"No, not tomorrow. The day after, we are free," Elizabeth answered. Her spirits were low, Darcy noted, hoping it was merely fatigue.

"Until then." Simmons turned his horse and rode off.

The dust settled before they walked to the manor, silent until reaching their chambers, where a welcoming fire glowed against the setting sun. Darcy poured a glass of brandy, one of the amenities his valet brought from London. He watched Elizabeth gaze out of the window and poured a glass for her. Taking a hefty gulp from his own, he strode over, silently offering the amber liquid. She looked at him as if not recognising him, then roused herself to take the glass.

"Thank you," she replied, subdued.

Darcy was uncertain how to proceed.

"So, that is your Mr Simmons," he said at length.

"*Was* my Mr Simmons." She took a long sip of brandy. "It was just so sudden. I was looking for you, had turned back to find you, and there he was. For so long, I longed to see him—and then, there he was. And all I felt was my need to find you."

Darcy was filled with both surprise and hope. She looked at him with confusion, and he led her to the sofa.

He sat beside her, his thumb drawing circles on her hand in a comforting rhythm. "Are you well?"

She nodded.

He inhaled deeply, willing away the question that had to be asked. "Do you regret marrying me?"

"No!" she turned to fully face him. Frowning at whatever she saw in his countenance, she caressed his cheek. "Apart from what you did for my family, I am glad, so very glad, to be your wife. Although our acquaintance is brief, I feel...what I feel is stronger for you than for any other I have known. We are meant for each other. I cannot explain it other than that. It is what my heart whispers to me."

He smiled and gave her a hesitant kiss. She leaned into him, and Darcy deepened the intimacy. Her hands slid from his arms to his hair, her fingers embedding in his wind-tossed curls. Relief washed over him until a thought wriggled into his brain. *What if she wishes to distract me from her regret? Or to convince herself?* He pulled back, hands cupping her cheeks, wishing to see into her soul. "You are sure?"

"Yes. Jamie is my past, but you are my future."

He sat, looking into her eyes, enjoying her reassuring smile. His hands caressed her skin, and his heart pounded. He pressed his lips to hers and she returned his kiss freely, fully. He pulled her closer, needing to feel her body yield to him. Opening his eyes, he saw love in hers. Her smile released the binds across his heart—restraints he was unaware had shackled his past. He kissed her again.

Later, they lay wrapped in each other's arms until sleep began to overtake them. Dusk settled around the fire, and the crackle of burning logs rippled in the silence of the room. As he surrendered to slumber, Darcy heard Elizabeth whisper, "He is mine and I am his."

THE THIRD DAY OF THEIR MARRIAGE SAW THEM CALLING on friends and relations, including Elizabeth's Aunt and Uncle Philips. Though their manners were appalling, Darcy could see their genuine care for their niece. Then there were the Lucases. Sir William was gregarious to a fault, and when he uncovered the fact that Darcy had been at St James's, his effusions bordered on the offensive.

Yet Darcy needed only to look at Elizabeth, her eyes infused with merriment, to relax and regale his audience with his adventures in town. From that family, he learned that Charlotte Collins, née Lucas, was Elizabeth's dear friend and married to her cousin, Mr Collins. She now resided at Hunsford with her husband, who was the vicar to Lady Catherine de Bourgh. Darcy frowned when he heard that.

Shortly thereafter, the Darcys made their farewells. Darcy held Elizabeth's arm as they walked back to Longbourn, his hand covering hers, yet he remained in thought.

"I wonder what has caused your handsome face to darken so?" she teased.

"Mr Collins, your cousin, has the living at Hunsford?"

"Yes," she said with a nod.

"Which is presided over by my aunt, Lady Catherine de Bourgh."

"Your aunt is Lady Catherine de Bourgh?"

He nodded.

"Why does this upset you?"

"It does not, in and of itself. My thoughts merely wandered to my most recent interactions with her." He rubbed her hand, resting on his arm. "She was very harsh to Georgiana and me. It is not a fond memory."

"Oh."

They continued in silence, maintaining their physical connexion. Rounding the corner to the front of Longbourn, they saw a horse being led away by a stable hand. Elizabeth stiffened and slowed her approach.

"What is it?" Darcy asked in alarm. When she looked up to him, he saw confusion in her eyes before she turned toward the horse. Guessing the identity of their visitor by her distress, Darcy squeezed her hand. "Come, Mrs Darcy, it seems we have a guest."

They walked, united, into the parlour, where Simmons was looking at the portraits of Mr and Mrs Bennet hanging over the mantel. They greeted him, Darcy seeing the longing in his rival's eyes, along with an emotion he could not name.

Simmons made polite conversation, speaking of his travels in the New World. Darcy was cheered considerably to learn of the man's upcoming return to New York. He wished to be merciful, gracious even, to Simmons, but then the man reached for Elizabeth, a longing in his gaze, and Darcy's fists clenched. He watched with disbelief and a growing rage as, after a surreptitious look in his direction, Simmons took Elizabeth's hand. Elizabeth tugged it back, but he held on, raising it to his lips, for a too-lengthy kiss.

Elizabeth turned, discomfited. Darcy strode to her and she gave him such a look of relief that he relaxed for the first time since their return home.

"Until tomorrow then, Mrs Darcy, Mr Darcy."

Darcy put his arm around Elizabeth, rejoicing as she relaxed into his embrace, and they saw their guest to the door.

BEYFORD WAS AN EFFICIENT, PROSPEROUS ESTATE, roughly ten miles from Longbourn. Mrs Simmons ran the estate during her son's absence, ensuring its smooth continuance for both the family and tenants. She adored her only child, and while civil to the Darcys, could not hide her disappointment.

"So, Mrs Darcy, where did you meet your handsome husband?" She turned to Darcy and added, "She always did have an eye for a good-looking man." Her gaze drifted to her son, seated across the table.

"Yes, I can see that," Darcy replied civilly.

"In town." Elizabeth glanced at her hostess.

Simmons watched Elizabeth, while she focused on her soup. "You would like America, Mrs Darcy," he said. "It would suit you, your spirit, your sense of adventure, your eyes, your laugh." He pushed an errant curl behind her ear.

She set her spoon down with decided force, her eyes fixed on his with displeasure. "Mr Simmons, I would ask you not to repeat yourself."

Simmons lowered his voice. "Oh, how I have missed you, Lizzy."

"Mr Simmons!" She looked away from his smirk to find Darcy's glare locked on him.

"Mr Simmons?" his mother chided. "Surely there is no need for such formalities. You have been friends your entire lives."

Elizabeth caught Darcy's increasing unease but turned her head sharply when Simmons touched her knee. Jolted by his touch, Elizabeth leapt to her feet, her chair crashing to the floor. She looked to her husband, who nodded at her unspoken plea. Placing his napkin on the table, he strode to her side.

"Mrs Simmons, I feel a headache developing, and must call this visit to a close," Darcy spoke with a forced calm to his hostess.

"Oh, no, Mr Darcy. Please." She scrambled to her feet.

"Elizabeth, shall we?" Taking Elizabeth's hand, Darcy led her to the door.

"Goodbye, Mr Simmons, Mrs Simmons, it has been a pleasure to see you again." Elizabeth and her husband departed, walking the short distance to the stables.

"What happened?" he asked her as soon as there was some distance from the house.

"Not here." She heaved a sigh of frustration upon seeing his ire. "Please, I just wish to leave this place. I promise, I shall share all with you." Looking him directly in the eyes, she relaxed her tensed shoulders when he nodded. She smiled, as a mother would with an exasperating child.

Elizabeth kept the pace brisk enough to forgo conversation. It was not until in the drawing room that she spoke. "You must promise that when I tell you my reasons for our premature departure you will remain calm. We leave the day after tomorrow and will not see Jamie Simmons again."

"Very well," he finally conceded.

"Good." She took a long sip of brandy. "He tried to get my attention, first by attempting to hold my hand and then…" She hesitated.

A scowl took control of his mouth. "And then?"

"He placed his hand upon my knee."

"I will kill him."

"No! Fitzwilliam, you promised."

"That was before I knew what that miscreant did."

"Which is why I made you promise before I told you." She grasped his arm, pulling him back. "There are more pleasurable things we can engage in to keep Mr Simmons in his place."

Elizabeth watched Darcy struggle to contain roiling emotions across his face, and especially in his eyes. He clenched his jaw so hard she heard his teeth grind. Finally, he cocked an eyebrow and asked, "Such as?"

Stepping closer, she pulled his face to hers. "This." They kissed until she was certain Jamie Simmons had entirely faded from his mind.

CHAPTER NINE

On their last full day in Hertfordshire, Elizabeth led Darcy down a road abutting Longbourn's east side. While she had taken great pleasure in showing him the wilds and wonders of the estate, this morning she kept to the main road, parallel to the fields.

'Tis a pleasant prospect, he thought, *but an unusual choice for our last ramble here.* Darcy startled when, upon rounding a bend, Elizabeth silently dismounted, tying her horse to a nearby tree. Seeing her struggle for composure, he scrambled off his horse. With a growing unease, he took her in his arms.

Looking up with sorrow in her eyes, she mumbled haltingly, "This is where my parents lost their lives."

Although Darcy knew she and her sisters were orphaned by a carriage accident, he was shocked it had happened so close to home.

"I miss my father," she wept. "He was...I just felt so

loved by him. With him, I was someone special, the best little girl there was. Just because I was me. He would soothe me when Mama's words hurt. I was never her favourite, you see. But none of that mattered because my father was there. Always there.

"And then, one day, he was gone. It had been raining —you know how wet the spring can be. I was walking one of the ponies, getting him accustomed to the bit, when I heard it—the crash. A wheel caught in a rut. It was the worst sound ever. I ran, completely forgetting my horse, but he followed me. And we found them. Roberts, our coachman, was dead when I arrived, as was my mother. Her neck…it dangled. But my father… I did not realise at first, but his back had broken."

She looked up at him. "He was in such pain. He was alive, but his breathing was laboured, and he could no longer see. I called to him, and he whimpered in pain and then said, 'I knew you would come. I love you, my dearest Lizzy. I always will.'"

Pulling her head to his chest, Darcy held her and struggled with his own emotions. *I too, witnessed my father die, although his lingering illness prepared us both. By the time he breathed his last, it was a relief, leaving only my grief. For Elizabeth and her sisters, there was grief and terrible shock.*

"I told him I loved him," Elizabeth mumbled into his coat. "That we all loved him. And then he was gone. I stayed with them until some men from Meryton came to help. Afterwards, all I could do was sit and stare. For weeks. I felt surrounded by ice—layers and layers of frozen air between me and the living, between me and the dead. I could hear and see everyone, but they were distant, unreachable.

"Sarmacia—she was the last mare bred with Papa's assistance—gave birth one night, about six months later. She had a terrible time and suffered so. I could hear her calling, her neighs like screams—wild, frightened, agonising. Her pain cut through the ice. Her heart, her need, touched me and I had to help. I went to the stables and stayed with her for two days until that foal was born, healthy and well. Her eyes are what saved me. Brown pools of love. In all the pain that horse endured, she still let me know she loved me, was grateful I had come to her. I was needed. As damaged and empty as I felt, she needed me, and I had to respond.

"When Sarmacia was stable, and Killarn, the colt, was as well, I collapsed and slept for three days. When I woke, I went to her. She nuzzled me, and as I looked into her eyes, I knew everything would be well."

Elizabeth looked up to Darcy. "And as you see, it is."

ELIZABETH WALKED TO THE STABLES ON THEIR LAST morning at Longbourn. The air, still cool from the night, billowed around her. She hoped it would not rain before they departed for London. *I have enjoyed being home, though I suppose it is mine no longer. Except Noah's Promise—that will always be mine. It was good to have Fitzwilliam look over my plans for the farm and the breeding charts. It felt nice to have another with whom to share my thoughts and hopes.*

She smiled, remembering their late-night discussion in front of the fire, a glass of wine for each as the wind howled outside their window.

"Surely your sisters will not mind?" He rolled his glass in his hand.

"Not mind? Not mind leaving everything they have ever known? Not mind uprooting what is left of their life, their sense of home, to traipse after me? I think they might, sir."

"Please be reasonable. What good is it to have two house-holds, when one will suffice?" Placing his glass on the rug, he tossed a piece of wood on the fire and turned to take her hand. "I am not asking for this to occur tomorrow, or even by the end of the summer. But your sisters are getting older. Jane will surely wish to marry and have a home of her own soon enough, and the others not long after. Please, think about it, that is all I ask."

Elizabeth looked at him, then into the fire. Closing her eyes, she hugged her knees. Longbourn was her home, where she felt most connected to her parents. She was not sure she could let them go.

"I shall think about it, that is all I can promise." She looked at her husband, casually arrayed before her hearth in only his shirt and breeches. Her fingers twitched with the desire to run through his tousled hair, but she withstood the temptation.

"Besides, it is not our decision alone, Fitzwilliam. We must discuss this with my sisters."

He nodded and smiled invitingly before pulling her into his embrace.

This morning she was far more disposed to Darcy's way of thinking: that the horses would like being moved to Derbyshire. *I hope he is right, and his stables can handle my babies.*

The sound of a familiar whinny pulled her back to the present, and Elizabeth looked to the clouds that still promised a storm. She hurried to calm Sarmacia, who was again in the last days of her confinement. The horse ambled over, lumbering her head over Elizabeth's shoulder. Elizabeth smiled and patted the mare's long, chestnut neck, whispering sweet nothings to her. The rest of the yard was quiet, with only one or two of the stable hands at their posts.

Sarmacia lifted her head in alarm. Turning, Elizabeth blanched as Simmons advanced with a smile, though his eyes were troubled. "Elizabeth, I am happy to find you alone."

"Good morning, Mr Simmons. What brings you out on such a turbulent morn?" Elizabeth grew concerned at the increasingly wild look in his eyes.

"You, of course." He stepped closer.

Sensing Elizabeth's distress, Sarmacia butted her head between them. Simmons smirked, batting her nose with a touch more force than was necessary. Elizabeth pulled the horse's head to her, soothing the pregnant mare.

"I was hoping you could explain some of the talk going about town."

Elizabeth glared at him.

He chuckled. "The old biddies are taking your name in vain again, my dear. All sorts of wild notions of why the clever Miss Lizzy suddenly married a man none of them had ever heard of until now." His eyes narrowed. "So, tell me. Why are you married to Darcy?"

Fists clenching, her reply was low, concentrated. "You have absolutely no right to ask me anything about my personal life, nor my motives. Not after disappearing without a word three years ago, to say nothing of your behaviour the other evening."

"It is not me who is asking, Elizabeth." He raised his hands in defence. "I care not why you married the man. It is the matrons of Meryton who abuse you so."

Elizabeth turned away, furious at the gossip running through town—again!

"What did you expect?" He stepped behind her, so close that she smelled his sweat mixed with stale alcohol. "While I do not care, I am curious why you chose Mr Darcy of Pemberley."

Elizabeth turned, giving him a sharp glare.

He smirked. "Oh, *I* know who Mr Darcy is. A man of his consequence is hard to hide. I tried to let the ladies of Meryton know of his position. Unfortunately, the information only fed their curiosity." His smirk widened into a wolfish grin.

Elizabeth recoiled, but caught a glimpse of something in his eyes, hinting at a deeper menace.

"So, how did you arrange the alliance, my dear? Although I definitely understand the draw on his part." He ran his hand up her arm, lowering his head to whisper in her ear. "No matter what woman lays beneath me, it is always you I see."

"Yet you left me with no word for *years*," she spat as she pushed him back.

He leaned closer. "I tried to forget you, but it was

impossible. I long for you, to feel you, to possess you. You are meant for me."

Elizabeth pushed harder, stepping back. Old feelings churned in the pit of her heart, darker feelings that no longer felt like love. "What right have you to speak this way to me?"

He grabbed hold of her arm, angered by her resistance. "Aye, such a fine lady now, are you, Mrs Darcy?" He pressed his body onto her.

"This has nothing to do with my being anything or anyone but me." She pulled back with more force.

"And you are mine." He stepped closer.

"No, I am not." She broke his hold on her by side-stepping his advance. "That was over long ago. Three years to be exact. When you left. I recall your words all too well. You said if I would not go with you then, you would not return for me. So why are you here? Why now?"

"I missed you."

She laughed. "After so long? No. I still want to know, why are you here?"

"A man is entitled to visit his home is he not, Miss— excuse me, Mrs Darcy."

"That is not my meaning. Again I ask, Mr Simmons, why are you here, at my door, at Longbourn? What do you expect after all this time?"

"I had to see you. I heard you had returned and came for you. You are unforgettable, Elizabeth." He ran his free hand through his hair. "You would love America, Lizzy. Come away with me."

WAKING TO AN EMPTY BED, DARCY THREW ON HIS breeches and shirt and, buttoning his waistcoat, went in search of his wife. Heading to the stables, he froze a moment, seeing that Simmons had come to call. He hardly had time to comprehend the scene before him when a slap against Simmons's cheek rang out.

"Even if I did not love my husband, I am not so without honour as to forsake my vows, made not a week past! Get away from here now."

Darcy ran forward just as Elizabeth turned away. Simmons, not seeing him, grabbed Elizabeth's arm, spinning her to face him and forcing her into his embrace. Elizabeth struggled, kicking him as he bent to kiss her.

"It will be over soon enough, but not before I have had my share."

Darcy grabbed Simmons's jacket, and punched him, unaware he still held Elizabeth's arm. Seeing her fall, he gasped as Simmons snatched at and ripped her bodice. As Simmons attempted to rise, he gaped at Elizabeth's uncovered flesh. Darcy growled and smashed his fist into Simmons' face, satisfied as the cur fell back onto the dirt, unconscious.

Darcy lifted Elizabeth in his arms, running them both back to Longbourn, calling to the stable hand. "Bind him, then send for the apothecary and the magistrate."

Gaining Longbourn's door, he rushed up the stairs, while calling out, "Mrs Hill, hot water, now. Please hurry."

Elizabeth blinked at him, in shock. "How could he? He said he loved me."

He halted his steps; her words cut like an assassin's blade. Anger and jealousy raged against each other in his heart. Gathering his courage, he continued to their bedchamber.

"Fitzwilliam? Please, look at me."

Darcy struggled to master his roiling emotions. Looking into her eyes, filled with the same love they had held earlier that morning, he gave her a half-smile.

"My distress is not born of my love for him, Fitzwilliam. It is that a man I thought I knew could turn so vile, so violent."

Mrs Hill arrived, a glass of sherry in her hand, followed by a kitchen maid with hot water. Elizabeth refused to let Darcy go, so he remained while she undressed, and he held her until she slept in his arms.

ELIZABETH WOKE HOURS LATER, A FIERCE WIND thrashing branches against her window. A banked fire cast a cosy glow around the familiar setting. She tugged her grandmother's quilt farther up her body, grateful for the familiar view from her window, as well as for Darcy's arms wrapped around her. He dozed, slouched against a pile of pillows, cradling her against his chest, where she had fallen asleep with the sound of his heartbeat in her ear. She cuddled closer.

Although just after noon, the storm cast dark shadows. Elizabeth felt no inclination to stir any further. She turned, placing a kiss upon his chest, needing to know he was still hers, that the morning had not diminished his love for her. She unfastened the buttons of his shirt, one by one, sliding her hand beneath the fabric. At first contact, he gasped. Looking up, she found him smiling.

"Please?" she whispered. "Let us implant new memories, your touch into my skin, into my soul."

It was a task he was apparently more than happy to fulfil. He whispered, "My love," as he kissed all the flesh she willingly offered.

Gathering her strength, she whispered in return, "I love you, Fitzwilliam Darcy, and I always will."

WAKING FROM THEIR RECUPERATIVE NAP, THEY DECIDED, rather than wasting the afternoon, to return to the library for any books Elizabeth wished to bring to Pemberley. Cataloguing the shelves, they discussed their favourite works and authors. While not surprised at the depth of his understanding, Elizabeth was pleasantly surprised at the respect he afforded her when they disagreed. She remembered her father saying that a sign of a true gentleman was the grace with which he allowed another to disagree.

Again, Darcy mentioned selling Longbourn.

"I shall think about it," she told him, "but you must see it is not my decision to make alone." He bristled, so she added, "I understand the legal aspects of this, that I no longer have as much direct say—"

"No, Elizabeth. This is your home."

She smiled. "I am glad you understand. Longbourn is our legacy and I shall not let it be treated as anything less." She spoke then of things beyond the yield of crops, horses, or tenants.

"It is not the house, is it?" Darcy spoke after a

prolonged silence. "It is where you lived, as a girl, with your family—together. After all you have done to keep your sisters together, here in your ancestral home. Now I comprehend. This, Longbourn, is your connexion to the people you love—both those who live, and those who live no more."

She nodded and smiled, grateful that he finally understood.

"What do you want done with Simmons?" he asked as he returned three first editions carefully to the shelves, though she could see that he watched her from the corner of his eye.

She picked up a book. "That is up to you, is it not? I am yours now, and he wished to take what belongs to you."

He turned to face her with a reluctant shrug. "In the eyes of the law that is correct, though I do not see it thus. Assault with the intent to…" He did not say the word. He did not need to. After a pause, he added, "There is always the way to settle things of this nature as gentlemen do."

"A duel? No. *You* would fight honourably, but after today, I am not sure he would."

Darcy kissed her forehead, and she lay her head against his heart.

"I shall speak to the magistrate before we leave tomorrow and see what must come of it," he said, then pulled back to look her in the eye. "Would that I had come sooner. I came to find you when I woke and you were not in bed." He sighed. "I was not quick enough, though I must say, the sound of your hand against his cheek was one of the most satisfying things I have ever heard. Along with the words you spoke. 'Even if I did not love my husband.' Hearing that was intoxicating, Elizabeth, and it took a moment, entirely too long, I regret, before it registered that the situation had taken a decided turn for the worse."

Elizabeth clenched her fists as her ire flared, but when she looked into his eyes, she found them filled not with braggadocio but with an innocence and such a need for reassurance that her anger melted. She held his face in her hands. "It happened so fast. I myself was unable to react sooner or more forcefully. And by then you were already there, and Jam—Mr Simmons—was on the ground, and I was safe. As I am now." She sighed. "I am glad he is returning to New York."

CHAPTER TEN

Although Elizabeth had been in Darcy House before, Darcy recognised her nervous habit of tapping her hand against her thigh. He watched her acknowledge Mrs Wilson and Giles, their housekeeper and butler. The grace with which she met the his household warmed his heart, and he joined her in giving each a brilliant smile, knowing all would be well in his home.

Over the next few days, while she seemed recovered, Darcy suspected there remained a deeper sorrow. He did not believe she mourned Simmons as a lover, but the loss of trust in a childhood friend. *Of all the circumstances in the world, this I understand. How ironic that Elizabeth has a Wickham of her own.*

"Fitzwilliam?" Elizabeth entered his study, pulling him from his thoughts. "When does Georgiana return from Matlock Manor?" She took his extended hand, giggling as he pulled her to his lap.

"I thought to have her return next week," he offered between kisses to her neck. "You think that unwise?"

Elizabeth bit her lip; he kissed it.

"Then, my dear, when would you suggest?"

"I should like to have the Gardiners and Jane for dinner later this week, if that is agreeable to you, and I should like Georgiana to attend. Do you not think she would feel more comfortable in her own home?"

"Yes, I believe she would." He toyed with one of her errant curls. "I just thought you would like more time to adjust to being my wife."

She blushed. "I appreciate your thoughtfulness. However, Georgiana needs our support now, perhaps more than she has in quite a while. I should like her to truly feel welcome here. That her home is, as it has always been, here with you."

"With us, Elizabeth." He tightened his embrace, one hand caressing her thigh, until Giles entered, announcing that lunch was served.

ELIZABETH WOKE SURROUNDED BY DARCY'S ARMS. His face still held a beatific smile, and she pressed delicate kisses on the flat, strong plane of his chest, running her hand lightly over his skin. She blushed at her abandon. They were utterly naked in his bedchamber. A candle flickered on the dressing table. Folding her hands on his chest, she perched her head upon them, contemplating her husband and the turn of her life in just three weeks. She chuckled, thinking how her uncle's problems were now resolved, and her future, which had at times seemed so bleak, was now filled with such dizzying emotion she could hardly account for it.

How have we come so far? What is it about him, about me, that makes me feel so wanton? With no compunction whatsoever! She reviewed what she of knew of him, from meeting his sister and his relations, to her uncle's enquiries. *He is a reserved man who flouts many of society's strictures, but he is neither vindictive nor cruel. Rather, a generous, just man, who speaks his mind after giving serious thought to his decisions. He is intelligent, witty even, among his intimates. Those who know him are loyal and recognise that he is the same. Yet, beyond all this, though our acquaintance is of short duration, my heart tells me this joining, this love, is right.*

Her thoughts turned darker, to Simmons's betrayal. Allowing her emotions to play through her mind, she realised that it was not any romantic feeling that lingered. Her dreams and ambitions had changed. *And then there is Fitzwilliam. And those Meryton hens can gossip all they want, it changes nothing. I am Elizabeth Darcy, and this I shall remain.* As her fingers idly skimmed Darcy's arm, she turned her thoughts to her time in London, and Blainard. *It was flattering, I suppose, that an earl offered his attentions to me. But to find his intentions, nay, his actions, were so depraved—of all the impudence! To devote so much time and effort, all for the sake of satiating his lust. How wicked some people are to seek the destruction of others with no thought, no care to their well-being!*

"Elizabeth, what is it?" Darcy embraced her, stroking her hair as it lay across her back.

Looking into his eyes, so filled with love and concern, she said, "Thank you for everything. For finding me, aiding my uncle, saving me from both Jamie and Lord

Blainard. Saving me from disaster." She exhaled and smiled up at him. "At times, I feel you have answered my prayers and made my dreams come true."

"It is no dream." He looked into her eyes. "This is how I feel, in truth, with you." He kissed her soundly, igniting a passion that lasted until dawn lit the sky. Exhausted, they slumbered once more.

THE NEXT MORNING, RATHER THAN A LETTER EXPLAINING his dealings in Meryton, Darcy's solicitor, Mr Mercer, requested a meeting. Darcy's ire was piqued at the unusual nature of his request, but he agreed.

"Mr Darcy." Mercer offered his hand. "May I offer you great joy on your recent marriage?"

Darcy thanked him, then gave his solicitor a wary glance. "What brings you to Grosvenor Square?" he asked, retaking his place behind his desk.

"I travelled to Meryton, as per your instructions. However, when I arrived, Mr Simmons was nowhere to be found."

Darcy's eyebrows shot up. "How can that be? We left but three days ago, and he was in custody on my charge!"

"Apparently, Mr Simmons has friends in high places. Very high places, sir."

"How high?"

"Unofficially, I queried the solicitor. It was Lord Vickers who initiated the petition for Simmons's release."

"For assault with the intent to… No. Impossible."

"The magistrate corroborated that the request originated from the Home Office." Pre-empting Darcy's next question, Mercer added, "He did not reveal anything further. I believe he merely saw the seal and complied."

"I see." Darcy released the breath he had been holding. "Thank you, Mercer. Is there anything else?"

"Only that once released, he did not return to Beyford, his estate. And no one has seen or heard of him since."

"Of course not."

DARCY SPENT THE GREATER PART OF THE AFTERNOON IN his study, deep in thought, while Elizabeth visited the Gardiners and Jane. He had sent word to his cousin and Henderson, who was quickly dispatched to find Simmons's current location.

A knock interrupted his thoughts. Colonel Fitzwilliam strode into the room, heading for the sideboard.

"By all means, Richard, would you care for something?"

"No, thank you, Darcy, one is enough."

Ignoring the glower Darcy levelled at him, the colonel took a seat opposite him. "What crisis do you wish me to solve for you that called me from my actual duties? All seems quiet on the home front." He placed a full glass on the desk.

Darcy let him have his moment of levity. "I need your advice."

"I could count on one hand the times you have asked me for advice, and none of them have been pleasant."

Darcy toyed with his drink. "Neither is this. Elizabeth—"

"Hold on now. I know something about women, nothing about wives." Colonel Fitzwilliam let out a nervous chuckle.

"It is not about my wife but rather a former suitor."

"What has Blainard done this time?"

Darcy sighed. "It is not Blainard."

"Elizabeth is a beautiful, vivacious woman. You would be a fool to think you were her first—"

"I shall thank you to keep your thoughts on that particular subject to yourself, and for reminding me I shall spend the rest of my days fighting off potential rivals for my beautiful wife."

"And how do you propose to do that?"

With a wicked smirk Darcy continued, "By keeping her supremely satisfied."

Colonel Fitzwilliam smiled. "Now, tell me truly, what troubles you?"

"Three years ago, Elizabeth thought herself in love with a man, a neighbour, Mr James Simmons. The man has been absent since, but he returned while we were at Longbourn. He appeared to accept our marriage at first, and that she was lost to him."

"Appeared to?"

"A few days later, he returned to Longbourn. He found Elizabeth checking one of her mares that was about to foal. He restated his feelings."

"And Elizabeth? How did she react?"

Darcy smiled. "Have you ever noticed how sweet the sound of a small hand striking the cheek of a large man can be?"

His cousin laughed outright.

"He *forced* his lips upon hers, and likely would have attempted more, except—"

"You stopped him."

"I did. I came around to the stables just in time to hear him clearly state that his plan was 'to have his share.'"

Fitzwilliam whistled, low and long. "Men have swung from the noose for less."

"We left Simmons in the hands of the magistrate when we returned to town. I sent Mercer to Meryton to persuade Simmons to leave the country."

"Damned merciful of you."

Darcy launched out of his chair to pace in front of the fire. "Mercer applied to the magistrate and found Simmons had been released in response to a diplomatic entreaty. His whereabouts is unknown. I have Henderson after him." He went to the sideboard and refilled his glass.

"Does Elizabeth know?"

"No. She is visiting her relations. I shall tell her upon her return. I intend on having one of our larger footmen escort her about town until further notice."

"What do you want from me?"

"I want to know why someone with diplomatic connexions would intervene on Simmons's behalf. Who protects him, and why?"

"Where did you say he is from?"

"Originally from Meryton, in Hertfordshire, the same as Elizabeth. Now, however, he lives in America. In New York."

Fitzwilliam studied Darcy. "I shall make enquiries.

What does the chap look like? Any distinguishing features?"

"Tall, broad in the shoulders, blond hair, tanned skin, and green eyes. Sits well in the saddle.."

"Very observant of you."

"Faced with a rival, one takes note of these things."

"Indeed!" Colonel Fitzwilliam gulped the remains of his glass. "Right then, I shall be on my way."

"You will not stay for dinner?"

"I shall not interrupt your honeymoon." He began moving to the door. "Although I understand Georgiana returns before the week is out."

"Yes, Elizabeth insists on it."

Fitzwilliam knocked on the door he held in his hand, "Good. I think being in Mrs Darcy's company will do her a world of good. Your wife has already raised *your* spirits to dazzling heights." With a twinkle in his eye, he exited before Darcy could berate him for his feeble humour.

When Elizabeth returned from the Gardiners' home, her smile failed to meet her eyes. Darcy noted this and tried to engage her, but she would not speak.

"Not yet," she said. "I need time to work things out before I speak to anyone. Jane would get so angry with me, but I cannot help it. It is simply the way I have always been."

Her smile melted his trepidation, encouraging him to speak. "Is it anything I have done?"

Taking his hand to her lips, she shook her head, then patted his hand. "No, my love, it is not you. It is all that has swirled around me before and after our marriage that causes me such…not pain, not exactly, but doubt." She sat, and he joined her on the sofa. "I simply cannot understand what I did to warrant such treatment."

"Nothing! You did nothing, Elizabeth. Blainard is a cur. He was born that way and will, undoubtedly, die that way. As for Simmons, I cannot say what brought about such shocking behaviour. But I know you are blameless."

"Am I?" she whispered. "I wish I could be so sure. Everything I thought I knew has been shredded by all this."

"Everything? Even us?"

"No, you have become the one constant in my life." She smiled. "How odd life is. Only one month ago we were not even acquaintances."

"Yes, strange and wondrous."

"Indeed." Their kisses delayed further conversation until the dinner bell rang.

Lying in each other's arms that night, Elizabeth noted Darcy's distraction. Running her hand along his chest, she worried when he remained in his thoughts. "This is not a good sign for our marital felicity."

"Of what do you speak?"

"My failure to entice you away from whatever burdens your mind. What is it?"

"My solicitor came to see me this morning. I had sent him to take care of the matter with Simmons."

She kissed him. "Thank you, my darling."

"When he went to the gaol, Simmons was gone."

She pushed up to a sitting position. "Gone? What do you mean, gone? How can he be gone?"

He pulled her back to him, but she resisted. "Someone wrote, petitioning for his release. Mercer was only able to trace it to the Home Office."

"That cannot be."

"According to the magistrate, I am afraid it is."

"But how? Who would petition for Jamie's release? From the *Meryton* gaol? How could they even know so quickly that he had been incarcerated?"

"I do not know. But I shall find out."

Nodding, she looked away, digesting the information. He sat up, closing the distance to run his hand along the line of her jaw. "Elizabeth, I shall not allow him to harm or even come near you. Until this matter is resolved, Robert and Steven will accompany you when you go out, agreed?"

"Agreed."

"Do not despair, my darling. Whatever is to come, we shall face together."

She looked into his eyes for a long time, till he opened his arms, and she settled into his warm embrace.

"No harm will come to you, Elizabeth. I could not bear the pain."

They held each other until the dawn dispelled the dark of night, and the only sound heard was the crackle of the dying fire.

CHAPTER ELEVEN

The morning was brilliant, the breeze full of the season's perfume. Lady Matlock looked at her niece as they rode back to Darcy House. Though Georgiana's face remained impassive, there was a nervous cast to her eyes. *Mayhap it is too soon to return her. It has been only three weeks since Darcy married, and to share living quarters with newlyweds? Although I believe Elizabeth will be brilliant in bringing Georgiana back to life, I worry how it will be until then. At least Elizabeth has met Georgiana and knows her history. I trust her to be kind.* In truth, that was all she could hope for.

Darcy and Elizabeth waited for them at the front door. Both offered wide, full smiles of welcome. With a telling look to his wife, Darcy descended to greet his relations.

"Welcome home, Georgiana. Aunt, it is good of you to see our sister home."

"Darcy, Elizabeth," Lady Matlock greeted her relations, filling her smile with gratitude.

Georgiana followed two steps behind. "Brother, Mrs Darcy," she offered, her voice dull, as if speaking was a heavy burden.

Elizabeth gave Darcy a quick glance. "We are very happy you have returned, Georgiana. I am especially glad, for while your brother attends to his abundant business matters, I am left to while away the hours. Now we shall bide the time together." She gave Georgiana a wide smile that reached her eyes. Taking the girl by the arm, she took her into the warmth of their shared home. Darcy offered Lady Matlock his arm, and together they followed the young ladies inside.

They settled in the morning parlour, the windows and doors open to the fresh breeze and gentle morning light. Georgiana took a deep breath upon entering.

"It is an eternity since these have been opened, Darcy. I am impressed," Lady Matlock said, looking purposefully at Elizabeth. "And surprised I did not suggest it earlier. It makes the room so bright and uplifting."

Elizabeth smiled. "When Darcy gave me a tour of the house, I fell in love with these rooms at first sight."

"There are matching doors to Lady Anne's—I mean, the mistress's study, are there not?" Lady Matlock asked.

"Indeed, there are," Darcy replied.

Georgiana finally sat, only to then jump up with a startled, "Oh!"

Elizabeth rushed to her side. "Georgiana, I am so sorry. Here, allow me."

"What is it, dear?" Lady Matlock took her niece's hand.

"My embroidery." Elizabeth blushed, holding the fabric in her hand.

"May I have a look?" Georgiana gently took the fabric from Elizabeth.

"Yes, of course, although I admit handiwork is not my greatest accomplishment. It is not very good."

"Oh, but it is. That is to say, this is lovely, Mrs Darcy, truly."

"Please, dear, we are sisters now. I hope you would feel comfortable calling me Elizabeth." In a low whisper, Elizabeth added, "When you feel comfortable."

Lady Matlock examined the pieces in Elizabeth's work basket. "My dear, these are strange garments for a grown woman to work on." She held up a smock large enough for a girl of fifteen.

Elizabeth blushed. "They are not for me. They are for an orphanage."

"I see." Her ladyship smiled approvingly.

"My aunt Gardiner has always said that giving a little beauty to those who have so little is a good thing. It is because of her that I continue on, feeble as my attempts are." She indicated the contents of the workbox.

Georgiana, examining one of the smocks, spoke in her soft voice. "How wonderful. You sketch in the design to fill in later with thread?"

Elizabeth nodded.

"Would it be too much trouble to teach me how to do the same?"

"It would be no trouble at all. Perhaps you would

help me create a new design? I admit, I have had just about enough of primroses and ivy."

They all laughed.

"If I may leave you, ladies?" Darcy interjected. "Business awaits. I shall see you at dinner, then? Aunt, will you join us?"

Looking at her nieces, Lady Matlock replied, "I must return home. I thank you for your kind offer, and return it in asking you three to join us the day after tomorrow for dinner?"

"That would be lovely," Darcy answered. He then left his female relations to themselves.

GEORGIANA SETTLED EASILY BACK INTO LIFE AT DARCY House. The last two years had taught her to rely on the whisperings of her heart to untangle the meaning of what was said and what was left unsaid. She detected an unease between Elizabeth and Fitzwilliam. Watching her brother and his wife from the corner of her eye, what she saw was distressing.

Elizabeth, when she seemed to think no one was watching, would sit, her embroidery inert in her listless hands, confusion clouding her eyes. Or she would look off in the distance, as though searching for a solution to an unnamed, unspoken problem. When someone caught her attention, she would smile, but more often than not, it did not reach her eyes. She also noted that Robert and Steven accompanied her sister whenever she went out, whether for walks in the park, visits to Bond Street and the book shops, or to the Gardiners' for tea.

Her brother's reaction was even more telling. When

sitting with Elizabeth, he appeared relaxed. They touched almost constantly, and he rarely let her out of his sight. It was the rare times Georgiana caught him reading a book or attending his correspondence that she could tell something was amiss. *He seemed so happy at his wedding. Now, he is preoccupied, distressed.*

Unsure of what she could actually do, the urge to help deepened. Especially Elizabeth, who had been extremely patient with her, never forcing her beyond that with which she was comfortable, always willing to laugh and make light of the situation. After gathering the courage to uncover what was bothering her sister, she found Elizabeth in her study. While struggling to contain her anxiety, Georgiana knocked on the half-opened door.

"Mrs Darcy, may I come in?"

"Of course, dear. Is there anything amiss?" Elizabeth walked over to her.

"No, I only wished to see you." She entered what had been her mother's refuge. "You have done a lovely job redecorating."

"It was your brother's work. He asked my aunt for my favourite colours and had the walls redone in a pattern he thought I would like."

"It suits you."

Elizabeth smiled. "Thank you. Come, sit with me. Tell me what brings you to me."

Georgiana took her seat, wringing her hands longer than she wished. After a brief lapse of anxious silence, she inhaled, nodded, and then spoke, her voice a laboured whisper. "I know you know of my past. I appreciate that you have never condescended to me, even that first afternoon we met. You, a complete stranger, came to me with no judgment. I do not know if you understand how precious that is to me."

Elizabeth nodded, her smile wider, her eyes softer.

"I have sensed there is something that troubles you, and I wish to be here for you, as you were for me... S-Sister."

Elizabeth embraced her. Overcoming her surprise, Georgiana relaxed and returned the hug. Pulling back, she was startled by Elizabeth's tears.

"Mrs Darcy—Elizabeth, what is it? Should I summon Fitzwilliam?"

Elizabeth shook her head.

"Will you not tell me what upsets you so?"

Elizabeth walked to the mantel, looking at her hands. "Georgiana, I have been such a fool."

Georgiana felt a pang of alarm, which Elizabeth seemed to comprehend.

"Oh, not with your brother. It is the treachery of others that burdens me."

"Will you tell me what happened?" Georgiana asked softly.

"I shall not lie to you. You are so young yet have such understanding, have carried such pain." Elizabeth took a deep breath. "Three years ago, I fancied myself in love with a neighbour, Mr Simmons. He told me he loved me and asked me to marry him, to leave England and sail to America with him. I could not. My sisters and I had only recently lost our parents. And our stables, Noah's Promise, were prospering. We, that is my sisters and I, after all we had endured...for me to abandon them—" Elizabeth's voice cracked. "I could not. Terrible things were said about me in my village, that I was heartless to lead him on only to spurn him. But it was not him I spurned, it was leaving my home, my family, what was left of it. I just could not."

She broke into tears. "They, his family, my neighbours, taunted me for weeks, ceasing only after he left, which was mercifully soon. Slowly, I began to put my heart back in order. The gossips moved on to the next hapless victim. Fortunately, my younger sisters were away at school and were spared the worst of our town's cruelty. Jane and I grew even closer, and we were both grateful the horses required frequent travel."

Georgiana looked confused. "Do they?"

Elizabeth smirked. "Many noblemen enjoy riding and consider themselves proficient, but, in truth, they are completely clueless about how to bring forth the best in their horses. They are willing to pay excellent money for us to instruct them and their groomsmen in our particular methods."

"Surely you and your sister did not, *do* not groom the horses yourselves?"

"No, not really. We breed them, of course, and work the colts with our own brand of training, acclimating them to receiving commands, that sort of thing. They stay with us until they are proficient with humans. We almost always accompany them to their new homes, to oversee their adjustment, as well as receive payment."

"Oh, I see."

"Our steward accompanies us. Each delivery became a holiday of sorts, one we all sorely needed. Jane and I would take in any historical sites, or any particularly striking views. Anything to keep us out of Meryton at that point, until the rumours completely ceased, which was not until six months after Mr Simmons left."

"I can understand your reluctance not to leave the comforts of your sisters and familiarity of your home to go with him at the time, but pray, what has you so distressed now?"

"He has returned to England and was there when your brother and I arrived at Longbourn. We met him on an afternoon ride."

"Oh no!"

"Oh yes, I am afraid. At first, everyone was civil, and I thought we would escape any unpleasantness. However, on the morning before we were to depart, Mr Simmons returned to Longbourn while I was at the stables alone."

When Georgiana squeezed her hand a bit harder, Elizabeth asked, "Are you sure you wish to hear this?"

Looking as intent and stubborn as her brother, Georgiana nodded. "Yes. If you were able to bear it, I am able to hear about it."

Elizabeth nodded. "He said he still loved me. After three years without one word between us and knowing that I was married. He asked me to leave with him."

Georgiana gasped.

"I told him that even if I did not love my husband, I would not, *could not* abandon him, or my vows. Words were exchanged, and he attempted to kiss me against my will. After I slapped him, of course."

"You did not!"

"I most certainly did. I was not raised to take such abuse, and perhaps all the anger from his leaving just exploded. He implied all sorts of terrible things. I do not believe that a kiss was all he desired." Elizabeth became quiet, and when she spoke again, she was subdued. "I struggled and tried to break away, but I could not."

Georgiana asked, gently, "Then what happened?"

"Your dashing, darling, wonderful brother, is what happened. He came, and he rescued me." She grinned. "Later, he told me it was the sweetest sound, hearing my hand connect with Mr Simmons's cheek." They shared a smile. "Physically I am fine," she said. "But I just wonder, why did this happen to me? I feel ashamed."

"You did nothing to be ashamed of," Georgiana said urgently. "He was an old acquaintance who abused your trust and your good nature. His misdeeds are not your fault."

"I know this in my mind, Georgiana." She turned her head. "Yet I feel it is my fault. That is what my heart tells me."

Georgiana put her arm around Elizabeth. "I know. Truly, I understand. As one who has stood in your shoes, I know how it feels." She offered a slight smile before looking away. "Believe me, I know how difficult it is to recall this small but incredibly important fact. But you must remember, it was not—it *is not*—your fault."

They embraced, eyes closed, hearts full of this new understanding of each other and themselves. When they pulled apart, their smiles were full.

"We shall have to remind each other often then, shall we not?"

"We shall indeed, Elizabeth."

"There is more, and I promise to tell you, but I would ask to postpone that for another day."

"Agreed. I believe one wound to heal per day is my limit."

"I am very grateful it was my turn today."

They smiled and rang for tea. Darcy soon found them, expressing his pleasure at finding them at ease with each other.

DARCY SPENT THE AFTERNOON IN CONVERSATION WITH Mr Gardiner, seeking advice on Elizabeth's behaviour and on handling Simmons. The older gentleman expressed his horror when Darcy briefed him on the events that had marred his honeymoon.

"There is more." Darcy looked to his new uncle who sat, pensively regarding him. "It concerns Blainard. It is he who encouraged and enabled Whitecastle to gamble so far beyond his means. It was he who recommended embezzlement to pay off the accrued debts."

"I will kill him. He recommended endangering my family!" Mr Gardiner pushed himself up out of his chair, marching to the sideboard. Pouring a glass of brandy, he drank it down, then offered one to Darcy, who accepted.

"Blainard aimed to use this to force Elizabeth's hand."

Mr Gardiner gulped down the rest of his drink and slammed the glass on his desk. Then, deflated, shook his head and asked weakly, "How do you know this?"

"You recall when we announced our engagement?"

Mr Gardiner nodded.

"I found his reaction…off. A man who aided me during the Wickham disaster, well, I had him trail Blainard. After a few drinks and a few nights of heavy gaming, his lordship revealed all. He was rather despondent that his plans had come to naught when Elizabeth accepted my hand."

"Thank God for that," Mr Gardiner said firmly. "I cannot fathom that he would go to all that trouble."

"Elizabeth is a rare jewel."

"That she is. But to ruin my family, and all those who are dependent upon us for their livelihood, all because he wished to bed…," Mr Gardiner cringed, his hands curling into fists.

"To Blainard and his ilk, it is a game. As you or I would move pieces on a chess board, he believes he can move people."

"Darcy, I do thank you for all you have done for me and my family."

"I may safely say that almost from the first time I laid eyes on Elizabeth, she was part of me. Since then, you, by extension, have been part of me, part of my family."

JANE BENNET AND MRS GARDINER ARRIVED AT DARCY House for tea the next afternoon. The windows and doors were open to the lovely spring day and the terraced courtyard. Elizabeth was finally ready to relay the pertinent events of her honeymoon. Her relations were as dismayed as she might have expected, but she hurried them past distress and weeping. She had done enough of it in the past days to last a lifetime.

"There is something else, something we must discuss as a family. Mr Darcy has raised the idea of selling or leasing Longbourn."

"What did you tell him?" Jane asked.

Looking at her sister, Elizabeth took her hand. "I

told him it was not my decision alone to make. Longbourn is our legacy and will be treated as such."

"Good girl," Mrs Gardiner said.

"He did discuss with Mr Hill the idea of leasing Longbourn." Elizabeth saw her sister grow distressed. "Jane, what is it?"

"Where would we go? I love you dearly, but I would not want to impose upon you constantly. And what of our sisters? Mary is almost done with her studies, and Kitty and Lydia? That is too much to ask, even of you."

"You would all come to Pemberley. Mr Darcy would find a small estate in the county and we would purchase it."

Mrs Gardiner interjected, "That is very generous of him, but—"

"No, not Mr Darcy, *us*, we Bennets. Legally, he is involved in the decision, but he has given me every assurance that it will be my, *our* family's decision. However, he does insist on having his say."

They all chuckled.

"But he recognises how important it is to us. He made the suggestion of leasing Longbourn. We could use the money from that, plus the savings we have accrued from Noah's Promise, to purchase something so we may all remain together. If need be, we can borrow from Mr Darcy and pay him back, as we did with Uncle Gardiner. Only this time, we shall have two, no, three sources of income instead of just the one."

Mrs Gardiner looked at her niece with approval.

Jane said, "Lizzy, once you remove to the north, there is not much holding us to Hertfordshire, is there? It is an idea with merit. I should like to hear more."

"Well, first we must find an estate that is right for us, then advertise that Longbourn is available, and of course, speak with our sisters."

"They will be home in another month. We could meet then."

"I was hoping that you would all consider spending some time at Pemberley this summer. It would give us all a chance to become acquainted and perhaps look around. I know it is much to consider, but just think about it, Jane. Aunt, you and Uncle Gardiner are invited to join us as well."

Mrs Gardiner arched a sceptic brow.

"For part of the time, at least. Perhaps you could turn it into a vacation. The Peak, I hear, is lovely."

Mrs Gardiner laughed. "Of course. I cannot imagine your uncle letting this go by without something akin to *his* say in the matter."

The ladies laughed, and this was how the gentlemen found them. Darcy brought Mr Bingley with him to the drawing room.

"Elizabeth, look who has come to call." Darcy came to his wife. "Ladies, you recall my friend, Bingley?"

"Mr Bingley was kind enough to call upon us at Gracechurch Street after your wedding." Mrs Gardiner informed them.

Jane's cheeks were covered in a furious blush. Elizabeth and Darcy looked at each other with raised brows, then turned their gaze upon their caller.

"Did you? I had no notion," Darcy said to his friend, whose blush echoed Jane's.

"I thought Miss Bennet might need some entertainment after losing her sister on such short notice."

"Indeed," said Darcy.

"Would you care for tea?" Elizabeth asked, and the gentlemen settled in for the visit. The afternoon was full of lively conversation and the making of plans to visit various galleries and museums in the coming weeks.

CHAPTER TWELVE

Georgiana trailed her fingers over the top of the armchair, to the edge of the side tables, to the soft velvet of the cushions casually tossed in the corner of the sofa. But nothing could calm her nerves. Today, she was venturing out of her home to Bond Street. Even though she was going to La Celeste, the modiste who had dressed her since she was a child, the notion of encountering the women of the *ton* as they shopped was enough to turn her stomach. Seeing Elizabeth's work basket, she picked up the half-finished smock. *Elizabeth is trying the bluebells.*

Her sister entered the room, moments ahead of their butler.

"The carriage awaits, Mrs Darcy," he informed them.

"Thank you, Giles."

He bowed and left.

"Are you well, Georgiana?" Elizabeth asked. "I shall

send word to postpone our appointment for another day."

"No." Georgiana gripped her hands together. "I am well."

"You are sure?"

"Yes. I wish to go."

"Very well." Smiling, Elizabeth linked their arms and they headed to the carriage.

When it stopped at a street Georgiana did not recognise, in front of a building she had never seen before, her eyes widened, and her breath grew shallow.

"I shall be but a few minutes, Georgiana. I must speak with Miss Adams. Are you sure you do not mind waiting?"

"Of course," she replied, looking about curiously. "Where are we?"

"St Magdalene's."

"Oh." Georgiana lowered her eyes. As her sister left the carriage, she looked about the well-appointed cabin, thinking of how much she admired Elizabeth for all she did and all she was unafraid to do. Tired of languishing in her own regrets and failures, Georgiana decided to obey her impulse. *Deep breaths, Georgiana. In*— she inhaled —*and out*. Then she placed her bonnet on her head, and with one more steadying breath, unlatched the coach's door, surprising the groom.

"Miss Darcy?" he asked, moving quickly to assist her.

Struggling against her desire to flee back into the carriage, she took a deep breath, pushed her shoulders back, and kept her head high. "I am going in. Mrs Darcy and I have an appointment."

Sending a sceptical look to the driver, the groom

aided her descent and followed her as she walked to the impressive door. It took her several minutes to reach it. *I am looking for Elizabeth. I shall not stay—they will not force me to.* With each passer-by, Georgiana jumped, feeling every eye upon her, judging her. *Get a hold of yourself! Honestly! You are a Darcy. And it is only a door.*

With that, she opened the heavy oak barrier, crossing the threshold onto a marble floor. While clean, the building was worn. Georgiana breathed in the cool air, smiling at the light-infused hall. The sounds of industry beckoned, and she headed to the hallway where women of various ages bustled about.

"Excuse me?" she finally spoke as a young woman passed by.

"Yes? May I help you?" the young woman asked. Her strawberry-blonde hair was piled austerely on her head. Her dress was not new or fashionable but flattered her tall frame. And she was pretty, with kind eyes, which, while a bit sad, still held the spark of life.

"I am looking for my sister, Mrs Darcy."

"Ah, yes. The Miss Lizzy that was." The woman smiled brilliantly, and Georgiana could see how she would catch the eye of a predatory male. She shuddered at the accident of birth that protected her from such a fate. The young lady placed a gentle hand on Georgiana's arm. "She is with Miss Adams. If you please, follow me."

They walked in silence past a room of young women sewing and another where a school of sorts was underway, then through a courtyard of various herbs and flowers. Finally, they arrived at the nursery, where the newly born slept or cooed in cots. Elizabeth, holding a swaddled infant, spoke with two women. The older, about the age of Lady Matlock, had her arm around the younger, to support her. All three looked at the babe, resting comfortably in Elizabeth's arms.

Georgiana stopped, overcome by the rows of cots filled with babies of all shapes and sizes, the result of these women's shame. Innocent, hidden away, just like the woman who stood alongside Elizabeth, looking pale and worn. *What do they discuss? Names for the child? Or where they will be sent?* Feeling her knees buckle, Georgiana reached blindly for aid, as the young woman whispered, "It is a bit much, the first time in the nursery."

Georgiana met her eyes and found understanding and compassion—qualities she was only just experiencing for herself. She nodded, and the woman smiled.

"Meredith?" the older woman called.

"Yes, Miss Adams. This young lady wished to see Miss El—I mean, Mrs Darcy."

Elizabeth looked up, smiling when she saw Georgiana. Coming over, she took her sister's arm, and with a warm, grateful smile, she said, "Thank you. This is my dear sister, Miss Georgiana Darcy. Georgiana, this is Miss Meredith Whitcomb."

The young women curtseyed to each other, then Miss Whitcomb took her leave. "The girls will need their lessons checked."

Elizabeth and Georgiana watched her depart. Elizabeth explained, "Meredith is now a midwife and instructs some of the women in the art. She has turned her tragedy into a source of strength. She gives these young women, like herself, the knowledge to return to the world with an honest trade, one of which they may be proud. They may even, in some cases, return to their families or reside nearby and resume lives within society." She then added, almost to herself, "They are all so very brave."

Georgiana nodded, agreeing wholeheartedly.

Elizabeth turned to Miss Adams. "I shall bring your concerns to my aunts, Mrs Gardiner and Lady Matlock."

"Thank you, Mrs Darcy."

"It is my pleasure. And now," Elizabeth said, "we must make haste. Madame Lestrat will be angry if we are late."

THE NEXT WEEK, GEORGIANA AND ELIZABETH WERE availing themselves of the refreshments after hearing the naturalist, Smithson, give a talk on Thomas Nuttall at King George Hall.

"Is it not amazing how exciting he made those rocks sound?"

"Exciting?" Elizabeth giggled. "I am unsure I would say that." She rolled her eyes at her sister's enthusiasm, but she was glad to have brought her, for it was one of the first times Georgiana had expressed a wish to go into society since she returned home.

"And how well he read the account of America," Georgiana said with a sigh. "Even though he has not stepped on its soil himself. It sounds so fascinating. Can you imagine what it must feel like to create a new society? Think of it—an entirely clean slate, a place where no one knows your past. Wondrous."

Wondrous indeed, Georgiana. Elizabeth bit her lower lip.

At least she is entertaining the idea of a new beginning. Is this not the first step to redemption? "Come, my dear, let us examine the natural wonders Mr Nuttall has sent to feed our imaginations." The two women meandered through the exhibition, marvelling at the strange plants and animals on display. Ahead of them were two women speaking in French.

"Clarice, cette fleur est magnifique! Est-ce un crocus? Il est parfait. Je vais l'intégrer dans mes creations de printemps." Madame Lestrat indicated a beautiful camellia blossom both on the small tree in front of her as well as the illustrations chronicling the plant's natural cycle.

"Oui, Tante Celeste."

"Madame Lestrat?" Elizabeth greeted the startled woman. "What a pleasure to see you. And Mademoiselle Clarice, is it not?" She smiled at the younger woman, giving her a welcoming smile.

"Oui, Madame Darcy." The older woman curtseyed. Elizabeth knew that Madame Lestrat had likely espied a number of her clients at the lecture but wondered how many deigned to greet her and her niece.

"Are you admirers of America?" Elizabeth asked.

"My niece is, madame." Madame Lestrat linked the young woman's arm with hers.

"Shall we continue together and brave the wilds of the New World?" Elizabeth asked.

The four women meandered through the exhibit, enjoying the displays, unearthing the surprising depth of knowledge the younger women had on the subject. Elizabeth offered an invitation to the women for tea.

"I am sorry, but we must return to the shop. It is only Clarice's passion for the subject that induced me to abandon my work these few hours. But thank you for your kind offer."

"Perhaps another time."

"Yes."

"Mademoiselle Clarice?" Georgiana hesitated.

"Yes, Miss Darcy?"

"Thank you for the list of books. I shall ask my brother to find them for me. Perhaps…" Georgiana bit her lip before continuing. "Perhaps we might continue our discussion again in the future?"

Clarice smiled broadly. "Yes, I should enjoy that Miss Darcy, very much."

Georgiana nodded, and her smile remained well past tea. Darcy remarked upon it later that evening, and she enthusiastically recalled the events of her day.

Taking Elizabeth in his arms, Darcy kissed her. "Thank you for taking the time to not only note Georgiana's interest but help her step back into society."

LATER THAT EVENING, AT BROOKS'S, MR OSWALD shared a bottle of brandy with Lord Blainard.

"Damn interesting lecture this afternoon, at King George's Hall," Oswald said, sipping his beverage.

"You know I do not share your enthusiasm for rebellious subjects or their savage land."

Oswald looked at his red-cheeked companion, whose condescending, sour expression did nothing to enhance his appearance. "A shame, really, for it was the most interesting crowd."

The earl replied with a disinterested grunt.

"The Darcy women were in attendance." He sneered

when Blainard's eyebrows shot up, and he readjusted himself in his seat. "It was...strange."

"Strange? How?" Blainard asked eagerly.

"She spoke, quite energetically, with that French dressmaker. Whom, it is rumoured, is related to Darcy's mistress."

Oswald noticed, with an educated eye, Blainard's reaction. *Lust or anger? I cannot tell. I have been his partner on too many an adventure and know the two emotions are well mixed in his being.* Oswald puffed hungrily on his cigar. "Shame that all fell through. I was quite looking forward to sharing Miss Bennet with you."

"I have a new prize in mind now," his lordship replied. "A piece of French pastry, sweet and light. It will only be a matter of time before I persuade her to my needs."

Oswald's eyes flared. "For a price?"

"For a price, my dear Oswald. Always for a price." Blainard smirked. "And as you know, I am a generous man who knows that sharing is caring."

Oswald smiled wickedly. "Well then, my friend, I wish you luck in capturing your French tart."

THE DARCYS EMBARKED ON THEIR ANNUAL PILGRIMAGE to Rosings Park at Easter to see their aunt, Lady Catherine de Bourgh. While never a pleasurable visit, since the *débâcle*, it had become an unbearable obligation. This year, the journey was marked by smiles and laughter. Elizabeth and Georgiana continued their handiwork, while Darcy read aloud from *The Taming of the Shrew*.

"How my sisters loved to call me Kate," Elizabeth chuckled.

"I do not believe it," Georgiana cried as she tied off a silk strand on a lovely shawl.

Elizabeth laughed. "But you have not seen me attempting to subdue two errant sisters from pulling at each other while Reverend Markham completed his sermon."

"You may have to employ those self-same skills when listening to Mr Collins," Darcy said.

"I was so hoping he had improved with time and the careful ministrations of my friend Charlotte."

"You are familiar with Mrs Collins?" asked Georgiana.

"Oh yes. Charlotte is my dearest friend outside of my family."

"How could you let her…" Georgiana stopped.

Elizabeth suppressed her giggle. "Marry my cousin?"

"Mr Collins is your cousin?" Georgiana asked.

"I am afraid so."

"This will be a most interesting visit, indeed," Darcy said, as the carriage filled with delightful giggles.

UPON THEIR ARRIVAL, THEY WERE GREETED BY A discomfited Colonel Fitzwilliam and the imperious Lady Catherine.

"Darcy! There you are. Welcome to Rosings," the great lady said. "We expected you hours ago."

Darcy handed out his sister, giving her an encouraging smile, then held tight to Elizabeth's hand. As she glimpsed his formidable aunt, she returned his grip, understanding his need for succour.

With a disapproving scowl, which Elizabeth had been told was Lady Catherine's usual expression, her ladyship addressed her guests. "Georgiana, how pale you are. Come now, you must get inside before you catch a chill."

"Yes, ma'am." She hurried to her cousin, who took her arm and kissed her forehead.

"Are you ready for this, Elizabeth?" Darcy asked in a low whisper.

Looking to her husband, then his aunt, she returned the whisper. "You know me, sir, my courage rises at each and every attempt at intimidation."

Ascending the steps, Elizabeth and Darcy were halted as Lady Catherine stepped in front of them. "And this, I presume, is Mrs Darcy."

"It is a pleasure to finally meet you, Lady Catherine."

"Aunt, may I present my wife, Mrs Elizabeth Darcy?"

Lady Catherine sniffed. "If you must."

Darcy's muscles stiffened under Elizabeth's hand. "If you prefer, madam, we shall save the servants the trouble of unpacking and depart at once."

Lady Catherine stared down at her nephew, who held his ground. Elizabeth looked between the two of them, relying on Darcy's understanding of the situation. Finally, the older woman relented and stepped aside.

"Come inside then, before we all catch cold." Lady Catherine quickly turned into the grand house.

"Where is Anne?" Georgiana asked, sipping the tea provided for their arrival.

An odd smile came over her aunt's countenance. "She is out, riding."

"Riding?" Darcy asked. "Alone?"

"Of course not. I am not so careless as to allow impropriety of any kind."

Darcy looked to Richard for enlightenment. "I do not know, Darcy. I arrived only moments before you. I thought Anne indisposed."

"Certainly not!" retorted Lady Catherine and, as if on cue, in walked Anne de Bourgh, flushed and smiling, on the arm of Lord Blainard.

CHAPTER THIRTEEN

"There you are, my dear." Lady Catherine gave her frail child a vacuous smile. "How was your ride? Do come and sit by the fire. Would you care for some tea? Lord Blainard, something stronger, perhaps? Darcy will fetch it for you."

The hair on the back of Elizabeth's neck stood on end, and she glanced at her husband, who glared at his aunt. Darting her eyes to Colonel Fitzwilliam and Georgiana, she found the same, hard-eyed glower on both. Even Anne looked embarrassed. Only Blainard wore a satisfied smirk as he walked to the fire before turning his predatory gaze upon Elizabeth. His hand went to his mouth, and he ran his forefinger between his lips, appraising her from her feet to her head. Elizabeth stiffened when his leer focused on her bosom. A panic grew in her heart when she noted a wildness in his demeanour —his cravat was rumpled, and he threw his head back then refixed his attention on her person. It was unnerving and hinted at danger.

"No, nothing, Darcy. Tea suits me. Along with the fair company, of course."

"If you will excuse me, I need to rest," Elizabeth announced, setting down her cup.

"Of course," said Lady Catherine, who appeared to have caught Blainard's wayward attention, for she was peering at him unhappily. Turning to her daughter, she said, "Anne, ring for Martins. He will show you to your rooms," she said to Elizabeth without looking at her. She waited until her daughter returned from calling the butler. "Anne, this is—"

"My *wife*, Mrs Elizabeth Darcy." Darcy's eyes bored into Blainard.

"A pleasure, Mrs Darcy." There was more warmth in Anne's response than Elizabeth expected.

"Thank you, Miss de Bourgh."

"Please, call me Anne. We are family, after all."

"Indeed," replied Elizabeth. "Then you must call me Elizabeth."

Anne's smile lit up her frail features. Elizabeth returned it, delighted by the sincere welcome from at least one of Rosings's residents.

Anne then went to her cousin and kissed his cheek and wished him joy. Elizabeth's heart swelled to see Darcy's surprise and pleasure.

When Martins entered, Georgiana, the Darcys, and Colonel Fitzwilliam voiced their desire to refresh themselves. Lady Catherine waved them off before turning her attention to Blainard, who took a seat near Anne.

With Georgiana and Elizabeth three steps ahead,

Darcy asked the colonel, "Did you know anything about this?"

"Not a clue."

"As I never imagined Blainard to be here in Kent, I let Robert and Steven return to their families. I want Elizabeth accompanied at all times by one of us."

"And Georgiana?"

"Let us hope she stays close enough to Elizabeth to make our lives easier."

The colonel snorted, earning curious glances from his female kinsfolk.

"ARE YOU WELL, ELIZABETH?" DARCY ASKED, ONCE THEY were inside their chambers.

She smiled, but she wrung her hands one in the other, as if keeping them under regulation. "As well as can be expected. I heard that you and the colonel were unaware of Lord Blainard's invitation."

"I was as shocked as you."

"I must say, I do not believe Blainard's sudden sociability is coincidental."

"Nor do I." He brought her hands to his lips one at a time. "But we have at least one advantage. He is unaware that we know of his involvement with White-castle and what his plans were. We are armed with that knowledge."

She crossed her arms and nodded.

"I want you to always have either me or Richard accompany you, wherever you go. If possible, I would prefer Georgiana be with you as well." Elizabeth arched her brow questioningly, so he added, "As you know,

Robert and Steven are with their families, so there are only Richard and myself, and your cooperation will make things much easier.

"How I hate this." She turned to face the window.

"As do I, my love." He came to her side.

"When will it ever end?"

He closed his arms about her and said, "I do not know. But I promise I shall do all in my power to keep you from harm. She tightened her arms around him and looked up. Her eyes drew his lips, and he willingly obliged.

DINNER WAS EXTRAORDINARY. BLAINARD, SEATED opposite Lady Catherine, held court, and her stupefied nephews gaped as her ladyship deferred to his opinions. Anne sat to his right, Georgiana to his left, with Mrs Jenkinson opposite Elizabeth, leaving Darcy and Fitzwilliam to flank the grand dame herself. Both gentlemen were stunned as Lady Catherine shouted across the length of her table to the man she most assuredly pushed at Anne. Anne, evidently basking in the attention, engaged in more conversation than Elizabeth had anticipated. A small, almost secret smile played upon her lips.

If I did not know better, I would think she has an understanding with him. Elizabeth sipped her wine and, feeling her husband's intense eyes upon her, looked up and smiled. She then looked to Georgiana's end of the table to assess her comfort, relieved to find her sister holding her own. As her eyes glanced over the table, Elizabeth met the lust-filled gaze of Blainard and froze. His eyes devoured her, and he slowly and deliberately licked his lips. Looking to Darcy for reassurance, Elizabeth caught his scowl at Blainard's reptilian leer.

Colonel Fitzwilliam broke the rising tension. "Aunt, I hear your parson has a new wife. Tell me, what kind of woman is she?" With steadfast charm, he led the conversation, for which Elizabeth was grateful, for it gave her time to regain her composure. She looked across the table, grateful for the concern in Darcy's eyes, and nodded.

THE NEXT MORNING, ELIZABETH AND DARCY DESCENDED to breakfast, remarking on the fine day. Knowing his wife's penchant for wild, deserted vistas, he guided her into the woods beyond the manicured gardens.

"It is so lovely."

"It is now, Elizabeth." He bent down to kiss the top of her hair. *A little farther and we shall be beyond the range of either Georgiana or Richard, should they ramble.* "There is a folly I wish to show you."

"Truly?"

Darcy looked up as a pair of falcons flew above them in intersecting circles. "A couple for sure. See how they hunt together, as a team. That is how I wish us to be—a team in all we do."

"Do you?"

"I do. I know it is a bit unconventional, but I have seen how beneficial it is for all concerned, as well as any children we may be blessed with."

"Do you wish for children, Fitzwilliam?"

"I do. Pemberley has been silent for too long. I long to hear the laughter of our children filling its halls."

"Tell me about Pemberley. Is it grand, like Rosings?"

Darcy led her farther through the woods. "No, not really. Here in the south, everything is cultivated, tamed. It is not so at Pemberley." He stopped then, grabbing hold of her to kiss her passionately. She returned his kiss, then broke free, running ahead, her laughter cascading back to him. After a moment to collect himself, he followed, his long legs making short work of the distance. Taking the lead, he ran to the stone temple on the top of a hillside. Reaching the summit, he doubled over, bracing his hands on his knees and leaning against one of the columns, his breathing laboured.

She ran up to him. Running her fingers through his hair, she smoothed his windswept curls. His breath remained laboured, but from a more carnal cause. Leaning into him, she pulled his head closer, his growl muffled by her body. Slowly, he captured her in his embrace as surely as she held him in hers. Their kisses rained over each other's faces, necks, shoulders, and anywhere else they found purchase. It was not until the sun was high in the sky that the lovers made their way back to the curated existence of Rosings.

As they ambled back to the gardens and pathways of Lady Catherine's design, two voices, off to the right, broke into their private bliss. A third voice joined the duo.

"Come, Anne."

Creeping closer to the source, the Darcys saw Blainard and Anne ride off in her curricle. Elizabeth drew Darcy's attention to a man, scurrying away from the estate on foot. Gaping at each other, the Darcys struggled to contain their amazement.

"What was that?" Darcy stepped toward the curricle as it crested a hill.

"It appears Anne has some explaining to do," Elizabeth looked off to where the unknown man had fled.

"Lady Catherine, a word?" Darcy beckoned his aunt into the library.

She agreed ungraciously. Her skirts swished impatiently and, for not the first time, he wondered at her vehement displeasure. *It has been thus ever since Wickham's exposure—no, perhaps that is merely when she dropped the pretence.* He watched her take a seat, her actions imperious, her irascibility evident in the crisp flick of her fingers as she grasped the armrests. Darcy studied his hands, wondering how to broach a subject he knew would be ill received.

"Lady Catherine, I feel it is my duty—"

"Duty? You dare speak to me of duty, Nephew? You, who have brought nothing but shame, disapproval, and disappointment and heartache to this family! And this latest round of shame—this chit—is she all you could afford? Is this what you have come to?"

Darcy reared back, astonished by her vitriol. "Madam, desist at once. I must tell you something for Anne's sake. Blainard is not a man of honour."

"How dare you doubt my judgment on a suitable husband for my daughter!"

"There is much about Blainard you cannot know."

"I know enough to know he is good enough for

Anne. This conversation is at an end." She left the library.

Darcy slumped into the nearest chair, rubbing his forehead with heavy hands. The door opened, and a woman's light step approached. Before he could draw another breath, Elizabeth knelt on the floor before him, her arms pulling him to her. Her hands held his with great tenderness, as one would tend a battle-weary soldier. Prying them from his face, her lips replaced them, as if washing away his pain, the loneliness, and the emptiness of failure. Darcy let her tend his wounds, accepted her kisses, her caress on his cheek, her gentle stroking, the pull of her arms as they wrapped around his upper body. His heart was heavy, and she wrapped him in her love, understanding, and her belief in what he tried to do.

"She would not listen."

"I know, my love, I know."

THE NEXT AFTERNOON, LADY CATHERINE SAT TOGETHER with Lord Blainard in the drawing room, enjoying a cup of tea.

"Your nephew married well, my lady."

Lady Catherine sipped her drink. "She is a pretty thing, I give you that, but what are they about, marrying so precipitously? What is this country coming to when members of the first circles do not follow the traditions of honour and decency?"

"Well, madam, as you say, Miss—I beg your pardon, Mrs Darcy is a beautiful woman. Most attractive."

Lady Catherine, placing a rather large piece of raisin

scone in her mouth, missed the lascivious gleam in her companion's eye as he continued.

"Perhaps there is a reason for their haste?"

Lady Catherine's face brightened. "Really? Do you think so, Lord Blainard?"

"I am not one to conjecture on matters such as these, madam."

"Do tell what you have heard."

"Nothing directly. However, it is known that Mrs Darcy has, of late, spent an inordinate amount of time at St Magdalene's Home for—"

"That den of trollops?" Lady Catherine's lips cracked into a smug smile.

Controlling their grimaces, and with fire in their eyes, the Darcys stared at the couple who were too engrossed in their conversation to note that the newly-weds had been standing in the doorway for the last five minutes.

ENTERING HIS WIFE'S DRESSING ROOM THAT EVENING, Darcy found his wife looking grim. "Elizabeth, what is it?" He sat at her side on the chaise longue.

"They are so cruel," she said with a sad shake of her head. "It is astonishing."

"I know, my love. And they are not worth your tears."

"I know it is but a taste of what the *ton* is capable of."

"Not when time passes and there is no inconvenient birth a month or two ahead of time."

She gave him a small smile. "I had not thought of that."

"Elizabeth, if that were the reason for our union, I would still be the happiest of men. Your love is worth more to me than all the gossip in town or the country."

"I agree. And our reason was just. I would rather have my reputation dragged through the streets than allow my uncle to suffer. Not after all he has done for us and the children."

Darcy arched his brow.

"And then if...if not for you, how he and the children, my dear cousins...they would have suffered for the rest of their lives, all because of that...that man." She looked at Darcy with such tenderness that courage flushed his chest.

Pulling himself back from the emotion in her eyes, he asked, "If you were with child, that would not be so bad, would it?"

Elizabeth's countenance softened, "No, not at all." His face did not quite express joy at this thought. "What concerns you, husband?"

"I simply wonder what kind of father I shall make. I am not good with..." He blinked at her laughter as she kissed him on each cheek. He grabbed her arms and hugged her. "Elizabeth."

She looked at him with delight in her eyes, and laugher in her throat. "Fitzwilliam, let me tell you the qualities I seek for the father of my children, shall I?"

He nodded.

"First, the man must be sound of mind."

Darcy gave her a quick kiss. "I may be able to manage that."

"Tall."

Darcy stood.

"Strong."

He flexed his arm.

"Courageous."

"I do my best."

She laughed again. "One who will stand up to the *ton*, willing and able to defend me against slander and disgrace."

He smiled warmly, regaining his position at her side.

"Kind, and of course, very, very handsome. And since all these qualities are abundant in the only husband I have at the moment, I intend to keep him."

Her laughter was silenced by the urgent kisses her generous husband bestowed.

LADY CATHERINE EXAMINED THE WOMAN SITTING IN HER parlour. *She is a pretty enough girl, in a rather alarmingly unconventional manner.* She watched as the woman focused on the embroidery in her hand. "What is it you work on, Mrs Darcy?"

"A smock, Lady Catherine."

"A smock?" she exclaimed, surprised.

"Yes, madam."

"Are you in the habit of wearing a work smock?"

Elizabeth held aloft the child's smock with lovely ivy embroidered on the collar.

Lady Catherine gasped. "You are with child so soon?"

"No. This, along with the others I work upon, are for St Magdalene's."

"The place for…for fallen women?" Her ladyship's lips were tight with fierce disapproval.

"For women importuned by unscrupulous men, yes."

"How indecorous of you, Mrs Darcy."

"I beg your pardon, but how is that so?"

"Those women are responsible for their own downfall. They deserve no charity."

Elizabeth gasped, then scoffed, "Surely you do not mean that?"

"I am not in the habit of saying things I do not mean. I can understand someone in your position feeling this way, but I assure you that families of the first set follow a more demanding standard."

"Yes, the merciless, cruel, hypocritical ones do!" Elizabeth muttered under her breath, but not quietly enough to prevent Lady Catherine from hearing it.

"Speak up. Clear speech is a sure sign of good breeding."

"As is holding one's tongue." Elizabeth returned her work to her basket. "I fear a headache coming, and a breath of fresh air is in order."

ELIZABETH STOOD, LADY CATHERINE'S EYES BURNING holes in her back. Exiting to the wide courtyard, she found Blainard leaning against a column, a gleam in his eyes.

"Ah, Elizabeth."

"It is Mrs Darcy, Lord Blainard. What a surprise to see you out of doors."

He laughed, keeping his eyes on her. "I was wondering how long it would take before you sought solace in the bosom of nature. Will you walk with me? Just a short stroll, perhaps?"

"I think not. I fear a headache forming. If you would excuse me."

"Come now, Elizabeth. A bit of fresh air will serve you well." He grabbed for her arm, which she swung away, but he took hold of her. "I have heard how you greet your former suitors." His eyes narrowed.

Elizabeth gasped.

Blainard chuckled. "I find old friends are the best friends, my dear. They know one so...*intimately*, after all. Making reunions all the sweeter."

Pulling back, Elizabeth broke his hold on her arm, her heart beating hard in her chest, she glared at Blainard as though he were a cockroach. Without another word, she turned and walked away.

From the second story of the great house, a pair of eyes carefully observed the pair before their owner rushed from the window.

CHAPTER FOURTEEN

Colonel Fitzwilliam passed the note to Darcy, watching his alarm grow.

"I apologise, Lord Darlington, an urgent matter requires my immediate attention." Darcy rose from the chair, placing the fine cigar and snifter of rare brandy on the side table.

"No, no." Darlington walked the younger men to the door. "As my visit was unexpected, I shall take my leave, with your promise to join me, along with your ladies, at Heatherton."

Darcy bowed.

"Thank you for the invitation," Colonel Fitzwilliam said. "I shall convey your best wishes to my father and mother."

"Excellent. Rumour has it that you have captured a beauty, Darcy, and a vivacious one at that."

"Mrs Darcy is a beautiful woman," Darcy agreed, unhappy to delay their departure. "But her appeal extends beyond her appearance. You may even find yourself charmed when you witness her wit."

Colonel Fitzwilliam added, "Undoubtedly."

"Then I double my plea. Surely you cannot deny an old man the few true pleasures remaining to him."

"We would not suspend any pleasure of yours, sir." Darcy looked fondly at the friend of his late father.

"Smart lad. Now, be about your urgent business. Must not keep the ladies waiting."

Darcy left the colonel to see their guest to his carriage.

DARCY TOOK THE MARBLE STAIRS THREE AT A TIME TO the parlour. Totally disregarding the bellowed invectives of his aunt, he surveyed the chamber for his wife, but she was not there. Giving Lady Catherine a curt nod, he hastened to their rooms, throwing open the door as a maid laid a wet cloth on Elizabeth's brow. Hearing his step, Elizabeth took the cloth from her head, agitation in her movements.

"I shall attend her. Leave the basin," Darcy said, his eyes seeing only his wife.

The maid curtseyed and departed.

"Blainard knows about Jamie," Elizabeth said before Darcy could reach her.

"What? How?"

"Of course, he did not mention him by name, but he spoke of reunions…and intimacy, and the way he looked at me, Fitzwilliam. He knew what had happened. I just know he knew." She took hold of his hand.

A knock on the door startled them, as the maid returned with a fresh basin of water.

"What shall we do?" Elizabeth asked.

"I am not sure." Darcy walked to the double doors that opened onto the balcony. "It bedevils me that he knows Simmons."

Elizabeth hurried to her feet, walking to his side. "Or of him."

"Or of him."

"And then there was his release from gaol."

"Yes." He looked into her eyes. "We must inform Richard. He has taken on more intelligence, or rather counter intelligence, work these last two to three years. When I mentioned that Simmons lives in America, his interest was piqued."

"There are rumours of war."

"Indeed. I believe he would wish to know this." He kissed her brow. "You are well? Please, tell me you are well. I could not bear it if you were harmed by that lout."

"I am well. I gave him the Darcy glare and left him. I assume Georgiana sent word to you?"

He nodded. "I am glad she did." Slipping his arms around her, he drew her closer to his heart, nuzzling her neck. "So very glad."

"Fitzwilliam?"

"Hmm?" he replied from behind her ear.

"I wish to retire for the evening."

"Alone?" He could not hide his surprise.

She shook her head, pulling his hand as she walked back to her bed.

His eyes widened, then flared, and his smile stretched his lips.

A wicked gleam filled her eye and with one brow arched, she gave him a seductive look. He growled and scooped her into his arms. They remained ensconced in their bed for the rest of the night.

"Not that I mind the diversion, but why the sneaking about? Would not a simple conversation do? Why leave a note in my chamber, employing a code we have not used since we were lads?"

Darcy shook his head at his cousin. "I would not leave Elizabeth. Hence the note."

"No, quite right. I assume your absence from dinner—"

"I could not trust myself should I encounter that miserable excuse of a man."

"What happened?" Richard stepped farther into the chamber as Elizabeth approached from within.

"Blainard knows about Mr Simmons." Elizabeth's eyes searched his for answers as she handed him a snifter of brandy.

"What? How?" Richard sputtered, looking between the two Darcys.

"Come." Darcy walked them to their chairs. "As you know, Blainard waylaid Elizabeth earlier."

"He spoke of reunions with old friends," Elizabeth interjected.

"Needless to say, neither Elizabeth nor I discussed our wedding journey in any detail with anyone in this house."

"No, I dare say not."

"He made a veiled reference to Mr Simmons and the assault," Elizabeth said.

Richard paced. "So, Blainard knew you were at Longbourn."

"He did not mention the attack per se, but he did speak of the joy in 'reconnecting with friends' and 'intimacy.'"

Shaking his head, the colonel continued. "And then, when this Simmons was charged and held in the gaol, a diplomatic request arrived with no precedence, clearing and releasing him."

They nodded again.

"And he has not been heard of since?"

"So far, no. But Henderson still searches," Darcy said.

"Smart to keep him on it." Richard returned to sit with them. "But the question remains, how does Blainard know of Simmons at all, and what are we going to do about it?"

"What do you suggest?" Darcy asked.

"I am not sure."

"I would prefer Lady Catherine remain ignorant of this, as much as possible," Darcy said. "Her vitriol is at a new pitch. Who knows what damage she could wreck with this?"

"Agreed," Richard and Elizabeth declared simultaneously.

"And yet..." Richard leaned forward, elbows on his knees, hands united. "To let the challenge go might embolden him."

"Perhaps a conference, man to man, is required," Darcy suggested.

His cousin held up his hand. "If, and only if, you can rein in that temper of yours. Lord Aubrey would be terribly interested in knowing the how and why of this connexion, and I would not have you ruin my chances of information with your fists."

"Aubrey? Your father's friend?"

"Yes, and my superior in my new...*field of interest*. It is too circumstantial that these two men of such diverse origins should converge within Elizabeth's orbit on the relative cusp of Wellington's visit to Longbourn."

"You think that is the reason?" Elizabeth asked, her shock evident.

"You think Blainard, who began his campaign to possess Elizabeth months ago, is linked to Simmons's return from America?"

"No, not initially. However, things are unsettled everywhere. The Americans grow more belligerent every day and, well, one can never be sure with the Tyrant. As such all unusual activity must be looked examined. When were the plans for Wellington's visit first proposed?"

"We presented the idea of giving him Roan a year ago, at her birth. She truly has the most promising bloodlines I have ever seen."

"And the presentation? When were those plans initiated?" the colonel asked.

"We arrived at a tentative date over three months ago. We were satisfied with her training, and your generals were fairly sure things would be quiet —relatively."

Richard nodded.

"It seems preposterous that all these machinations are centred on a horse," Darcy said. Turning to Elizabeth, he added, "Regardless of how glorious her bloodlines."

"I agree," she said with a sigh, leaning back against his shoulder.

"As do I," said the colonel. "It could be happenstance. However, that Blainard knows of Simmons at all, to say nothing of his attack, bears investigating. I do not like it at all." After thinking on it a moment, he said, "I think Darcy and I should interrogate Blainard—set him straight about the happenings at Longbourn, see if we can uncover the connexion. Let us act surprised that he, an earl, would concern himself with a man like Simmons. I believe that should to the trick."

BLAINARD WAS STANDING, READING A MISSIVE, WHEN Darcy and Richard entered the library. Startled by their appearance, he tucked the fob watch he had been fondling between his thumb and forefinger away into his left waistcoat pocket, then folded the letter into fours.

Darcy began first. "Mrs Darcy informed me of your earlier conversation."

"How very daring of her."

"What is your game, Blainard?" Colonel Fitzwilliam asked, leaning against one of the overstuffed and underused armchairs scattered about the library.

"Game?" The earl smirked. "Of what do you speak?"

"Beyond your obvious and pitiful obsession with my

wife," Darcy said. "Why bring up a painful experience for her? Why impose your presence on her at all?"

"To ensure she is well, when her husband would not protect her. Where were you when this reprobate Simmons assaulted her in such a base manner? If she were mine——"

"But she is not and never will be," Darcy spat, his brows drawn and his eyes pinning the earl where he stood.

Blainard tucked his fingers in his waistcoat pockets, rubbing his left index finger, as if stroking the silk stirred his courage. "You are so sure of yourself, Darcy. A knight riding in to save the fair damsel in her hour of need. So predictable." He shook his head. "You are insufferable in your self-righteous posing, and one day very soon, you will understand how little it truly signifies. Oh, your day will come, when your high-minded do-gooded-ness will be shown for the useless tripe it is."

"What a dismal portrait you paint, my lord," the colonel said.

Blainard scoffed. "Say what you will, Fitzwilliam. But while men of such noble mien lead us to wars on foreign soil, there are counter currents uniting like-minded men of vision. Men connected beyond the paltry boundaries of country."

"To what end?" Darcy asked.

"Why do men ever exercise their talents? To refashion the world to their desire." Blainard settled in a nearby chair. "And with the right connexions, I have found it possible to refashion events to achieve my desires."

"Take pains, my lord, that these desires have nothing to do with my wife." Darcy gripped his hands into fists.

Blainard gave Darcy a nod as if acquiescing, though his eyes taunted. "As you wish. Do recall that Elizabeth has been my concern for well over a year—longer than she has known you, Darcy. As such, I am well informed on all the currents moving in her world." He smirked. "It is only natural that I utilise my connexions to arm myself with information to protect her. Now, as lovely as this little chat has been, gentlemen, I believe I shall retire. I bid you goodnight."

He left the library, and the cousins could only pivot from watching the door close to gaping at one another.

THE NEXT MORNING, DARCY, ELIZABETH, AND Georgiana walked along the wooded paths, wanting to clear their heads before visiting Charlotte Collins at the vicarage. Darcy had agreed to escort them but refused to spend the morning with Mr Collins. "I mean no disrespect, but I cannot hear that man blather away all morning." Elizabeth had laughed merrily at his distress, soothing away the furrow of his brow with kisses. It was why they had been twenty minutes late meeting Georgiana.

Turning their direction towards Hunsford, the Darcys heard a sentry's half-contained call. "Make haste, someone comes."

On instinct, Darcy drew his women behind him and stepped forward. Proceeding stealthily, they followed a rustle of movement to their left. Boots pounded the soft earth as the creaks of a vehicle being entered filtered through the bushes. The crack of a whip followed, and the Darcys hastened to the source. Darcy ran after the vehicle until he realised Elizabeth had run in the opposite direction after the lone runner. He stopped, turning to search for her.

"Where is she?" he whispered, more to himself than his sister. Pulling Georgiana along, he retraced his steps, until Elizabeth returned to the clearing, barely out of breath. In her hand, was a man's glove, which she examined.

Georgiana giggled when Elizabeth brought the leather to her nose, wrinkling it in disgust.

"Odious mixture to be sure," Elizabeth pondered.

"What is?" Georgiana enquired.

Darcy interrupted all discussion by taking Elizabeth tightly by the shoulders. "Do not ever do that again! Do you hear me?"

Georgiana stepped back in fright at her normally composed brother; Elizabeth froze. Seeing them pulled Darcy from his panic. He pulled her into a tight embrace. "Elizabeth, forgive me, I was so frightened when I could not see you."

"Frightened? I do not understand."

"I turned, and you were not there."

"I knew the riders in the curricle were Anne and Blainard. I wished to know the identity of the third party."

"How do you know it was Anne and Blainard?" Georgiana asked, surprised.

"It is not the first time they have ridden out together," she explained. "Even Lady Catherine knows this. She favours the alliance, for reasons that escape me. I daresay she will be surprised when Anne announces her engagement to another."

"Another?" asked Georgiana. "I thought, with all the looks sent to Lord Blainard, that it was him. If not, then who?"

"And on what do you base this supposition?" Darcy asked.

"As to who, the man is missing his right glove." Elizabeth smiled at Georgiana while stretching the glove between her two hands, before turning to her husband. "And as for how I arrived at this conjecture, it is by plain and simple observation, Husband." She continued walking.

Darcy growled, coming up beside her, "Elizabeth!"

She giggled, took his arm and gave it a squeeze. "It was Blainard's voice we heard. He was the watchman. The lookout, not the lover. Now we must detect what precisely these secret rendezvous signify."

Georgiana blushed. "You think Anne has taken a lover?"

"Why else would she meet so secretly in the woods? They certainly did not count on our early morning rambles." Elizabeth smiled up at her husband.

He coughed. "What concerns me, apart from the impropriety of it—"

"But they are chaperoned," Georgiana said.

"That is my other concern. That Blainard is the chaperon. That he is involved is disconcerting."

"But why?" Georgiana asked.

"That someone of his character would impose himself into Anne's life in any regard is an abomination."

"It is apparent you dislike the man, Brother, but why?" Georgiana asked. "Your reaction is marked."

Darcy clenched his jaw.

"Because Lord Blainard attempted to harm my family," Elizabeth explained, "so that he could appear as our saviour if I gave myself to him, only without the sanction of marriage. Fortunately, your brother heard of our distress and offered for me before Lord Blainard could enact his plan."

The three continued in silence until reaching the parsonage gate, whereupon Darcy addressed his sister. "Georgiana, no one knows of this, and we ask that it remain so."

She nodded just as Mrs Collins was heard calling out to her friend. Elizabeth waved, then kissed Darcy quickly before releasing his hands and taking Georgiana by the arm.

"Elizabeth, either Richard or I shall come for you in an hour."

"Two," she replied.

Shaking his head, he nodded, and the two women joined Mrs Collins for a lovely morning tea, staying on through the midday meal.

AT DINNER THAT EVENING, COLONEL FITZWILLIAM looked to Elizabeth. "I understand Wellington will be coming to collect his horse from Longbourn."

"You mean Roan?" Elizabeth asked. Pretending not to notice that Lord Blainard had locked eyes on her, she nodded to Fitzwilliam. "She was doing well when we looked in on her, before coming to Kent."

"You abandoned such an auspicious animal?" Lady Catherine accused with her words and her eyes.

Replacing her glass of wine on the overly fine tablecloth, Elizabeth replied, "The grooms are more than capable of caring for her, madam."

"Indeed," Blainard mumbled, focusing on his wine glass.

Elizabeth allowed her glance to travel the table. Anne seemed preoccupied, and Elizabeth wondered, not for the first time, what she was about. *That Blainard is involved can only mean ill. But what of the third voice, who is he?*

"I look forward to seeing Longbourn for myself," the colonel added.

"You travel to Meryton, Richard?" Darcy asked, clearly surprised.

"I mentioned the presentation to my commanding officer, General Lessing, and we shall both join the festivities." He shot a glance at Blainard.

"Excellent, Colonel!" Elizabeth said. "Will you be able to stay with us? Or will you billet with the general?"

"Most likely with the general."

"Pity." Darcy sipped his wine. "You will miss a house full of females."

"Females with a penchant for red coats," teased Elizabeth.

Georgiana blushed, while the colonel looked confused.

"My sisters return from their studies two weeks before the anticipated presentation, I believe."

The rest of the evening passed in almost pleasant discussion as Lady Catherine offered her seasoned opinion on the intricacies of horse breeding, a subject on which she held no knowledge. She also spoke on the illustrious equestrian lines in residence at Rosings, Matlock, and, of course, Pemberley. Elizabeth continued watching Anne, who seemed most anxious to get away. Elizabeth supposed her preoccupation had more to do with her morning rendezvous than her lack of interest in horse flesh.

After another of Anne's furtive glances, Darcy asked loudly, "Tell me, Lord Blainard, when do you wed your dear cousin, Lady Bleary?"

Lady Catherine, who had also been smiling at his lordship, scowled at the untimely mention of her daughter's rival. "Yes, well, we know how well those things turn out," she murmured.

THAT NIGHT, A LONE HORSEMAN RODE ACROSS THE FIELDS of Rosings Park. Before he came to the finely manicured gardens, he dismounted and walked to a small gazebo. A figure emerged from the shadows. Silently, they mounted the single horse and rode off. Their laughter echoed through the otherwise silent night.

CHAPTER FIFTEEN

The next morning, Elizabeth and Darcy took their time going to breakfast. Fortunately, only Colonel Fitzwilliam was at the table, though he looked haggard. When Darcy approached with a wide smile, after seating Elizabeth, he remarked, "If I did not know better, old man, I would think you had been out carousing."

His cousin shot him a dark, unforgiving look. "It is not I who was actively engaged last night. *All* night, I might add. You may think the walls here are as thick as Pemberley's, but with the warmer weather, many of us left our windows open, and were subjected to quite a bit of noise—of a particular kind."

Elizabeth turned beet red; however, Darcy was unrepentant. With an arched brow, he sipped his morning coffee. Before anyone could reply, the trio heard a commotion upstairs, and momentarily, a breathless Georgiana hurled herself into the room.

Elizabeth leapt to her feet. "Georgiana, what is it, dear?"

"Anne is gone," she said with a gasp.

Ten minutes later, fifteen footmen were marshalled into a search party led by Colonel Fitzwilliam. Before joining them, Darcy checked with his wife and sister, who were searching Anne's chamber.

"You will be well here, Elizabeth?" he took her hand in his.

"Yes." Elizabeth nodded towards Georgiana who was surveying the bookcases. "We shall remain in Anne's chamber looking for any clue as to where she may have gone."

"And Lady Catherine?"

Elizabeth rolled her eyes and smiled, then kissed the knuckles of his hand. "We shall see to her as well."

"You mistake my meaning, Elizabeth. I am afraid she may be more...obstreperous than usual."

"Her daughter is missing. Both Georgiana and I shall bear this in mind when dealing with her." She smiled. "Now go. The sooner you begin, the sooner you may return, errant cousin in hand."

"That is my intention." With a final kiss to her lips, Darcy made to depart.

"Fitzwilliam?" Elizabeth called as he crossed the threshold.

"Yes?"

"You will leave word in which direction you are headed in case we find something?"

He took a moment to consider this and nodded, "Of course."

Once the men left, the ladies focused on dissecting Anne's chamber. "Georgiana, we must think like Anne, adding to what we know about the situation."

Georgiana asked, "How do we do that?"

Elizabeth took a lingering look around the chamber, which was singularly devoid of personality. "I was wondering that very thing myself." She walked to the dressing table, found nothing of note, and flopped into a chair. Then she jumped up. "Her maid!"

"Randalls!" Georgiana called out, pulling the bell to summon her.

"Yes, ma'am," came the tremulous voice of the lady in service to Anne de Bourgh.

"Come and sit. You look a fright," Elizabeth said with great empathy.

"Yes, Miss, I mean, Mrs Darcy." The woman took the seat Elizabeth indicated.

"Would you like some tea, dear?" Elizabeth asked.

"Yes, thank you."

Georgiana went to ask her personal maid to arrange for tea and cakes to be sent up. When she returned, Elizabeth began the questioning.

"Was anything amiss last evening?"

"Amiss?"

"Yes, odd—strange."

"Did Anne do or say anything out of the ordinary?" Georgiana persisted. "She seemed in fine spirits this visit."

"I could not say, Miss," Randalls replied.

Elizabeth and Georgiana exchanged surprised looks.

"Why not?" Elizabeth asked.

FOR THE DEEPEST LOVE

"I have only come into service these past three months."

"I had no idea you were so *very* new," Georgiana replied. "But then, Rosings endures a great deal of turnover."

"I can imagine," Elizabeth replied, and all three women smiled. "Randalls, do you know what happened to Miss de Bourgh's last maid?"

The young woman took a sip of tea. "Well, my mother, who is Mrs Collins's cook, said that she— Maggie, her name was—were called away all of a sudden-like."

"Called away?" asked Georgiana.

"A letter came, and the next thing anyone knew, she was packing, and my mother said it was my big chance. So I came to speak with the housekeeper, and here I am."

"Before Maggie left, all was well?" Georgiana enquired.

"Oh, yes. She were the talk of all us servants."

"How so?" asked Elizabeth.

"Because she lasted the longest with Miss de Bourgh. It seemed they actually got along, meaning no disrespect."

"None taken," Georgiana replied, clearly embarrassed for her relation's behaviour.

"Did Miss de Bourgh's disposition improve when Lord Blainard arrived?"

"Oh, yes, ma'am. It did." She seemed enthusiastic to finally have information to contribute. "She stayed in her chambers all afternoon reading her letter."

"Her letter?" Elizabeth asked.

"Lord Blainard wrote her a letter?" Georgiana echoed.

"More likely brought her one." Elizabeth drummed her fingers on the armrest of her chair, considering this information.

"From a mysterious, one-gloved man," Georgiana said.

Elizabeth nodded, then said, "Randalls, I understand you have not been in service to Miss de Bourgh for very long but perhaps you know where she hides her special things? Tokens? Any trinkets that might mean something special to her?"

She nodded and walked over to a wardrobe, though, upon reaching it, she frowned and said, "This is odd."

"What is?" Elizabeth and Georgiana asked in unison.

The maid walked around the tall piece of furniture, examining it. "It belongs against this wall, but it should be... over there." She pointed half a foot farther along the wall.

Sharing an excited glance, Elizabeth and Georgiana joined her in pushing it away. There, built in the middle of the wall, was a small bookshelf, perhaps three feet high. A thick layer of dust covered most of the area, save for six inches that were swept clear.

"It was there yesterday!" Randalls cried.

"And do you know what she kept there, on that shelf?"

"There were two boxes. The first was older. She said she had it since she was a child."

"Did you ever see what was in either of them?"

The maid nodded. "Yes. Miss de Bourgh was ever so

eager to share." She looked to the two women. "I think she was lonely." Taking a deep breath, she continued. "The first had her baby clothes."

"Baby clothes?"

"Of when *she* was a babe," the maid blushed. "She kept her best baby clothes, and a rattle she was fond of. Said they reminded her of her father."

Elizabeth thought long and hard before speaking, bouncing the knuckles of her curled fist against her pursed lips. "Her father has been gone a long while?" she asked Georgiana.

"I barely knew him," she replied.

"So, she was raised solely by Lady Catherine?" Elizabeth asked.

Georgiana nodded.

"Randalls, did Miss de Bourgh look at these clothes often?"

"At least once a week."

"Indeed." Elizabeth said with sympathy for her wayward cousin. "Did you ever get a glimpse of what she kept in the other box?"

"Yes, ma'am. Her memory box."

"Pardon?"

"Her memory box is what she called it."

"And she shared these with you?" Georgiana asked.

"Oh, yes, ma'am. As I mentioned, Miss de Bourgh used to be ever so eager to share its contents with, well, I believe anyone who showed interest."

"And what were the contents?" Elizabeth prodded.

"There was a small portrait of the late Sir Lewis and a few medals with ribbons. A bit of fabric. Not much else. Oh, and a few bundles that looked rather business oriented, if you know what I mean."

"Did you notice any new additions of late? Even in the few weeks you served her?" Elizabeth asked.

"A few letters."

"Who were they from?" Elizabeth asked eagerly.

"I do not know. When the first one came, about a month ago, she stopped sharing her box with me. Said those memories were not yet made."

When Elizabeth and Georgiana returned downstairs, a rather unperturbed Lady Catherine was biting into a scone topped with clotted cream.

"Lady Catherine?" Georgiana asked. "Are you...? You must be very worried about Anne."

"Not at all," her ladyship replied. "She and Lord Blainard have obviously gone to Gretna Green."

"No!" Georgiana clasped an adjacent chair to steady herself.

"Oh, yes, I am sure of it."

"Forgive me, Lady Catherine, but how can you be so sure that was their destination?" Elizabeth asked.

"Because just the other day, I overheard Lord Blainard, the dear boy, enquiring from my coachman about the distance between Rosings Park and the Scottish border. He wanted to know of the best reposting establishments. And the irrefutable fact that both my daughter and Lord Blainard are not here at Rosings."

At that moment, Lord Blainard entered the breakfast room, announcing that he was hungry for his morning meal. The only sound heard after that was the shatter of china, as Lady Catherine's coffee cup hit the floor.

As Georgiana and a footman attended to Lady Catherine, Elizabeth turned her attention to the man selecting his breakfast from the sideboard. "Lord Blainard?" She controlled her vitriol. "Exactly who was in the woods with you and Miss de Bourgh yesterday morning and on your many rides about the estate?"

"Why, whatever do you mean, Mrs Darcy?"

Blainard's mischievous gleam irked Elizabeth. From the corner of her eyes, she saw Georgiana quietly leave room.

"I shall ask you again, Lord Blainard, whom did you meet? Who accompanies Anne?"

"Has Miss de Bourgh gone somewhere?" He blithely placed a scone on his plate.

"You know very well that she has."

"Oh my! Without prior notice? I say, Rosings Park is rife with scandal, is it not?" Placing his plate on the table, he took his seat as Georgiana returned, plucking a small but hefty candlestick to hold behind her back.

Elizabeth narrowed her eyes. With a chilling calm in her voice, she said, "Rather her scandal than your infamy, my lord."

He started at that, then without warning, lunged across the table at Elizabeth, who, reacting quickly, stepped out of his range. "Perhaps you wish to reconsider your answer, Lord Blainard?"

"Why should I wish to do that?"

"Rather than having your involvement in the ruination of a member of the nobility sent to the papers—"

"No decent paper would publish that tripe."

"I speak of the rumour mills feeding their slander, so attractive to the habitué of the gambling dens."

They glared at each other.

"I am a woman of many resources and connexions and am not afraid to use them."

Blainard looked between Elizabeth and Georgiana, both pinning him with their glares of contempt. He drummed his fingers nervously on the table as he weighed his options, finally saying, "Merriweather."

"Of course!" exclaimed Elizabeth.

Lady Catherine roused herself from her faint with an indignant groan. "The man to whom I refused my daughter's hand?"

"And your part in this, sir?" Darcy entered the room, Colonel Fitzwilliam behind him.

"Me?" Blainard hissed. "I am but the simple agent that encouraged Merriweather to elope with the woman he loves. Miss de Bourgh is of age, and he was more than receptive."

"You blackguard!" The enraged Lady Catherine flew out of her chair, lunging at the stunned peer. Surprised, he lost his balance and the two crashed to the floor. Blainard gained the upper hand, flipping Lady Catherine on her back. Georgiana, the closest, lifted the candlestick in her hands, smashing it forcibly to his head. The earl looked up briefly, seeming surprised, before collapsing.

Colonel Fitzwilliam rolled him off Lady Catherine and chuckled. "Well done, Georgie, you saved both our aunt and Blainard from a horrible fate." On the questioning looks the others directed his way, he added, "It is scandalous to be in such an attitude on the floor, a widow and a bachelor. They would be forced to marry, no?"

Lady Catherine awoke to the unfettered laughter of her younger relations filling the chamber.

CHAPTER SIXTEEN

L ord Blainard departed later that afternoon with his head bandaged, complaining of a tremendous ache behind his eyes. The Darcys trimmed weeks from their stay, remaining at Rosings only long enough to ensure Lady Catherine was recovered from the entire *débâcle* with as much dignity as possible. Uncharacteristically subdued, she left the Darcys and Colonel Fitzwilliam to their own amusement.

The day prior to their departure, they received word that Anne was now Mrs Merriweather, and the foursome took one last romp through the estate's meadows and woods. The men tried their hands at fishing, while Elizabeth and Georgiana strolled along the stream. Walking in silence, they revelled in the sunbeams glinting off the waters flushed by the spring's rains. In the bucolic environment, Elizabeth broached the topic of their newest family member.

"There is a great chance we shall encounter them in London."

"I know you and Fitzwilliam worry about me." Georgiana picked up a stone, turning it to catch the sunlight. "But I am relieved, in a way. Lady Catherine was wrong to separate Anne from Mr Merriweather." She skipped her pebble into the babbling stream. "I mean, it was not that suitors rushed to Rosings to court Anne. And she truly cares for him. She wrote of him to me, just after my aunt's refusal, and was distraught at her mother's humiliation of him." She threw another stone into the brook. "When news of my...George Wickham...when that was made public, Anne sent a long letter saying how sorry she was that things had turned so wrong."

Only the water tumbling over the river stones broke the growing quiet. Elizabeth looked at the tears glistening on Georgiana's cheeks. Rather than a handkerchief, she held out a smooth rock. After a long pause, her sister reached out her open palm, into which Elizabeth dropped the cool stone. Georgiana rubbed her fingers along the smooth surface as she admitted, "As difficult as the last years have been, so desolate and alone, I cannot feel they were not beneficial."

They looked at each other.

"I have changed, become something unforeseeable. My brother has changed. We have both found the courage to be ourselves—who we are without the trappings with which society had bound us." Georgiana kept the stone in her hand but kicked another into the water. "I am well, Elizabeth. More than well."

Elizabeth smiled at her sister, and they continued

meandering along the stream until it was time to return. They would leave for London on the morrow and wished to spend a little time with their aunt.

"It is done." Lady Catherine slumped into her imposing chair at the head of the table, its ornate frame dwarfing her sunken shoulders. "Once you depart I, too, shall leave Rosings, perhaps for the last time."

Darcy and Richard exchanged a startled look.

Lady Catherine waved her hand at their unasked questions. "I cannot imagine Mr Merriweather welcoming me to his new home."

Georgiana extended a hand towards her aunt, "I am sure Anne—"

"Are you?" her ladyship snapped. "Do not speak of my daughter. It is your fault. If you had behaved with the decorum of your mother's family, he"—She gestured at Darcy —"would be my son, and I could remain here at Rosings."

"Enough, madam." Darcy stood.

"Sit down," Lady Catherine commanded. "I will have my say. I have held my tongue long enough. It is not enough that Georgiana disgraced herself with the son of a servant, for God's sake. But you allowed it to be known!" She banged her hand on the table, rattling the china. "Look how we have fallen. You are married to this girl, who has little respect for her betters, and I am abandoned by my own flesh and reduced to nothing. We are the laughingstock of society."

Elizabeth wiped her lips before replacing her napkin on the table. "You have said enough, madam." She nodded to Georgiana, who scrambled to her feet. The colonel did the same. Darcy had ignored his aunt's instruction to sit down and remained standing. With a small smile to each of them, she addressed Lady Catherine. "Rather than blame my husband and sister for their courage and strength, you should examine why Mr Merriweather felt the need to revenge himself upon you in the first place." Then, as one, her family followed her from the room.

SETTLED BACK IN LONDON, THE GROUP RECONVENED IN Darcy's study, windows open to the late afternoon of an enticing spring day. The ladies sipped some sherry, while the gentlemen enjoyed their port.

"What I fail to comprehend is why Blainard involved himself in Merriweather's cause," said Richard, studying the prism cast by his cut crystal snifter.

"I admire his tenacity," Elizabeth offered. Aware of the unexpected silence that greeted her words, she added, "Merriweather's, not Blainard's."

"Tenacity?" Darcy asked.

"To defy Lady Catherine twice in one's lifetime indicates a certain tenacity, you must agree?"

"I see your point." Colonel Fitzwilliam grinned, lazing in his chair, swirling the rainbows cast by his glass.

"While I concur with your assessment, Elizabeth, the material point remains, why?" Darcy traced his finger along her wrist. "Why would someone of Blainard's ilk bother with Merriweather's romantic inclinations?"

"Perhaps he is a romantic?" Georgiana said. All three of her companions' jaws dropped.

"What do we know of Blainard?" asked the colonel.

"That he is despicable, unscrupulous, deceitful." Elizabeth crossed her free arm across her chest.

"Yes, he is all that. However, I was speaking of more mundane qualities. Such as, with whom does he associate? Who are his friends? His relations? Merriweather is second cousin to some duchess, is he not?"

"I cannot recall exactly who," Darcy said as he paced the room.

"Yes, but what would that signify?" asked Georgiana.

"There must be another, more recent connexion," Darcy said.

"Such as?" Elizabeth leaned back, watching her husband.

"School? A club?" Darcy suggested.

"Illicit pursuits?" Colonel Fitzwilliam added, almost as an afterthought. All eyes focused on him. He took another swallow of brandy and explained, "After the incident at Longbourn, I made some enquiries regarding Simmons in town, and found that he, along with Merriweather, Blainard, and a gaggle of other well-heeled reprobates, are frequent guests of Madam Praxton's." Looking at the women, he added, "Which is an infamous den of iniquity—gambling."

A knock on the door announced the butler, bearing an express addressed to Elizabeth. With a raised brow, she took the unexpected letter, breaking open the seal. All conversation stilled until she announced, "It is from Jane."

May 12, 1812

Dearest Lizzy,

I hope you and Mr Darcy are in good health. I have heard from our sisters, and they are eager for their return to Longbourn. I want you to know, I have given the prospect of relocating farther north a great deal of thought. It is difficult contemplating leaving home and all this place holds for all of us. It is nearly impossible. To that end, I have decided that even with the removal of the stables to Pemberley, I shall remain in Hertfordshire.

Mr Bingley has been very kind. He was in Meryton recently, looking at estates with the idea of settling in the area. As you know, it is one of his fondest wishes to find an estate to call his own. Netherfield appeals, but as the current tenant holds the lease until after the harvest, he remains uncertain.

Lizzy, since writing the above, something of a most distressing nature has occurred. This morning, Mr Hill found a man loitering about the stables. They exchanged words, and the vagrant attacked him before any of the stable hands could come to his aid. The man escaped in the confusion, but Lizzy, Mr Simmons was seen riding out of town with a stranger. Since Mr Hill was unable to verify if this was our trespasser, we have only conjectures to work with.

I confess, I am shaken by this and have spoken with Mr Hill about hiring an extra hand or two, to increase my sense of security. For the first time in my life, I am uncomfortable being alone here at Longbourn. A part of me believes I am safe, but after all that has happened, I am torn between remaining here to defend our home and fleeing to London until a better defence is in place. But I am not you, and so I shall join you or Aunt Gardiner in town by the end of the week.

Your loving sister,
Jane Bennet

Elizabeth leapt from her chair, looking to her husband.

"What is wrong?" Darcy asked, taking hold of her arms.

"Read this." She handed him the letter to read, then wrung her hands. "Jane says she will hire another hand, hopefully a burly lad, but what can this mean? I do not want her there alone. What can we do? I must go to her."

"No. Elizabeth, she is coming to town."

"But…" Tears stung her eyes. "The thought of Jane coming to harm…"

Darcy pulled her into his arms.

"Who? Who will hurt Jane?" Georgiana asked.

"Simmons has returned to Meryton," Darcy informed her.

Elizabeth answered her sister's question. "I do not know if he would attack Jane, but who is this stranger he was with? The thought she might be in danger terrifies me."

"Of course it does. I shall send Robert and Steven to Longbourn immediately to guard our sister. They can remain until we better understand what this signifies." Darcy looked to his cousin, who nodded in acknowledgement. "That will buy us time to sift through this and find the right solution."

"Thank you, my love," Elizabeth said.

"What think you, Richard?" Darcy asked over her head.

"Wellington."

Darcy watched. "Surely you do not believe one, two men—"

"That we know of. Knowing that Simmons has an accomplice indicates there is more in this."

"Why else would he be there?" Elizabeth asked. "It is known I shall not return prior to the presentation, so it cannot be for me. It must be related to Wellington's arrival."

"I agree," said the colonel. "Two agents familiar with the stables and the people behind this could do irrevocable damage."

WHILE THEY WAITED FOR JANE'S RETURN TO TOWN, Elizabeth and Georgiana divided their days between St Magdalene's, the Gardiners', and Madame Lestrat's. Encouraged and supported by her family, Georgiana agreed to attend an upcoming ball given by family friends. Preparing for her first social appearance since her disgrace, she worked on remaining calm and brave enough to face the ton. Her gown, chosen with great care, flattered but remained within the bounds of decorum. Elizabeth's gown was outstanding, Madame Lestrat having draped her two professed 'favourite customers' as the nobility she insisted they were.

Georgiana spoke with Clarice, Madame Lestrat's

niece, indulging their mutual curiosity over the wilds of America and the freedom of a new society.

When the gowns were nearly complete, Clarice sat alone with Georgiana. "I wished to tell you how brave I believe you to be, and how much...how much I admire you."

Georgiana blushed deeply. "I assure you, I am not so brave, nor admirable."

"But you are! You are like the phoenix, rising from the ashes created by that man."

Georgiana looked away. *Will it ever end? Will I never be free from this?*

Clarice spoke in a very small, very timid voice, barely above a whisper on the wind. "When I was but a babe, a man returned to our village...to my mother. She thought she was safe, that he had done his worst, but he returned to... His intention was to do again what he did before I was born. That is when she... After she died, my aunt took me in, and we came here, to England. So, you see, I too know the heartlessness of man."

Georgiana extended her hand, taking Clarice's trembling one. "Thank you for telling me. While not wishing anyone to suffer, it gives me great strength to know I am not alone, and that others have recovered enough to find happiness. And, might I hope, peace?"

"You must not let the *ton* intimidate you, Miss Darcy. They are nothing to you! Their airs are...like dust. You are true quality. Graciousness and strength are what signify. Do not bow your head to anyone. There is no one superior to either you or Mrs Darcy. You have proved beyond measure the goodness of your characters. My aunt and I have said so many, many times."

Georgiana blushed again and changed the subject to the latest books they had read on America, until Elizabeth came to fetch her for their return to Darcy House.

AS GEORGIANA GATHERED HER PELISSE AND GLOVES, Elizabeth moved to Madame Lestrat. "I am glad they are becoming friends."

"I, as well," she replied.

"It is best, I believe, that they remain unburdened by their family history."

Madame Lestrat took hold of her hand. "Bless you, Mrs Darcy."

"How is Mademoiselle du Marché?" Elizabeth whispered.

"She is…adjusting."

"Do you think she would like to make my acquaintance?"

Madame Lestrat gaped.

"I just worry she may feel she has lost a friend. But I could be another."

Madame Lestrat assessed her customer, then looked to the young ladies still speaking in hushed tones. "I shall keep them entertained. If you take the back stairs, you will find her in the room overlooking our courtyard."

"Thank you." Elizabeth smiled before heading down the hall. Knocking on the door, she waited for the muffled permission to enter. "Mademoiselle?" she asked as she entered the chamber.

"*Oui?*" A beautiful blonde woman turned from her worktable.

"I am Elizabeth Darcy."

Antoinette clutched her hands together. "Madame!"

"I wished to make your acquaintance, and—"

"To see your rival?"

Elizabeth started. "To see whether we could be friends." She held her nerve until Antoinette's façade crumbled.

"Forgive me, Madame Darcy." She kept her eyes lowered, as if in submission.

"No! I mean, yes, of course." Elizabeth crossed the room but maintained a small distance. "I know Darcy has kept his distance, but it will not last. He only wishes to reassure me."

"But there is nothing, really, not anymore. He does not want my love."

Elizabeth hesitated. "Perhaps not in that vein, but he, as always, extends his friendship. And remember, you are his cousin."

"Too distant to love." Antoinette focused on Elizabeth's eyes. "But he is a good and steady friend."

"He is."

Antoinette smiled.

A knock preceded the door opening, and Madame Lestrat entered. "They are getting restless, Mrs Darcy."

"Of course. Good day, Mademoiselle du Marché."

"*Au revoir*, Madame Darcy. And thank you. I am pleased to have made your acquaintance." She curtseyed.

Elizabeth smiled, then followed Madame Lestrat through the door.

"Do not let anything Antoinette says upset you, Mrs Darcy. There was nothing romantic between her and your husband. He is one of the most honourable man of either of our acquaintance, and sometimes I think she needed to believe a good man could want her."

"Thank you," Elizabeth smiled, weakly, then joined her sister in the carriage.

ELIZABETH, DARCY, JANE, AND MR BINGLEY SAT SIDE BY side in their box at Covent Garden. The Darcys exchanged a panicked glance seeing Lord Blainard seated with the former Miss Anne de Bourgh, her husband, Mr Roger Merriweather, and Miss Caroline Bingley. Elizabeth turned to see Mr Bingley send a steely gaze to his sister across the auditorium. She focused on Miss Bingley as well, noting an edgy quirk in her behaviour as she ravenously searched the grand hall. Mr Oswald entered with glasses of champagne for her and himself. She appeared to sneer when he leaned into her ear, reaching behind the chair for her opera glasses. Taking them from him, she perused the boxes of the quality and stilled with an unnatural stasis upon finding the Darcy box occupied.

"Excuse me." Mr Bingley headed to the door. Elizabeth noted that all members of their party were focused on the box across the theatre, and she watched as Miss Bingley focused the glasses on her. Within moments, the door to Blainard's box opened, and Mr Bingley arrived within, bending to address his sister. He appeared to be speaking with uncommon anger and grabbed Miss Bingley's hand before bending on his knee to whisper in her ear. His sister only shook her head.

Anne and her husband rose. Reluctantly, Mr Oswald did as well, indicating to Miss Bingley their evening was over. Mr Bingley exited the box with the two couples, leaving Lord Blainard alone. From this distance, Elizabeth could just make out a strange smile crossing his lips.

Mr Bingley returned to the Darcys' box, informing them regretfully that he needed to see his sister home. Jane expressed her relief that he was seeing to Miss Bingley's distress. Only ten minutes later, the door of their box opened again, and Bingley stepped inside.

"When I returned to the lobby, they were gone! I dare say Caroline will be home when I return, or with Mrs Merriweather. In either case, it was *extremely* impolite of them to leave when I had expressly stated that I would accompany Caroline. She was in quite a dither."

Shaking his head, he sat down again.

CHAPTER SEVENTEEN

The room at St Claire House was brilliantly lit, reflecting the jewels adorning the pampered attendees. All three Darcys, along with Miss Bennet and Mr Bingley, made their way through the maddening crowd. Elizabeth wore an ethereal gown of lilac, its organza overskirt dotted with embroidered flowers. Amethysts hung about her neck, interspersed with diamonds. Her smile was broad, her heart full of life and love. Those who approached were kind, some even sincere. The Gardiners, their equilibrium restored by the restitution of the renamed Gardiner and Associates, attended as well. The evening was a great success, socially and personally, until the end of the festivities, when Mr Simmons sauntered over to Elizabeth, who was waiting for her husband's return.

"May I have this dance?"

"I think not, sir." Elizabeth's eyes darted about the hall for her husband.

"Miss—I mean, Mrs Darcy, surely there is no harm in one dance."

"That depends upon one's understanding of the word harm."

"As your husband still has his fun with his French tart, I see no harm in your indulging me." Simmons tipped his head to the right, then grasped her hand, evidently meaning to drag her onto the floor as the musicians struck up a quadrille. Her next words halted him.

"You might have escaped last time, but do not think it impossible for me to see you prosecuted for assault with the intent to rape me. My husband is a powerful man related to other powerful men, and your connexions might find themselves less willing to save you next time."

"I have no idea what you mean," he said, his eyes taunting her.

"I mean, you have already tempted fate and the justice of either the magistrate or my husband's sword at dawn. I should not try it again if I were you. Let this be the last time you importune me, Mr Simmons, or I shall see to it myself." She turned on her heel and walked away.

Simmons, wiser than was his custom, turned and walked off in the opposite direction.

DARCY RETURNED FROM THE REFRESHMENT TABLE, looking for his wife. His eyes widened as Elizabeth walked off the dance floor, abandoning Simmons. Struggling to contain the surge of anger at the scoundrel's presence, he turned to Elizabeth, moving towards her before he knew what he was about. With each step, his concern for her overpowered his drive for revenge. She smiled, and when she took his offered hand, her touch relaxed him. He led them to a private balcony. The night's breeze refreshed their troubled souls.

"You are well, Elizabeth?"

"Yes, Fitzwilliam. He was odious but not harmful, and I reminded him of what information we possess that could yet be a problem for him." Elizabeth placed a hand on her husband's cheek. "We leave London soon, and he will fade from us like a bad dream in the morning's light."

Darcy kissed her hand, then bent and kissed her lips. Playfully, she bit his lower lip and he pressed her to him. She welcomed his embrace.

"Madam, I believe I would enjoy one more dance, and then perhaps to return home?" he said with a little nibble of her earlobe. She gave a little shiver which seemed to inspire him, and he drew even closer, his lips more insistent, lowering to her neck.

"That seems very agreeable to me," she replied softly. Straightening their clothes, they re-entered the grand hall, which thrummed at the late arrival of the guest of honour.

Jane and Bingley were waiting for them. "Darcy! Wellington is here!" Bingley blurted. Both Darcy and Elizabeth shared a smile, caught in the growing excitement for their nation's champion.

"General Waring is here as well, Lizzy. He wishes to offer his felicitations to you—"

"Personally, if I may, Mrs Darcy?" A distinguished looking middle-aged man bowed from behind Jane, beaming in amusement at her being caught speaking of him. "Forgive me for startling you, Miss Bennet, but I knew you were the shortest route to Miss Elizabeth—I mean Mrs Darcy." He took Elizabeth's hand to his lips, offering a gentlemanly bow. "Congratulations, madam, on your recent marriage. I wish you all possible joy."

"Thank you, sir," Elizabeth replied with a beaming smile. "May I introduce my husband, Mr Darcy. Mr Darcy, General Waring." The men bowed.

General Waring offered his hand. "Congratulations, Mr Darcy, you have captured an amazing woman, a rare jewel."

"Thank you, sir. I agree wholeheartedly," Darcy replied with a wide smile.

"If only my colonels would be so compliant, sir! With that attitude you would go far in the military."

"Oh, I think not. My cousin, Colonel Fitzwilliam, tells me often that I would not last a day."

The men chuckled.

"Fitzwilliam?" the general asked. "Ah, yes, Matlock's boy. Fine man, excellent commander."

"Thank you, sir, we are all very proud of him."

"Is he here this evening?"

Darcy shook his head.

"A shame, but well, duty and all that. Still, the evening is enchanting." The general then turned to Elizabeth. "Mrs Darcy, may I present you to Lord Wellington? He has specifically requested the introduction."

Elizabeth nodded, feeling the thrill of such a distinction. "It would be an honour, sir."

He offered his arm, and with a quick look to Darcy, she accepted. "Come, all of you, the general will not bite anyone. None, that is, save the French." He chuckled at his own joke, and the merry party strode across the room to a mélange of people gathered around the medalled leader. When there was a brief interlude in the conversation, General Waring intruded.

"Sir, if I may?"

"Yes, Waring, what is it?" Wellington said in a booming tone. Side conversations stilled.

"You wished to meet Mrs Darcy?"

"Ah, yes, the filly mistress."

"Mrs Darcy, may I present to you Lord Wellington. My lord, this is Mrs Darcy, the former Miss Elizabeth Bennet of Longbourn."

"And this is her lucky husband, I presume?"

Darcy stepped forward and bowed.

"Ah, well then, may I kiss the bride?" Wellington asked before leaning in and placing a chaste kiss on Elizabeth's cheek. "Congratulations, madam. May I wish you and Mr Darcy great joy."

"Thank you, sir," Darcy replied, and the gentlemen shook hands. "It is a great honour."

"Yes, yes, the honour goes to our troops, man. Finest in the world."

Darcy nodded.

"Tell me, madam, how fares my filly?"

"Very well, sir. She awaits you impatiently."

"Excellent. Contrary to public opinion, female horses are best in battle. Very little unsettles them. Lycea —Chestershire's mare—remains exceptional. I thank you for her."

Elizabeth blushed. "I believe Roan will please as well, sir. She shows great spirit."

"Splendid. Waring?"

"Yes, sir?" said he.

"I wish to have my horse as soon as may be," he said. "Arrange the details, will you? And now, Mrs Darcy, if you will excuse me, I believe I must dance the next with my wife. It has been a pleasure." He bowed and strode off in search of Lady Wellington, while General Waring took Darcy's card. The Darcys were then left to dance the last set as well. Bingley requested the same from Jane.

Simmons, leaning on a pillar, gazed at the twirling couples gliding across the floor.

HALFWAY THROUGH GEORGIANA'S FITTING WITH MADAME Lestrat, a great commotion could be heard in the back of the shop. Elizabeth shared a look with her sister, then both looked to the dressmaker.

Visibly chagrined at the disturbance in the midst of fitting two of her favourite clients, Madame Lestrat dropped the hem she was inspecting. *"C'est incroyable!* I shall have someone's head for this!"

A knock sounded at the door. One of the shop assistants nodded at the ladies then said, *"Pardonnez-moi, Madame Lestrat, mais c'est une circonstance critique, et la votre présence est exigée."*

Madame Lestrat nodded, then said to Elizabeth, "Please excuse me. There is a situation I must attend."

"Of course," Elizabeth replied. "We shall still be here in awe of these creations."

"Merci, Madame Darcy. Perhaps you would help Mademoiselle Darcy out of this gown and into that

one." She pointed to a beautiful periwinkle-blue linen gown. "We are done with this one."

"Of course." Elizabeth went to her sister. When she turned back, Madame Lestrat was gone.

The sisters marvelled at the second gown from every angle, then, having exhausted ideas for possible alterations, they looked to the still-closed door. Elizabeth's impatience and concern soon became unbearable, so she went to investigate. She searched through the various rooms until she found Madame Lestrat's private office. She knocked twice before opening the door, unprepared for the scene within. Stretched on a divan, nearly unrecognisable, Antoinette lay, bruises disfiguring every inch of her visible skin. They were angry bruises the width of a leather strap. Madame Lestrat stood, staring in shock at her cousin.

"Have you summoned an apothecary?"

Madame Lestrat's eyes darted between Elizabeth and Antoinette. "No."

Elizabeth left the room, returning a few minutes later, a shop girl hard on her heels bearing a basin of fresh water. She knelt at Antoinette's side, bathing her face and arms with the cool water. Madame Lestrat took the cloth when Elizabeth was done, squeezing her hand.

Elizabeth inhaled to speak in a soft voice. "I am so sorry. Who did this to you?"

Antoinette's eyes remained closed. "I was fooled by another man, Madame Darcy," she wheezed, and when she next spoke, her voice was reduced to a raspy whimper. "He asked to meet me. I thought he wished to be a patron for the shop." She began to weep. "He thought I was…Darcy's. He wants to punish William." She grabbed Elizabeth's hand. "He will come for you next."

"Who?" Elizabeth whispered, her skin prickling with dread. "Mademoiselle du Marché, who beat you like this?"

Though it evidently cost her greatly to do it, Antoinette opened her eyes and whispered, "*Seigneur* Blainard."

DARCY ENTERED LA CELESTE, IGNORING THE ASTONISHED looks from ladies entering and leaving the surrounding shops. Clarice led him to an unused dressing room, and he sighed with relief at finding Elizabeth waiting for him, her sadness and distress evident in her eyes.

"What is it? Is it Georgiana?" he asked immediately as she crossed the room and fell into his arms.

"No, I sent her to Lady Matlock. It is Antoinette."

At her unexpected reply, he froze. She placed her hand on his forearm. "She is upstairs, on a divan, beaten nearly to death."

"What? How? What happened?"

"Blainard beat her. Because he wants to hurt you."

"What?"

"That is what she said. He must still believe she is your mistress."

"The devil! I swear, I will kill him."

"No. You shall do no such thing, Fitzwilliam." Elizabeth's voice was low, yet full of fury. "Would you leave me a widow? The wife of a murderer?"

"No, I would not." He shuddered, then straightened his spine.

Elizabeth nodded, then said, "I should like to take Antoinette home with us."

"No. Absolutely not."

"She cannot remain here. She must be protected. It is my fault Blainard attacked her."

"Elizabeth, Antoinette cannot come to our home."

They looked at each other, locked in a standoff, until Darcy relented with a sigh. "Not only would it fuel the rumours, but she might interpret it as more than our caring for her, as one would for a friend and relation. And what would we tell Georgiana? It is simply not done, Elizabeth. It would bring unwanted attention to both her and us. However, I do agree with you, she cannot return to her residence." He paced, thinking through the arrangements. "We shall find her a safe haven for her recovery."

"I shall go with her."

"Impossible."

"She needs care!"

He stared at his wife, recognising the set of her chin, the flint in her eyes that was evidence of her iron-clad resolve. "What of that place?" Darcy waved his hand. "The one you and Georgiana visit."

"St Magdalene's?" Her eyes lit up. "That is a brilliant notion. I shall send a message for them to expect us."

Darcy followed her to the door. "She will be safe there, Elizabeth. I shall see to it."

Elizabeth paused, turning to look at him. "That is good of you."

"I could do no less." He ran his hand through his

hair. "It is my fault. I let the rumours of Antoinette as my…"

"Fitzwilliam." Elizabeth rushed to him.

Embracing her, anguish filled his voice. "I never thought Blainard would take things so far."

She stroked her palm along his cheek with such great tenderness that Darcy pulled her even closer. An approaching clerk, requesting Elizabeth's return to Madame Lestrat's office, recalled them to their place. Darcy remained in the dressing room till she returned. "How bad is she?"

Elizabeth took a deep breath, her hands gripping his arms that still encircled her. "She rests now, but he marked her badly. From what I can see, he took a strap to her arms and her face. When she fell, he kicked her, repeatedly."

Darcy's façade crumbled, imagining the beautiful woman he knew, now laying beaten and bruised. Guilt for abandoning her fired his instinct to hunt Blainard down and kill him, both for hurting Antoinette and for his threats to Elizabeth. Gaining some control of his emotions, he looked at his wife. "Do what you can for her."

She grasped hold of him before pulling back, eyes locked onto him. "We must be careful. Lord Blainard is rich, but vindictive, cruel."

Darcy saw the fire in her eyes and knew his spirited wife would not let the blackguard destroy her. "He will not win, this I promise you, love. You have my word."

LATE THAT NIGHT, DARCY STARED AT THE BURNING FIRE long after his man, Henderson, departed. Rubbing his hand over his eyes, he tried to clear away the strain of the day, which had begun with such delight when Elizabeth bestowed her favour upon his eager soul, yet had turned into a day of further trauma.

Leaning his head back, he stared at the ceiling. *I am eternally grateful I kept Henderson tailing Blainard. He was surprised when I summoned Elizabeth to hear his report. I had to, though I admit I did not wish to at first. But she was adamant. And I am glad. She needs to know how unstable Blainard has become. Positively unhinged!*

He scowled, pounding the armrest. *Blast his fortune! It hides a multitude of sins. Even the magistrate would not hear of this latest offense. Despite Henderson stating that more than one young girl had gone missing after receiving his attentions. And if his word was not good enough, Blainard's cousin believes the rumours, and has ended their betrothal.*

Darcy shook his head. *Antoinette vacillates between life and death in St Magdalene's from her wounds, which are now infected and bring a fever. It is my fault. If I had acknowledged our blood ties years ago, there would be no confusion or degradation to her reputation. I took the coward's way, allowing a fragile woman to protect me from the harpies of the ton. We did what we could to protect her from her French abuser, but how could we have foreseen Blainard and his unnatural need to have Elizabeth?*

It was only a game to the likes of Blainard. Gardiner was nearly bankrupted in Blainard's plot to ensnare Elizabeth, a scheme Darcy had, thank the Lord, foiled. *So, believing Antoinette was my lover, Blainard attacked.* He propelled himself out of the armchair to pace in front of the fire, hands clasped behind him. *What will he do next?*

How do I protect her? If he did this to Antoinette, what would he do to Elizabeth? She is the object of his obsession, and it is her safety in jeopardy.

Murderous thoughts clouded his vision, and he approached the door. "Giles?"

The butler quickly answered his master's call. "Yes, sir?"

"Do Archer and Mills still accompany Mrs Darcy? And Baker still guards Miss Darcy?"

"Yes, sir. Of course."

"Good. I want them accompanied at all times. Do you understand? Even in the house."

The butler nodded.

"And I want the men armed."

"Yes sir. Anything else, Mr Darcy?"

"Keep your eyes open, Giles. No harm must come to either my wife or my sister."

CHAPTER EIGHTEEN

Elizabeth, Georgiana, Darcy, and the Bennet sisters waited at the portico as Wellington's entourage turned onto Longbourn's drive. Mr Bingley stood behind Darcy, near Jane, having arrived with them three days before. Georgiana and Elizabeth's three younger sisters had ploughed through their initial shyness to discover areas of mutual interest and fascination. Elizabeth did not think Georgiana was quite as taken as Lydia and Kitty with the red coats and gold braid that had invaded Longbourn, but she seemed well pleased as she watched the Advance Guard bustling about, focused on their duty. If they noticed the pretty young women multiplying around them, they schooled their features not to betray any interest.

Colonel Fitzwilliam and his commanding officer, General Lessing, arrived as part of the procession, leading it directly to the front of the house. Wellington dismounted and strode to greet the Darcys. Taking Elizabeth's hand, he placed a gentle kiss on her glove before turning to her husband and shaking his hand.

"Welcome, my lord. We are most honoured." Elizabeth curtseyed.

"Thank you, madam. Ladies, gentlemen." He bowed to the gathering. "I am all anticipation to meet my new filly." Extending his arm to Elizabeth, he turned with her towards the stables, pausing to steady her when her shoe caught on a divot, and she stumbled.

When they reached the paddock, the earth burst apart, smoke billowing everywhere as clods of packed earth rained back to the ground. Picking themselves up from the dirt, the startled soldiers rushed through the haze to Wellington, pulling him and Elizabeth farther away from the now gaping hole.

With relief, Elizabeth saw Darcy and Mr Bingley run to help her sisters. Through the confusion and clearing air, she also saw a lone, masked rider barrel towards them and toss a lit torch at the stacked bales of hay, igniting them instantly. The flames jumped from the bales to the barn, sending the horses into a raging panic. They bucked and bayed, eyes wide and crazed as the stable hands scrambled to open the gates. Snorting and stamping, the horses broke free and as one, jumped the fence, racing into the open fields.

Pandemonium engulfed the yard; women shrieked, and men ran back and forth. Being led to safety, Elizabeth turned back, blinking at the destruction. As she wiped the smoke and tears from her eyes, a sobbing Lydia ran to her. Behind Lydia, a horse trampled through the chaos. Shock shot through Elizabeth as the rider pulled a pistol from his side, aiming at Lord

Wellington, who was shouting orders to care for the women a few feet ahead.

Pushing Lydia away, Elizabeth grabbed a thick clod of earth and launched it at the head of the horse running straight at her. The horse recoiled and reared, nearly unseating his rider. Elizabeth threw herself at Wellington as a shot rang out, and her right shoulder exploded in pain.

THE RIDER, REGAINING CONTROL OF HIS MOUNT, surveyed the carnage with satisfaction, until he saw a bloodied woman protecting his target and soldiers charging towards him. With bullets flying past his head, he kicked his heels into the horse's side, spurring him to breakneck speed away from Longbourn. Thundering through the open fields, the officers still more than half a field behind, horse and rider jumped the stone fence at the edge of the wooded coppice. "That is it, laddie. Just a little farther and we'll be free."

He urged the horse to go faster. "When I jump, you run free." He patted the horse's neck, and as they approached a large branch, he jumped, the horse barrelling on alone. Watching the stallion fly through the glade, he took a minute, smiling beneath his mask. Chuckling at the beauty of the plan, he climbed higher as the beating hoofs of the calvary thundered ever closer. Watching the soldiers ride beneath his feet, he plastered himself against the trunk until the posse rode by.

· · ·

GEORGIANA AND JANE FLEW TO ELIZABETH'S SIDE WHILE
Darcy scooped her into his arms. Jane applied pressure
to her shoulder, staunching the blood flowing down the
clammy skin of her arm. Jane glanced at her sister,
hissing at the pallor spreading over Elizabeth's face.
Wellington's personal surgeon, Major Tidwell, rushed
after them. Having seen many such wounds in combat,
he ordered the dining room table cleared. Sending a
Lieutenant Stilton for his tools, he prepared his patient
for surgery.

Clean linens were laid under Elizabeth, once Darcy
was convinced to release her from his embrace. He
stayed by her side, holding her hand, wiping her brow
with his handkerchief until Mrs Hill brought fresh, cool
water and soap to clean her face. He aimed at keeping
her comfortable, while Mary cut the sleeve off her
shoulder and Jane ever so gently cleaned the blood from
her skin. Unheeded, tears fell from them all, save the
physician. While none of them dissolved into hysterics,
the sight of their Elizabeth, helpless and unnaturally
pale, with pain in her eyes, slashed at their hearts.
Prayers were whispered, and as news of the fire spread
through the village, people came to Longbourn, offering
whatever they had to help.

Elizabeth struggled to breathe. Darcy held her firmly,
yet gently. Wave after wave of agonising pain shook her
upper body. Daring a look, her head jerked back, horri-
fied by the ruptured skin and exposed muscle, and her
breathing deteriorated. Sweat beaded her forehead, and
her mind grew hazy. "There is Mary, and Jane, but I
hear them not," she mouthed. "I feel distant from them.

Even Fitzwilliam. I see him, but we are a universe apart."

She screamed as someone or something pressed her shoulder.

"We need to stop the bleeding, my darling," Darcy whispered.

"Lizzy!" Jane cried out as Elizabeth's tears soaked the cloths beneath her head. She took another to Elizabeth's fevered brow. "Lizzy? Lizzy, I am here!" Over and over, Jane drenched clean cloths to cool Elizabeth's face, while Kitty pressed firmly upon her sister's wound.

Finally, the lieutenant returned with Major Tidwell's bag, and the surgeon prepared for his grisly work. After giving Elizabeth a generous dose of laudanum, he picked up a pair of elongated, pointed tongs, poised to pick pieces of gunshot from Elizabeth's shoulder.

"You cannot mean to use that on my sister?" Mary asked.

Glaring at her, the surgeon replied, "I do. I must."

"I think not." Mary grabbed a towel, wrapped it around his implements, and rushed to the kitchen, giving the bewildered surgeon a parting rebuke. "For cleanliness is next to Godliness, Major. Mrs Hill! Boil some water."

"Stop!" the major commanded as Mary disappeared. "Stilton!" he bellowed. "Go in there and retrieve my instruments."

Lydia ran to the door, blocking the soldier's passage. "We clean the implements we use on the horses, and you want to use those filthy things on my sister?"

"Young ladies," Tidwell said. "Every moment we waste—"

"Will be more than made up for by Lizzy avoiding an infection or fever once you are done," Jane said.

Tidwell held up his hands. "So be it, but I shall not be held responsible for the consequences of the delay."

Mary bustled in with the now boiled instruments. "Fortunately, Mrs Hill knew what to expect and had the water ready." She lay the towel near the doctor as Mrs Hill entered with another basin of steaming water, a bar of soap floating in it, and a clean towel on her arm.

"Here you are, sir," she said.

"Beg pardon?"

"To wash, Major."

"Wash?" he queried, aghast.

"Do as she says, man, and get to work," Darcy ordered.

Jane stepped up, fished out and handed the surgeon the soap. "It reduces the risk of foreign material entering the wound."

He gave the soap another glance and quickly washed his hands before searching for and retrieving fragments of gunshot and granules of stone and earth from the tear in Elizabeth's shoulder. Each piece clanged against the porcelain bowl Stilton held at the ready.

Jane winced when Tidwell fished out a good-sized pebble from Elizabeth's shoulder, making her cry out.

"She's lucky, our Mrs Darcy," the surgeon remarked, dropping another fragment into the basin.

Darcy shuddered as it clanked against the porcelain. "Lucky?"

Without giving him a glance, the doctor continued. "The bone is intact and, more importantly, the bullet missed the major artery. A few inches up and over and her aorta would have been severed. Then there would have been nothing I could do."

Darcy's knees buckled.

"Stilton?" the surgeon called out.

"Yes, sir," the young officer replied.

"I am nearly done here, prepare the kit."

As Stilton handed him the needle and thread to close the wound, they were all startled when a roar erupted outside the window. Rushing to the kitchen door, Mary asked the nearest person what was happening.

"The fire's out!"

"Thank the good Lord," Elizabeth mumbled before her eyes closed.

"IT IS DONE?" SIMMONS CAUGHT THE REINS OF THE young man's horse, steadying the highly strung beast. Looking up at the guilt-ridden eyes of the rider, his heart beat faster, his eyes assessing the wooded glen of their appointed meeting grounds. "No one followed you, did they?"

"No. I did exactly as you said." The young man struggled against his agitated horse. "I jumped to the branch, watched those fools fly by. I then found this fine filly, rode through the fields, not too fast, like you said. Oh, and I changed my waistcoat and jacket—"

"And cravat?"

"And cravat. Then I rode back at a slower pace to meet you here."

Simmons nodded. "Good man, good. What happened? Just the facts."

"You did not mention that...hoyden—"

211

"You," Simmons jabbed an index finger into the assailant's thigh, "watch your tongue about Elizabeth, boy."

"If it were not for her, my bullet would have found its mark, instead of her——"

Simmons pulled the reins that he held tighter still. "You missed your target, and you shot Elizabeth?"

The rider rolled his eyes. "She nicked the horse as I pulled the trigger. He reared. The shot went wide."

"Going wide does not mean shooting a lady in the heart."

"I did not hit her in the heart!" He scoffed. "Her shoulder I believe."

"You believe?" Simmons's voice threatened.

"I did not tarry, as you might imagine. I high-tailed it out of there, Simmons."

"You left your target alive, and a woman bleeding in the dirt?"

"What did you expect?"

"Better than this." Simmons retrieved a pistol from an inner pocket, and before either drew another breath, shot the would-be-assassin through the heart. "There, there," he soothed the bucking horse as the young man slid from his saddle, his astonished eyes wide as he hit the ground. Giving the body a hard kick, Simmons mounted the riderless beast. Looking down at the corpse, he snarled, "'Tis more than you deserve." He straightened in the saddle. "If the Masters heard of your incompetence, this would be a mercy. They abhor loose ends." Kicking his heels into the animal's sides, he rode off.

CHAPTER NINETEEN

Colonel Fitzwilliam nodded at the officer guarding Longbourn's icehouse to unlock the door. Inside, he breathed in the frigid air, smirking at the ragged horse blanket preserving the deceased's modesty, whose clothes had been removed to search for hidden clues. As he walked around the old door on which the body lay, examining the stiffening limbs, his attention fell on a small ribbon tattoo on the inner side of the man's left arm. Bending closer, he puzzled at the oddly familiar string of Ts. "If I did not know better, I would think our man here was a templar knight," he scoffed. "As if he was worthy of such a claim."

Arms folded across his chest, the colonel stared at the well-built, but lanky man. Seeing the bullet wound, he pursed his lips. "That was from close range. Very close. But only one set of boot prints in the ground." He stroked his cheek as he pondered. "When you left here, you were on horseback. We found the hoof prints."

He walked to the back of the room, pulling a long wooden box to a cleared space. He then pulled a small notebook from an inner pocket of his coat. Checking his notes, he positioned himself in front of the box and to the left. "You were found here. Boot prints were here—and only one set. And the hoofprints were there. There was only the one set, and it showed that one man arrived, then man *and* beast walked around to stand here."

He recounted the route, checking his notes. "Three feet." He held out his hand, raised it and smiled. "To hold the reins. Of course! You arrived, someone was waiting, took hold of the reins. Why? Are you not a horseman?"

He assessed the body again. "You look as though you kept busy, but you are not from here, are you? None of the locals recognised you. So you needed an accomplice, someone to do the reconnaissance, learn the lay of the land for you to plant the explosives and know how best to start the fire."

Colonel Fitzwilliam acted the part as he worked through what must have transpired. "This local agent took hold of the reins and walked you around. But you did not dismount. Huh." He shifted his weight and crossed his arms. "Words must have been exchanged as the deed was not done, and Elizabeth was injured by mistake. There is no mistaking this second man's aim, here, either. Simple, direct...deadly. A heated exchange to be sure, but was it the plan to kill the killer? Or was it his failure that induced such a reaction? Or the third, elusive, option?"

He returned to circling the body. "While you are unknown in these parts, Hill claims you may be the person found on the premises a few weeks ago. In the presence of Simmons. Which would answer so much. But I cannot allow theory to configure evidence. Evidence must create its own theory. So," he pointed to the dead man. "Simmons, your accomplice, must be furious that you failed to kill Wellington. But when he learned that you shot, perhaps killed, Elizabeth, he pulled out a gun and shot you." He again held up his hand, as if to hold the reigns. "Slipped his hand beneath his coat, pulling his own pistol from its shoulder holster, and aimed it up, where the heart of the rider would be. And you have a wound with the right amount of powder and ferocity to shred the fabric of your clothes to imbed within your flesh." Fitzwilliam leant over the man's chest, eye level with the injury, hands on his thighs.

"Now, where do you come from, lad? And why would you strike against the head of our army when we are challenged on two fronts? Are you a traitor to your country, or an enemy agent sent to kill our best general?" He dropped, squatting on his heels, eye level with the corpse. "No identifying marks, save those silly Ts, and nothing to indicate your identity. Did you ride in today? Earlier? There has been no activity at Simmons's estate, Beyford, so where did you come from? Where did you stay?" He straightened, moving to the bench where the man's clothes were neatly folded. Taking each piece, the colonel methodically examined every pocket, seam and lining for a clue.

"Nothing." He threw the shirt on the bench and picked up a boot, examining it from every angle. Shoving his hand down the shaft, he traced the sole down from the heel to toe. He looked at the external sole and heel. "Rather new, on an old pair of boots." He double checked the age of the shank compared to that of the heel. Examining it closer, he ran his fingers along its outer edge. Grasping the heel, he twisted it and smiled as it swivelled in his hand. With a rush in his blood, he turned it further, revealing a small compartment. Taking a deep breath, he pulled out the slip of parchment lodged within. With mounting excitement, he turned it over.

Matthews. Red Hen Inn, Rumbridge

Faster than a skittish colt, Colonel Fitzwilliam was out of the door, shouting orders. Less than ten minutes later, he was riding towards Rumbridge, ten miles west of Meryton, with four of the best men in Wellington's escort.

DARCY REMAINED IN THE MASTER BEDCHAMBER, STARING out of the window, hands tightly clasped behind his back, tension humming through his body. A half empty glass of brandy stood on a side table. Silence hung in the room until he whispered, "I cannot lose her."

Sighing, he leaned against the window frame. "What is happening? We scoffed at Richard when he thought Simmons was here to harm Wellington, only it was not

Simmons, but a man called Matthews who rode into Longbourn, setting fire to the stables and exploding—" His voice blocked from emotion. "He could have killed us all."

He crossed his arms. "But he knew what to do, and how to execute his attack to the greatest advantage. One must know the lay of the land, as I do Pemberley, to achieve such precision. And this Matthews is not from here—but Simmons is. He is involved somehow. I feel it in the depth of my soul."

Elizabeth stirred in her sleep, commanding his attention, and Darcy pushed all thoughts of Simmons from his mind.

HAVING POSTED SAUNDERSON AT THE DOOR, COLONEL Fitzwilliam entered Matthews's chamber at the Red Hen. The sitting room was clean and well-appointed, with comfortable chairs and decent rugs scattered about the room. "This is definitely not what I expected. Even Darcy would stay here." He scratched his head. "Right then. Where to begin?"

He paced about the outer room, but there was not much there; no personal items, not even a valise, only— "Hello!" He smiled at the travelling desk, tucked behind a chair, but rifling through the papers revealed nothing. He threw them down. "All blank. Or are they?" Lord Aubrey had told him once that it was possible to make visible that which wished to remain invisible. He collected the scattered pages and stuffed them back in the desk, then rummaged through the drawers instead.

Opening the bottom drawer revealed a velvet pouch. Reaching in, he retrieved two sticks of sealing wax, one silver and the other blue, and two bottles, one of ink, the other containing a clear liquid. About to open it, he recalled Lord Aubrey's first instruction when he explained his new counter-intelligence responsibilities: *'Do as little chemical work in the field as possible. These special cases require a comparable scientific mind. Especially instances that are beyond the ordinary.'* Fitzwilliam slipped the implements back in the pouch.

When an examination of the chifforobe and leather portmanteau revealed nothing out of the ordinary, he walked into the bedchamber. Brushing past a table on his way, he heard the plunk of metal hitting the floor. He bent, searching for the lost object. "What have we here?" he said, examining the two-inch pewter piece retrieved from the rug. "Funny, this reminds me of Matthews's tattoo. If you turn it right side up, this cross becomes a T." He brought it closer to the candle to inspect it further, but to no avail. "Damn, not enough light."

Giving up on the strange object, he looked around the chamber, taking in its unexpected luxury. "Espionage and murder pay well. Very well," he huffed. Then he espied the bed. "Strange." He looked about the room. "All else is neat and tidy, and yet," he pulled back the coverlet, revealing the bed linens, "these are in disarray." He brought the sheet to his nose, then pulled back. "And in need of changing. Peculiar."

In a flash he was on his knees, reaching beneath the mattress and running his hand underneath it. "Ow!" he cried, pulling back, staring at the drops of blood on the side of his palm. Using his unharmed hand, he pushed away the mattress. There lay a leather packet, with eight shaving razors protecting its perimeter, two at a time bound together like double edged axes. He sucked the blood off his hand, shaking it to relieve the pain, before binding it with his handkerchief. Then, taking a quick, pre-emptory look for potential hazards, he broke the seal on the packet and undid the wrapping. Embedded in the leather were a series of needle-like protrusions, and he vowed to take extra precautions in everything to do with this Matthews from here on in.

He colonel picked the packet up, transferring it to the desktop. Tilting it released a bundle of papers, which he read until the candle burned out. Gathering them up, he noticed a small oval, drawn on the left corner of the third page. With a shrug, he stuffed the bundle inside the travelling desk. Issuing strict instructions to both seal the room and note any enquiries after Matthews, he made haste to Netherfield, where Wellington and his entourage were encamped, to make his report. If the look on his face as he secured his saddlebags and mounted his horse matched his thoughts, then it was dire expression indeed.

DARCY SHOOK HIMSELF AWAKE AS A LOG CRACKLED behind the fire screen. Rubbing his neck, he sat up in the chair, looking to Elizabeth, who still slept. Unable to help himself, he ran his hand gently along her brow, pushing back a stray curl. He smiled at her peaceful features. "Dear God, let her be well." He took up her uninjured hand to his lips. "I cannot take another loss. Not her. Not when she has only just come into my life. Keep her well.

Please, please heal her and bring her back. I swear I shall love her all the days of my life."

He remained at her side throughout the night.

COLONEL FITZWILLIAM ENTERED THE DARKENED STUDY, Matthews's travelling desk tucked under his arm. His commanding officer , General Lessing, nursed a brandy in the flickering light of the crackling fire.

"How go things at Longbourn?"

"Mrs Darcy sleeps, sir. She has a slight fever, but they are hopeful it will pass by morning."

He grunted. "We are all upset, of course, by her injury. Our thoughts and prayers are with her and your cousin, in particular. They are newly wed, are they not?"

"Yes, sir."

The two men looked at each other before returning their eyes to the fire. General Lessing broke the heavy silence first. "Before we get to your reconnaissance, what is your assessment of the day's unfolding?

"This was well planned, for one."

"Agreed. Who has access to the stables?"

"Mr Hill, who is the steward and the stablemaster. The grooms and stable boys are all present and accounted for, and according to Miss Mary Bennet, all have been with Noah's Promise since the beginning. My initial guess was that Mr James Simmons was responsible. He and Mrs Darcy have—"

"A past association."

The colonel gathered his thoughts and his temper. "He attempted to impose himself—"

"Yes, to kiss her?"

"'Twas a bit more nefarious than that, but it was avoided. But, considering his past history with Mrs Darcy, and his familiarity with the area, he could have hired Matthews to do the dirty work, giving *him* the date with the hangman."

"But?"

"But…" He paused. "Why kill Matthews?"

"Indeed. I suppose what you brought from the inn sheds new light on things?"

"I believe it does." Colonel Fitzwilliam grew serious. "Prior to entering the chamber, I believed Simmons to be the leader and Matthews—though I do not believe that is his real name—to be the subordinate."

"And now?"

He pulled a leather ottoman closer, setting the travelling desk on top and pulling the leather portfolio from within. "I found this beneath Matthews's bed."

Lessing nodded, picking it up.

"Careful, the entire thing was rigged." He held up his bandaged hand.

The general frowned. "Did you take care of it, as I taught you?"

"Yes. Miss Bennet cleansed it, and I used the preparation Aubrey provided."

"Cannot be too careful with these things. What else did you find?"

After showing him the pin-laced interior, Colonel Fitzwilliam pulled three particular pages from the portfolio and replaced it in the desk.

Lessing grunted as he read them, glancing between the two columns on each page. "While it is disconcerting to see so many familiar and illustrious names on this list, it is the code"—he pointed to the second column—"that provides context. I shall have Aubrey take a look at this. Is this a list of future targets whom this Matthews intended to assassinate? Allies? Or contacts to convert?"

"Convert?"

The general looked to the fire. "What I have to say goes no farther than this room. Secrecy is of the utmost import."

"Understood, sir."

"For over a year or so, there has been chatter, rumours through the unconventional channels, that an alliance was forming. A smattering of individuals, leaders of one sort or another, in various fields of expertise, in nearly every sector of society. Transportation, banking, politics, industry of every stripe. Even the military. All men and women of promise."

"Promise?"

Lessing nodded. "Those who are not leaders in their field are still positioned to, with a word or suggestion in the appropriate ear, change the course of world events."

"But those names." The colonel pointed to the papers. "They are of the best families. Highly placed individuals."

"They are." Lessing took up the papers, perusing them once again. "They are. However, they are second sons, a few newly elevated." He read the third page. "And often heads of diminished standing."

"Prime to be bought."

Lessing looked up. "Or open to an advantageous offer. One such misalliance of which I have knowledge began with an exchange of introductions to the man's social circle."

"That is it?"

"That is but one way it begins. The requests became more onerous, until the chap felt uneasy. It was a demand that he relay an overheard conversation between his uncle in the Admiralty and the Prime Minister that prompted him to contact us."

Colonel Fitzwilliam shook his head. "Why have you not acted to stop whoever was responsible?"

"The contact boarded the next ship back to America. We were left with nothing but our man's testimony. And no, his name is not on the list."

"Indicating it is not a hit list."

Lessing shrugged. "Possibly not, but is it a list of people yet to be contacted or of willing accomplices?"

"I see." The colonel digested the question, then reached back into the desk, retrieving the blank pages and handing them to the general. "These might hold some answers. I recalled Lord Aubrey's demonstration of invisible ink and what it takes to unmask it." Then he pulled out the velvet pouch and the two vials from the desk. "And his rejoinder to do as little chemical work in the field as possible."

"Good work. Very Good." Lessing opened the clear vial, sniffed, and pulled away. "One is never sure what it could be." He re-sealed the bottle. "Take this with the other things to Aubrey. Let him decide what to do with it."

"Your guess?"

Lessing shook his head. "I have learned the hard way to avoid these types of conjectures until the evidence is before me. Let us see what Aubrey comes up with. That will give us real evidence with which to build our theories."

Colonel Fitzwilliam sat, taking it all in.

"Is there anything else, Colonel?"

About to say no, he reached back into the desk for the metal object. "There is this." He handed it over to the general, who pulled a small magnifying glass from his waistcoat pocket, his smile growing with excitement.

After another moment, he looked up. "Your thoughts?"

"I believe it is a wax seal."

"Yes, yes. And?"

"It is made of pewter and appears to be a family seal —or, more particularly, a variant of a family crest. An eagle's head with crossed arrows in its beak. And here, along the edge, the border is made of these crosses."

"Oh?" Lessing re-examined it with his magnifier. "Yes, I see."

The colonel scratched his ear. "I can barely give it credence, as I find it hard to link this Matthews to the Knights Templar."

"Why would you say that?" General Lessing demanded.

Taken aback by the force of the reply, Fitzwilliam inhaled. "The assailant had a tattoo on his arm."

"Which arm?"

He thought a moment. "His left."

"Oh, ho!" Lessing clapped his hands together. "Fascinating. I want these brought to Aubrey at first light. He is to drop all other work and recover these blank pages."

He repacked the desk. "You are not to let this," he patted the box, "out of your sight. Under no circumstances is another to touch, open, or investigate this. Understood, Colonel?"

"Yes, sir."

"Good. And good night. Off with you. Do not return without Aubrey's analysis."

Colonel Fitzwilliam saluted, turned, and, box in hand, left the room.

CHAPTER TWENTY

After the initial night of fever and laudanum, Elizabeth's recovery progressed to the satisfaction of Major Tidwell and Darcy's personal physician, summoned from London. Though fear for her recovery had long passed, Darcy hovered, insisting she take things much slower than she would like. Fortunately, her doctors agreed with her, and she was allowed to walk the grounds within a week, once she assured them that she would comply with their prescribed limitations. Between Darcy and her sisters, Elizabeth's time was rarely her own.

She pushed her blanket away, placing her feet on the floor. Even though both physicians had deemed her well enough to walk, she took care, testing her strength with every step. Donning a simple gown, she made her way to the kitchen, where, though disapproving of her appearance, Cook fastened the last few buttons and handed her a muffin. Giving her a grateful smile, Elizabeth wrapped her shawl about her shoulders and opened the kitchen door.

Pausing, she smiled at the soft light of dawn that glistened in the dew still clinging to the grass. Breathing deeply, she closed her eyes and opened her ears. Birdsong called to her, and she opened her eyes again. Determined, she followed the path to the burned-out stable, but paused when the charred remains assaulted her senses. The scorched timbers were stacked for removal, and while the stench of burning was faint, it clung to the air, and she wiped tears from her eyes. Looking to the resettled ground, her head spun as images of the explosion flooded her mind and she grasped for purchase, relieved when the strong arm of her husband slid protectively around her waist, supporting her trembling frame.

"Elizabeth," he murmured in her ear. "What are you doing out here?"

She looked into his eyes, her own brimming with tears. "I had to. To show myself I could."

"Oh, my darling," he clasped her to his chest, careful of her shoulder. "I understand, I do, but to do this alone? I would have come with you."

Hearing the pain in his voice, she gave him a soft smile. "I know. And I love you all the more for that. But it was something I wanted to do on my own."

Darcy held her gaze and nodded.

Elizabeth looked to the unsalvageable piles that once held her dreams and sighed. "It is gone."

"The horses are all well at Netherfield."

She nodded. "But here… What once was is gone."

"We can rebuild."

"No." She shook her head. "We are to Pemberley, eventually. To rebuild here would be redundant." She looked over the abandoned corrals out to the fields, then turned to her husband. "Will you help me back?"

"Of course."

COLONEL FITZWILLIAM DEPARTED FOR LORD AUBREY'S London home two hours before dawn. His lordship's reputation was legendary, and though honoured to call on him, he felt—as he did each and every time the venerated man visited his father—as a schoolboy called into the headmaster's office. He knew only the most daunting cases were referred to Aubrey, who had bested French intelligence more than once.

Aubrey's butler opened the door, ushering him into a wood-lined study.

"Ah, Colonel Fitzwilliam. Good of you to come."

"Lord Aubrey." The colonel bowed.

"Come." His lordship indicated a fine table partially covered by books and journals. "Coffee? I admit I am already on my second pot. If it is not to your taste, I shall call for tea."

"Coffee would be most welcome."

Aubrey poured two cups. "How fares Mrs Darcy?"

"She is well, sir."

"Thank heavens. And…Longbourn, is it?"

"Yes, it is Longbourn. And it is still standing, thankfully."

"And the stables, Noah's…?"

"Promise, yes. The horses are stabled presently at Netherfield, the nearest estate."

"Ah. Good."

Returning his cup to its saucer, the colonel fidgeted under the older man's gaze. As the silence grew unbearable, Aubrey spoke. "As you know, you are here at General Lessing's request. I understand that you are heading the enquiries into the attempted assassination."

Colonel Fitzwilliam nodded.

Aubrey took his time over another sip of coffee. "Then, before I ask about your endeavours, Lessing suggested I share what I know about those we believe to be the perpetrators and their operations here in England. They are a group of oligarchs, often referred to as the 'Olees'."

"I have heard of them, but here, in England? I thought they were colonials?"

Aubrey shook his head. "While they are primarily active in the Americas, their network of like-minded individuals now extends to our own shores. These are men—and some women—of fortune. Often great fortune, from a number of sources, nefarious and legitimate. Their aim, it appears, is to mould governments to their own will, but not directly. They prefer being the shadow's shadow. They influence policy, law, public sentiment, amassing as much control as possible without the responsibility of actually governing."

Colonel Fitzwilliam clutched his hands. "I wondered who these people were, agitating here in England while Napoleon's terror still reverberates on the continent."

Aubrey shifted, his eyes radiating intelligence and intensity. "These people are at the top of their game, and their game is domination. Just think what would have happened if this Matthews was successful."

He nodded his agreement vehemently. "Killing Wellington would strike a blow. The army would be shaken, and it would take time to reorganise the command and counter the fear such an assassination would create. A general's nightmare."

"Not only would our military have lost a master tactician but think of the morale of our people!" Aubrey leant forward. "The populace is the foundation of every government. With the will of the people, great things are possible. But when they lose faith in their leaders to provide the basics—security, opportunity, order, stability —that is the root of all internal trouble. Revolution, sedition, civil war."

The colonel pushed back in his chair and considered. "I have never heard it stated quite like that."

"Young men are not generally taught these things. That would lead to questions those in charge would prefer were not asked." Aubrey reached for a portfolio on his desk, searching through a cache of documents and handing one to the colonel.

He read through what was a list of random events: a change in a politician's position on various issues, the withdrawing of funds from another man's bank account, the building of a factory in America, the commissioning of a ship. He looked up. "What is this?"

Aubrey smiled knowingly. "These events, on three continents, occurred at the behest of known oligarchs."

"But to what end? I have not had a chance to study it extensively, but at first glance I do not see a connexion."

Aubrey clasped his hands together. "We believe the

coming hostilities with our former colonies will be decided on the seas. Take that commissioned ship. It experienced a number of changes that tied up the shipyard for months. The same shipyard at which two of our frigates were to be built. The delays meant we had to use our second choice of shipyard. Beyond being irksome, they were incapable of implementing the required modifications. We believe that all these random events are aimed at destabilising England's dominion of the sea."

He gaped at Aubrey's audacious statement.

"Absurd, I know. However," Aubrey said, "keep in mind, a total collapse is unnecessary. A shifting, just enough of an opening, gives the 'Olees' the advantage."

"In what sense?"

"This is not a military battle, my young friend. Most wars serve an economic end. For what else is national security but the ability to protect a nation, a people's economic viability. If we cannot take in raw materials or export products, what happens? People lose their livelihoods, they grow hungry, ragged. That is what sparks civil unrest, that is what enables the oligarchs to dominate the political landscape and manipulate governments into doing their bidding, and that is how they advance their interests."

"Who are these people?" the colonel asked, exasperated, "and how did Simmons, from the miniscule town of Meryton, come to be involved in such a vast and devilish conspiracy in the three years he was in America? Enough to have a diplomat at his disposal to free him from gaol?"

"That is the quintessential question. We know they are prominent figures from all facets of life, from agriculture to ship building, who have banded together to benefit each other. The way I explain it to myself is to see it as a brotherhood of sorts. Aimed at keeping each of them at the top, to be the most prominent in their various fields." Aubrey went to his desk. Rifling through his papers, he offered another sheet to Colonel Fitzwilliam. "This is a list of those we believe are members."

The younger man was surprised to recognise many of the names on the list. "Matthews's papers contain many of these same names, sir."

"Excellent. Make a note of those, will you?"

He nodded, then returned to the document. As he did, his eye was drawn to an object on the desk. "What is that, Lord Aubrey?" he said, pointing to it.

"Ah, I meant to show it to you earlier. It is the only semi-reliable identifier of the 'Olees'. All the men on that list have one of these in their possession." He handed the fob to the colonel. The fabric was a plain field of blue stars, and it was edged with a familiar circle of Ts.

Colonel Fitzwilliam looked up at him. "I have seen this before. Matthews had a tattoo on his left arm—a ribbon of these Ts. I thought they were the Templar crosses."

Aubrey crossed his arms, his right hand stroking his chin.

"And on this seal." He reached into his satchel, pulling out Matthews's seal.

Aubrey's eyes flashed with excitement. He brought out a small, round magnifying glass and lit a candle to melt a bit of wax. He took the seal and eagerly pressed it into the wax, waited half a minute, then pulled it free. Grabbing the paper, he rushed to the window, shaking with excitement. "Yes, yes, they are the same."

Colonel Fitzwilliam took the paper. "Aye, they are. The rest look like a family—no, a personal seal."

"Not a family's crest?"

He shook his head. "No. The elements are too modern. It is more likely the amended crest for a second or third son."

"Yes. That makes sense, but the Ts are more prominent. I wonder at the replication of the design from the fobs on this." Aubrey pointed to the seal. "And in a tattoo." He shook his head in thought.

"Perhaps it is more aspirational than indicative of membership?"

"It could be." Lord Aubrey picked up the fob. "Whereas this remains the strongest indicator we have. I have seen it myself. They wear it." He leaned on the arm of his chair. "Unfailingly."

THE YOUNGER BENNET GIRLS AND GEORGIANA DIVIDED their time between nursing Elizabeth and debating Longbourn's future. While the main house was left unscathed, the tragedy had scarred their sensibilities. They longed for change and adventure. Georgiana, Mary, and Kitty walked, sometimes with Elizabeth, sometimes on their own, discussing which concerts they wished to attend, the exhibits they would see, and the masters they would enjoy together. Mary, finished with her studies, decided to spend the coming autumn with the Darcys.

Faced with the defection of her three youngest sisters, and to relieve Elizabeth of another concern so far from Derbyshire, Jane eventually capitulated, agreeing to lease Longbourn—for the time being. In the interim, she vowed to spend as much time as possible enjoying the treasures of her home, starting in her sanctuary, the herb garden.

Lost in thoughts of harvesting seeds and transporting plants to Derbyshire's unfamiliar soil, she did not hear footsteps on the gravel path leading from the manor until the last moment. Surprised when a shadow fell about her, she looked up to see Mr Bingley. Noting his nerves, evident in the strong grasp of his hat, she found a warmth in his eyes and his smile. Jane wondered what could be of such importance so early in the day.

"Mr Bingley! How good to see you, sir." She returned his warm smile, wiping the dirt from her hands.

"Miss Bennet."

Jane's heart beat brighter. Not only had his kind attention in London eased her acceptance of Mr Darcy, but she found her appreciation had blossomed into thoughts of his handsomeness—his eyes, his neck, how the fabric of his waistcoat moved when he breathed— that made her blush.

"Miss Bennet? Would you walk with me?"

"Of course." Jane offered her hand, and he pulled her to her feet, then stepped closer.

Mr Bingley's hand slid up her arm, where he held her gently, but firmly. "Jane," he whispered. "There is so much I wish to say."

Glancing at the sitting room windows, she took his

arm, returning his whisper. "The orchards are in bloom and are really quite lovely."

"As are you."

"Shall we?"

"Indeed, we shall." He released her arm, only to take her hand and thread it back through his arm. "I have some news. My sister has announced the date of her marriage to Mr Oswald."

"Really? Elizabeth will be as surprised as I am. We thought, surely, they would never actually marry."

"The happy day will be in September."

They continued to the small apple orchard where the sisters had played as children. The blossoms perfumed the air with the joy of spring. Jane breathed in their heady scent.

"I have heard," Mr Bingley said hesitantly, "that good things come in threes. I was wondering if you thought that…"

He trailed off, and Jane waited with her hands clasped in front of her.

At last, he continued. "Since we met almost two months ago, you have been constantly in my thoughts. And these visions of you, your beauty, your eyes as they look at me, they warm my heart. I love…I love you and beseech you to have mercy and say you will be mine. Please marry me. To live without you would be my undoing."

Jane offered him her hands, and he grabbed them. His eyes locked onto hers.

"Yes, Charles. Yes. I love you and will, most whole-heartedly, be your wife." Before she could inhale, he crushed his lips to hers. Moving closer, Jane grabbed hold of his arms, ran her hands up to his cravat and revelled in the strength of his neck. Her knees buckled as her fingers touched skin. He clasped her by the waist, and she raked her fingers through his silky hair, teasing out the curls at the end. She moaned as their kisses redoubled in intensity. Each was jolted by passion, and their bodies pressed closer into each other. She leaned into him, and he almost stumbled back.

"Jane? Jane?" Mary called from the garden. "Where are you? Mrs Hill is out of Lizzy's tonic." Mary reached the border between garden and orchard, her voice full of urgency. "Jane? Where are you?"

The lovers pulled apart, guilty grins upon their lips.

"I shall ride to London to speak with your uncle," Bingley whispered, before releasing her from his hold.

"There is no need. He and my aunt arrive this afternoon."

"Excellent!" He grinned like a cat. Offering her his arm, he said, "Shall we, my dearest beloved?"

She smiled, and they emerged from the orchard to bear with happy hearts the scolding of her younger sister.

FELICITATIONS WERE MADE ALL AROUND AT THE GOOD news, and Elizabeth and Darcy immediately offered to host a midsummer's ball at Pemberley.

This works to my advantage, Darcy thought as he looked at his new sisters. *I shall speak with Bingley about purchasing an estate in Derbyshire. We can keep Longbourn to lease and settle the younger Bennets between us.*

"What amuses you so, sir?" Elizabeth asked.

He only smiled.

She wrapped her arms around her body.

"What is it, Elizabeth?"

"I only wish Antoinette could be so happy."

Darcy's head snapped up.

"Oh, no, you are mine." She gave him a seductive smile, then sighed. "But is it so wrong to hope she could find a way? A new beginning, away from these awful rumours circulating, away from Blainard and his obsession? If only…"

"If only, what, Mrs Darcy?"

"It is just… Georgiana was asking about the Canadas, because Clarice wishes to travel there."

"Does she?" he asked.

"She does."

"It would be rustic, but Antoinette did well in Derbyshire, away from town."

"What are *you* thinking, Mr Darcy?"

"What if we were to finance their journey there? Quebec has some society, enough to support a dress shop."

"She is extraordinarily talented." Elizabeth's enthusiasm grew.

"She is."

"It would be a new beginning for her."

"And for Clarice."

Elizabeth nodded.

"Let us speak with Celeste."

"Oh, Fitzwilliam, how I love you." She walked into his arms.

"Which would leave us free to dwell on the pleasure that *two* sets of newlyweds, happily situated, could bring." Leaning close to his wife's ear, he smirked as his breath ruffled the curls at her neck. "In Derbyshire."

"I am all astonishment, sir. How your mind does turn."

He chuckled again before brushing his lips to hers.

CHAPTER TWENTY-ONE

Antoinette took her first walk around the
grounds of St Magdalene's without assistance.
Although her wounds were healing, her spirit
remained fragile, even under the care of the women
among whom she now lived. While she drew strength
from their example, the brutal attack had shattered the
emotional and physical shelter she had created for her
survival. The inflammation and redness across her face
had faded, but one look in the mirror told her that her
days as a beauty were over.

She looked up as her cousin and Clarice entered the
courtyard.

"Antoinette." Celeste kissed both her cheeks. "I am
so glad you are feeling well enough to come outside."
Her smile grew, encouraging Antoinette to smile
with her.

"We have such news," said Clarice, bouncing on her
toes.

"Oh? Does our *petite* have a beau?" Antoinette teased the younger woman.

"No, no," Clarice blushed. "Much better than a beau."

"*Ma, non*? What could be better than a beau?"

"A life." Celeste's voice grew hard, catching Antoinette's attention.

"Of course." She looked away, shamed.

"Clarice has a future dependent on her own talent," her cousin continued. "She will make her own way in the world, independent of the whims of men."

Antoinette nodded.

"But," Clarice said with a sly look. "Should a handsome man—"

"Of good character," Celeste insisted.

Rolling her eyes, Clarice smirked. "Of good character, yes, but should a handsome man happen to fall in love with me, I should not be averse to marriage."

The two older women shook their heads, but smiles graced their lips.

"But what of this new life?" Antoinette asked, looking to Celeste.

"The Darcys have written. They are convinced the Colonies could use a little sophistication, and Clarice does have a natural sense of things." She smiled fondly at her niece. "They propose a dress shop in the New World—well, Quebec."

"But to go so far!" Antoinette cried, dismayed.

"That is why we are here."

"Yes." Celeste clasped her hands in her lap. "While I am truly thrilled with the opportunity for Clarice, I am concerned for her traveling so far alone. I have come to ask if you would consider accompanying her."

"Me?" Antoinette asked, startled.

Clarice grabbed her hands. "Your work speaks for itself. Between the two of us, our success is guaranteed. We shall be partners."

"Partners?" Antoinette whispered, looking between the hopeful eyes of Clarice and her cousin. "No. No, I could not."

"You would be doing me a favour, and it is a chance for new beginning." Celeste held Antoinette's gaze.

"Yes, but—"

"It is settled." Clarice jumped from her chair to embrace Antoinette. "*Merci, merci, merci.* And we may speak French again. All the time."

Miss Adams appeared at the edge of the courtyard. "Oh, there you are! Pardon my interruption, ladies, but the young lady wished to see the puppies, and their mother has finished feeding them."

"Oh," Clarice exclaimed. "Aunt, may I go?"

"Go," Celeste shooed her off. "Ten minutes, Clarice. We must return to the shop. I have an afternoon fitting."

"Of course." Clarice and Miss Adams left the two alone.

"Antoinette," Celeste said, "this is a good thing for you and her."

"But we would be so alone."

"No, you would be together."

Antoinette shook her head. "No. It would not be good for her. To live with a woman who locked herself away from the world."

"A woman who worked hard to bring success to us

all," Celeste pleaded. "Darcy is sending letters of introduction, and a letter of credit. You would be safe. The
man you fear would not find you there."

"Yes, we would be safe." Antoinette looked into her
dearest friend's eyes. "But I would miss you, Celeste. So
very, very much."

COLONEL FITZWILLIAM RODE INTO THE GROUNDS OF
Oxford College, carrying Matthews's travelling desk.
Lord Aubrey had instructed him to present it to a
Professor Quartermaine, apparently an expert in such
devices.

"Thank heavens you did not have to force this open,"
the white-haired academic admonished, examining the
exterior with great intensity. Placing the desk on his
workbench, he headed to a glass cabinet, and began
rooting around inside.

"Why is that, Professor?" The colonel looked around
the chamber, more of a laboratory than a residence.

"Because," said Quartermaine, popping his head out
of the cabinet to answer, "a year or so ago, we examined
another container from these deviants. Resorting to force
earned us a spray of acid. Decimated the hands and
most of the face of my assistant."

"What?"

"Oh, yes. The last one of these I heard tale of had a
spray of three feet." He paused. "Poor Maxwell—
another assistant. If he had not been wearing his glass
shield, he would have lost his eyes." Coming back from
the cupboard, Quartermaine emptied the contents of
the travelling desk on the table. "Whoever creates these

little jewels is clever." He ran his fingers along the sides of the box. "Ah ha, here it is!" Placing the upside-down box on the table, he pressed the back corners of the box simultaneously until a click reverberated in the room. "My, how these devils do like their gadgets."

Colonel Fitzwilliam glanced again about the chamber, where, scattered about like toys in a nursery, were devices for concealing daggers, explosives, and sleeping draughts. "Looks as though they are not the only ones. Unless you are working for both sides, Professor."

"No, er, well, I suppose his majesty's government is able to afford the latest innovations as well. Now, shall we discover a secret?"

"Secret?"

"Yes," Quartermaine said. "There is usually a hidden compartment to carry that which is best to conceal. And this," he picked up the pewter piece the colonel had brought with him, "in all likelihood, will be the key."

"The seal?"

Quartermaine held it up for examination. "An innovative design, denoting the eagle of America, along with the oak of England, with, I surmise, the mark of oligarchical ambition."

"Aubrey and I wondered about that."

"Only members obtain the fob. Here, the Ts are on the perimeter—a border indicating aspiration to join, not conferred membership."

"Like the tattoo?" Colonel Fitzwilliam rubbed his left bicep.

"Precisely. You do catch on. Good to know Lessing is still reliable in his assessments. Aubrey was not so sure."

He gaped at the revelation. "But did you not say the seal is the key?"

"Unusual quality in this particular piece of pewter." Quartermaine leaned conspiratorially towards him. "The magic of it is, it is magnetised.

"Clever."

"Indeed." Quartermaine wiggled his brow. "And so satisfying to foil." Retrieving two pairs of oversized spectacles and leather gloves, he passed one set to Fitzwilliam. "For your protection. And now, let us discover what these 'Olees' wished to conceal." He picked up the box.

Hoisting the glass in front of his face, Colonel Fitzwilliam watched as Quartermaine moved the magnetic seal left to right at one corner, then its mate. An audible click filled the silent room. He gave the colonel a boyish smile and adjusted his own shield. Pulling the piece of wood away from its frame, he called out. "Duck!" Five sharp, quarter inch, iron quills catapulted three feet from each corner.

"Ah." Quartermaine peered at the now inert desk, then pulled out a drawer from underneath.

"A hidden bottom."

"Or side," the professor replied, studying the mechanism. With a pair of long copper pincers, he reached inside and picked up a felt sack. He shook it, looking surprised at the distinct jingle of coins. The curiosity sparking in his eyes turned to panic as he dropped the bag on his work counter and ran to open a window. Then, gesturing at the colonel to follow him, he ran to the door.

"Out!" he shouted. "Quick, boy."

Seeing an expanding haze emanate from the bag, Colonel Fitzwliiam all but ran from the room.

"What was that, sir?"

"A gas. A diabolical invention of the Americans. It must have activated when I shook the bag. It would have rendered us unconscious in a few moments." He sighed. "Unfortunately, I do not think we shall learn anything more about the contents of the desk today. Even with burlap masks, I could not guarantee we would be safe." He locked the door, pocketing the key. "There. Now, no one will enter until tomorrow. With the windows open, it should be safe to go in then."

Colonel Fitzwilliam looked longingly at the door.

"Do not fear. I shall make a detailed inventory of its contents and send you a report once I am able to re-enter. Now, off with you. I am a busy man."

He nodded and turned to exit the laboratory with haste.

WITH THE APPROVAL OF DARCY'S LONDON PHYSICIAN, they returned to town. Elizabeth wore her arm in a sling fashioned from lengths of silk selected by their sisters to coordinate with her gowns. Darcy ensured she followed Major Tidwell's exercises to strengthen her arm, but when walking about, he bound her arm to her body.

Within the week of their return, Darcy felt comfortable enough to let Elizabeth go about town and she headed to St Magdalene's. As the carriage turned onto Coleman Street, near the old London Wall, she planned her attack. *Miss Adams sent for me, so this cannot be good. I, too, am worried for Antoinette. The rumours have been relentless, no doubt fuelled by Blainard to draw Fitzwilliam to retaliate. But I shall not let him win.*

The door opened and Miss Adams's greeting drew her to the present. Stepping inside the cool, fresh foyer, Elizabeth took a deep breath, smiling at her hostess. The ladies of St Magdalene rushed to her, fussing over her sling, tending to all her needs, and shooing Archer and Mills into the kitchens for a cup of tea.

"Ladies," Miss Adams schooled her companions. "Allow Mrs Darcy space to breathe."

"Oh, forgive me," each of the five women tittered, stepping aside, allowing Miss Adams and Elizabeth to proceed to the small room where Antoinette sat at an easel. Looking about the space, Elizabeth found sketches of different gowns strung on a wire like laundry. She marvelled at the colour, variety and elegance in the dazzling array.

"Antoinette, these are magnificent! Your talent is astounding!"

"Madame Darcy!" Antoinette scrambled to her feet, hesitating when she saw Elizabeth's bound arm. "*Mon Dieu!* What happened?" She rushed forwards, guiding Elizabeth to a chair. "Not Lord Blainard?"

Saddened by the fear and guilt in Antoinette's eyes, Elizabeth clasped her with her free hand. "No, not at all. Rest assured, this was from an entirely different source."

"I do not know whether to be grateful or not," she said with a smirk.

"My sentiments exactly." Elizabeth smiled and crooked her eyebrow. Their shared amusement broke any remaining tension in the room. Then suddenly, Elizabeth noticed the lady was weeping.

"What is wrong?" She kneeled in front of the distraught woman, trying to calm her.

"It is nothing," Antoinette finally gasped.

"I beg to differ," Elizabeth soothed. "Antoinette, please, tell me what troubles you."

"Your friendship and kindness are too much. I do not deserve them."

"Of course you do," Elizabeth insisted. "It is because of me that you are in this position, and even if it was not, you are as deserving of kindness as I am."

"No, no, it is not so."

Elizabeth quirked her eyebrow, but remained silent as Antoinette's tears flushed the turmoil from her heart.

"When I see you, Madame Darcy, I think of what my life could have been if things had been different."

Elizabeth reared back.

"No, no." Antoinette studied her hands. "Celeste has convinced me that William and I could never be; he never held those feelings for me."

She then looked Elizabeth directly in the eyes. "And I realise that I longed for the love of a good man, a kind man. Your William is such a man, but he is not mine. I am ready and able to see that now. And release that infatuation."

"I am glad. Now, free from that encumbrance, perhaps you will find a happiness of your own."

"In Quebec? Are you, too, here to convince me to take such a risk?"

"It is more than just a risk. It is a grand opportunity to create a life on your terms. Antoinette, I believe that as long as we live and breathe, we have the chance to redeem, reform our lives, if we have but the courage to do so. St Magdalene is a testament to this." Elizabeth adjusted herself in her seat, hearing the truth of her words ringing in her own heart. "Of course, it would not be easy, but you strike me as a resilient woman."

Antoinette let loose a rueful laugh. "*C'est vrai.*"

"Then think of the possibilities! Quebec is French-speaking but is an ocean apart from the continent and London. You would be free from the danger of both."

Antoinette clenched her hands.

"If not Quebec, what is it you wish to do with your life? My husband, as you know, is a very generous man."

Antoinette blushed, but remained silent.

"Forgive me, but I would have thought the chance to accompany Clarice would be acceptable to you. You would not be alone, and Darcy has hired a man, Mr Bastillon, to ensure your safety."

"But who would look after Celeste? And Darcy?" She turned her head, attending to her tears.

"I shall look after Darcy—and Georgiana. And the three of us shall see to Madame Lestrat. And Quebec is not so far that the post cannot be delivered."

"You would write to me?"

Elizabeth took her hand. "Of course. And I do not think we could restrain Georgiana from corresponding with Clarice. She is in raptures that she might have a first-hand witness to the New World."

Antoinette chuckled. "You are very persuasive, Madame Darcy."

"Please, call me Lizzy."

Antoinette looked to her work, hanging about the room. "Shall I show you my designs then, Lizzy, which, it appears, will dazzle Quebec so?"

"Then you accept?" Elizabeth perked up in her chair.

"Yes." Antoinette nodded with caution. "There is little here for me anymore. It is time to take my fate in my own hands and make it mine."

"Wonderful! I foresee only good will come of this."

Antoinette shrugged, then moved to the first drawing. When a young girl entered with a tea tray, Elizabeth and Antoinette were in earnest conversation laying the foundation for the French women's future.

COLONEL FITZWILLIAM SAT AT THE WORKTABLE IN Darcy's library, studying an enlarged sketch of Matthews' seal.

"There you are," Darcy strode into the room.

The Colonel looked up but remained quiet.

"What are you working on that has you so dour? More so than usual," Darcy chided.

Pushing back from the table, the colonel snorted. "Avoiding your feeble attempts at humour, cousin."

"May I?" Darcy held out his hand.

"Why not?" He held out the document but changed his mind. "I must insist on your utmost discretion."

Darcy gave him a quelling look.

"Duty required I ask." He handed the paper to Darcy, who studied the design.

"What is this?"

"An enlargement of the seal found at this Matthews's lodgings."

"What does it signify?"

The colonel shrugged. "That is what I am

attempting to work out. What it means, and whether or not it matters. Though it is the border, those Ts, and not the interior of the thing, that is significant."

"Oh?" Darcy took a closer look at the paper.

Nodding, the colonel continued. "According to the papers we discovered in that box I mentioned the other night—"

"Yes, the gaseous case," Darcy chuckled.

He gave Darcy a glower. "Yes, well, they provide the evidence to establish a link between the conspirators here in England with those in America, where this diabolical plot seems to have originated. And of course, Matthews." He leaned back in his chair.

"So," Darcy replaced the paper on the table. "Did this Matthews come from America to contact people who might welcome the embrace of those…what did you call them? 'Olees'?" He took a seat across from his cousin.

"Yes. Fortunately, one of Quartermaine's men untangled their code, because of course it was in code. And thank heavens he did, otherwise the list of names found in Matthews's bed would have been absolutely useless. A rotating frequency was what they used, apparently, that revealed nothing until matched with the papers locked in that infernal box. What we do know is that these Olees had this well thought out."

"And it would have worked, save for Elizabeth." Darcy traced his index finger along the table, looking to the Colonel.

"I beg your pardon?"

"If she and I were not wed, you would not have been involved in Wellington's accepting of the horse, no?"

"No."

"He would have been attended by only the honour guard, which you have mentioned on more than one occasion are ceremonial at best."

"They were rather useless in the pandemonium."

Darcy shook his head. "Hopefully *someone* would have pushed Wellington out of harm's way."

He leaned forward, "But if you had not been there, who would have taken up investigating those involved and what this all portends?"

"Thank the good Lord for Elizabeth."

"And for my prescience to marry her."

"Yes, there is that." The colonel shook his head. "With her one, small act of courage, the plans and efforts of these mighty oligarchs fell to nothing. Wellington is alive and back in London, surrounded by loyal, battle-hardened troops, who would—and have—followed him to hell and back. He is untouchable there."

Darcy placed both hands on the table, his eyes filled with excitement. "Which is why Longbourn was the logical setting for the attack. Wellington was less guarded, and..." His eyes darkened. "It cannot be coincidence that Simmons has returned. He *knows* Longbourn."

Richard hunted for the slip of parchment taken from the assailant's heel. "We have but one name for two suspects. One could be the corpse buried in Hertfordshire's potter's field. Or Simmons. But the name we know is Matthews, not Simmons. Why would Simmons take a room at an inn so close to his estate?"

"Because he would not bring this business home to his mother," Darcy offered.

"Of course! He used this alias, Matthews. The note was *to* the assassin—the name of his contact and where to meet. Not, as we first assumed, the name he was to assume in the area and where to lodge."

"Jane did say Simmons was seen leaving the area with a stranger."

Richard rubbed his chin. "Could it be that simple? The Red Hen is on the opposite side of Meryton, not fifteen miles from Beyford. And Simmons has been gone three years. That is a long time to remember a man that may or may not have visited but a few times when he did live here. And if this hired assassin shot Elizabeth, killing him would make sense to Simmons. From what Lessing, Aubrey, and Quartermaine said, these Olees do not make mistakes. They expect the best from their underlings. Removing the assailant permanently may have been part of the plan from the beginning, or an act of the moment, or a contingency in the face of failure."

"But what will he do now?"

Richard shrugged as Darcy tidied up the papers strewn across the table. Picking one up, he glanced at the names, smirking at the bottom of the page.

"What is this?" Darcy jutted the paper towards his cousin.

"What?"

"This...egg? At the bottom of your notes. I did not know you had an artistic flare."

Glowering, the colonel grabbed the paper. "This, for your information, is a faithful rendering of a design I found on one of Matthews's papers. Not from the *box*."

"Odd place for a drawing. What do you think it signifies?"

"I have not a clue."

A knock and opening of the door startled the men. Darcy hurriedly collected the rest of the papers.

"Pardon, gentlemen. Colonel, this just arrived." Giles held out a silver salver upon which lay an official summons. Richard glanced at the letter. With a snarl, he nodded to Darcy, then left the room in a rush.

CHAPTER TWENTY-TWO

T he sun had barely risen when Elizabeth, Georgiana, and Darcy arrived at the dock. The large passenger ship bustled with sailors and footmen loading trunks, stores, and sundry last-minute preparations. The party sought out their friends who were embarking on the voyage of their lives. Mademoiselles Antoinette and Clarice, along with a trusted manservant, waited closer to the plank to board. Madame Lestrat waited with them.

Darcy clasped Bastillon's hand before bowing to the ladies. "*Au revoir*, Cousin." He kissed Antoinette's hand, then they quickly embraced. "Be well and let us know how you fare."

Wiping away tears, Antoinette smiled, nodded, then turned to Elizabeth, who opened her good arm and embraced her. "I am so grateful for your recovery, Mademoiselle, and pray for your happiness."

"*Merci*, Madame Darcy. And I for you and yours."

Both women composed themselves, and as the warning bell rang, Madame Lestrat ushered the émigrés onboard. Remaining on the pier, waving as their friends walked up the plank, Darcy stood beside Elizabeth, his arm pulling her close, his lips kissing her brow.

"I love you, Elizabeth Darcy, with all my heart. I always will. Your kindness humbles me." She looked up at him, until Georgiana alerted them that Madame Lestrat was returning to the dock, surreptitiously wiping her eyes.

"*Mon Dieu,*" she said as she approached. "I never thought it would be so *trés difficile* to part with that little chick. And Antoinette. They are all I have left, you know?"

Elizabeth put her arm around the saddened woman, giving her shoulder a squeeze.

"May we take you somewhere, Madame?" offered Darcy.

"*Merci.* That would be most kind."

They waited until the ship set sail from the dock, lost to the horizon of its journey. Then they headed to the waiting Darcy carriage. A man, swaggering and sloppily dressed, approached, blocking the entrance to their coach.

"Blainard," Darcy hissed, seeing all three of his companions tense. Noting his footman was alert to potential danger, he gripped his walking stick, dropped Elizabeth's arm, and stood in front of the women. Behind him, Elizabeth gathered the ladies and moved them back one step.

"What do you want?"

"Oh, I believe you know what I want, Darcy."

Blainard swayed, using his own stick to steady himself. "The question is what I shall accept in exchange for my little French pastry escaping before satiating my pleasure. What have you to offer to appease me?"

"Enough! This ends now, once and for all."

"No!" the three women cried out, dismayed.

"In two days' time," Darcy said. "My second will contact you."

Blainard gave an exaggerated bow. "I await his arrival with bated breath." He stumbled back as Darcy's walking stick struck his chest. Darcy stepped closer to him as the ladies hurried into the carriage. "Be on your way," he said, his voice shaking with controlled rage.

Blainard tipped his hat and turned, swaying down the street with unconvincing nonchalance. As he turned the corner, Darcy relaxed and entered the carriage, while his footman kept watch. Darcy looked to the women, noting a silent exchange between Madame Lestrat and his wife. Seeing Georgiana trembling, he stretched out his hand, pulling her to sit by his side as the coach moved forward.

AFTER LEAVING THE DARCY CARRIAGE, MADAME Lestrat strode through her shop, shedding her bonnet and pelisse into the hands of surprised apprentices. She ordered tea on her way to her office. Reaching her desk, she ignored the list of expected fittings for ball and wedding gowns to locate a sheet of parchment and a quill. By the time her head clerk knocked on the door with her tea, Madame Lestrat was reviewing her hastily composed note. She accepted the tea and ordered the note's delivery to a less reputable quarter of town.

She leaned back, grasping her hands across her waist. *That monster is nothing but a drunken abomination. What he did to Antoinette is a crime. A crime! And if there is one thing I know of men, it is that unstopped, the carnage will continue. They are ruthless and insatiable. Antoinette is out of danger, oui, but there are others. So very many others, unprotected and vulnerable. Non! The world will not mourn the loss of one such as he.* She slapped her hand on the desk. *What is done, is done, and for the best.*

THAT NIGHT, PROWLING THE RIVERFRONT FOR HIS NEXT amusement, Lord Blainard chanced upon a quartet of men. Undaunted, he dismissed their muttered insults with imperious taunts of his own. The quick thrust of a fist crushed his jaw, sending him reeling from one into another of the men, who pushed him onto the blade of a third. The long, thin stiletto split his jacket, waistcoat, and silk shirt, slicing between two ribs into his left lung. The fourth man jabbed it further, into Blainard's heart. As the last light slipped from his lordship's eyes, one of the men grabbed him by the hand, smirking as he pulled the signet ring from his finger and then let him drop like a dirty rag into the dark water of the Thames.

THE NEXT MORNING, MADAME LESTRAT SAT uncharacteristically still, eyes focused not on the gold signet ring, but on the past, to the man who had loved her sister, so many years ago in France, before a cruel nobleman destroyed their lives. She shed tears of relief that the threat to her dear niece and their friends, the Darcys, was gone. Finally, the hell that was Lord Blainard was over.

COLONEL FITZWILLIAM STRODE INTO DARCY'S STUDY, momentarily startled to find his cousin examining the open portfolio he had left there the day before. He slowed his stride. "Darcy."

Elizabeth entered, followed by Giles, who carried a tea service. "Good morning, Richard. I am so glad you have returned. I hope your business is resolved."

"Yes," he drawled, watching the butler set the tray down and leave the room. "A bureaucratic mishmash."

"No threat to our national security then?" Elizabeth teased, but a ripple of true concern laced her voice.

"No, nothing so dramatic," he dissembled.

"Good to know." Darcy turned over the page flashing the enlarged seal.

"Oh." Elizabeth walked to the desk, hand outstretched. "What are you doing with that?"

"I beg your pardon?" Richard rushed to take it from her, but she turned, eluding his grasp. "You recognise it?"

"I do. Is that significant?"

"Yes, it is."

She took another look. "Well, it is not quite the same, but very like the Simmons's family crest. Only this is an eagle, is it not?"

Fitzwilliam nodded.

"The Simmonses have a falcon." She handed the

page back to him. "It was an homage to Jamie's great uncle. He was infamous in Hertfordshire."

"Because?" Darcy smiled at her.

"Because his great-uncle Matthews was Hertfordshire's one and only highwayman." She handed the sheet to the colonel.

"Matthews?" Fitzwilliam stepped closer. "You are sure?"

"Oh, yes. The great highwayman Matthews was the hero of many of my childhood adventures." She retook the folio he still held. Examining it more closely she bit her upper lip. "These are new—the border crosses. But otherwise, yes, it is the same."

Darcy took the sketch from her. "Curious. Oswald, Miss Bingley's intended, his seal has them in the design. And they are Ts—I checked. They were unexpected, so I asked about them."

Fitzwilliam sat thinking for a moment, then said, "This sketch is from a seal found at the Red Hen Inn with the assassin's belongings. We thought the rider was in charge, but what we found indicates that it was—"

"Mr Simmons," Elizabeth concluded. "But what does this all signify?"

"That is what we will discover."

LATER THAT AFTERNOON, A STREET URCHIN APPROACHED the Darcys as they entered their carriage. The boy stuck out his hand, holding a sealed letter. "This be for ye, sir."

Darcy took it, as Elizabeth slipped a coin into his free hand, which he gave to the lad.

"Thank you, sir." The boy tipped his cap and left.

Darcy directed Elizabeth to continue to the carriage without a word, waiting until they were moving before breaking the nondescript seal. He fumbled to catch the gold band slipping from the unfolded letter.

"What does it say?" Elizabeth asked as she examined the ring.

Darcy, feeling more than a little perturbed, handed the note to his wife in exchange for the ring, which he threw out of the carriage window.

"Blainard! He is—" she gasped. She lifted the page. "From whom?"

Darcy did not answer, for she would see soon enough that it was not signed. He shrugged, retrieving the note and tearing it to pieces. "I know not, but we are spared a duel." He scattered the shreds out of the window, and they rode on to the Gardiners for tea.

WITH ELIZABETH HAVING BEEN DECLARED PERFECTLY HEALED by no less than three physicians, preparations began in earnest to not only remove home and horses to Pemberley, but to prepare for a late summer celebration of Jane and Mr Bingley's engagement.

The first stop was Longbourn. Now that her sisters had mutually decided to spend the summer in Derbyshire while they searched for a suitable home, leaving Longbourn was less emotional than Elizabeth had imagined. The fire, and Mr Simmons's betrayal, fuelled her and her sisters' desire to leave. When Mr Bingley expressed his desire to find an estate in Pemberley's vicinity, the decision was made, and together, they boxed up their memories, marked the furniture, and began their journey.

Those grooms who were willing to relocate, as well as Mr Bingley and Darcy, rounded and readied the eighteen horses chosen to make the move. The size of the large caravan slowed the journey to six days rather than its customary three. Jane and Elizabeth rode in the Darcy carriage, while Georgiana joined Mary, Kitty, and Lydia in Mr Bingley's. It was a merry party with the women watching the men and horses, admiring the ripple of muscle as they galloped after an errant animal, or their rugged return each evening, caked with the dust of the road over their well-hewn physiques.

Arriving at the inn, Elizabeth and Jane ordered hot baths, while the men settled the horses for the night. The younger women escaped to their rooms. Elizabeth added some of her special liniment to the large tub in her and Darcy's room. To counter its medicinal smell, she added lavender water, recalling Darcy's preference for the scent. When he entered, stripping off his jacket and waistcoat, his eyes sought hers. She smiled, and he grinned, indicating his mud-caked, grimy clothes. Taking in his strong form, she advanced, and he watched her hungrily.

"Something about riding in the saddle all day makes a man long for his woman." Darcy wrapped his arms around her, possessive, and irresistible. She crushed her body against his, unleashing the buttons of his shirt and pulling it from his chest. He bent forward and kissed her with a growing passion. She pulled back, pouring her love into him, and his smile lit the room. He yanked his boots off and then his breeches.

Elizabeth turned, walking towards the still steaming

tub. Looking over her shoulder, she gave him an impish smile, pointed to the tub, then untied her robe. Darcy stepped closer, pushing the silk from her shoulders. She dipped her toes into the water, then slid in. Darcy swallowed, then slipped into the hot, relaxing water behind her. Lavender steam swirled around them. Elizabeth twisted around and straddled his hips. He moved lower in the water, making room for her, and she eased each and every one of his aches.

As the water cooled, Elizabeth traced its rivulets down his chest. Darcy wrapped his arms around her and kissed the top of her head. She dragged her nails across the width and length of his chest. Both smiled in satisfaction, remaining as they were until the chilled water forced them to move.

LADY PRAXTON'S SALON, ON THE OUTSKIRTS OF ONE OF the more fashionable sections of London, had not been in her late husband's family for centuries, as was her father's. Yet, it served in being closer to her customers, men and women of quality, who sought the stakes at her table or needed an unobtrusive meeting place for unscrupulous assignations and alliances. Diversions of all sorts were available in the upper rooms of the grand house, with the unspoken understanding of anonymity. The men and women who frequented Lady Praxton's might not have acknowledged each other in the light of day, but come twilight, the great leveller of vice neutralised rank and privilege. More than one upstart ruled the available tables, enthralling peer and rake alike.

Colonel Fitzwilliam crossed the threshold, the guest

of his brother on this particular evening. In the two years since his last visit, much had changed in his perception of the gambling den. Recalling the list of names revealed in the Simmons documents, he grimaced at how many were in attendance—and were at their ease, as if this was their usual meeting house. Which, he realised, it probably was.

Striding to the garden, he gulped at the fresh air to cleanse and refocus his mind. He overheard the studied laughter of a woman change into the unmistakable sounds of coupling. He shook his head at how some enjoyed their passions spiced with the lure of discovery or even observance. He was about to head back inside when the woman's next words caught him.

"Oswald," she begged, petulant between the male's grunts. "Tell me you will not marry that awful woman. I know what you need, and she is not it."

"Oswald!" called a third, strident voice, which Richard vaguely recollected, its owner bursting through the bushes to interrupt the ultimate moment of intercourse.

"Vick!" The first man gasped, and the thud of a body hitting the ground brought a sardonic smile to Richard's lips. Glancing around the vacant balcony, he found refuge behind an unruly topiary shaped like a naked woman. Using the side view of the sculpted back-side, he peered around to observe from beneath her breasts, and was rewarded with a plain view of Caroline Bingley's future husband.

"Leave!" the second man commanded.

"But—" the woman whined.

"Go!" Oswald dismissed her.

The woman rearranged her skirts, departing with an attempted kiss. Oswald pushed her off and turned to the other man. "Could you not have waited another—"

"Minute?"

Fitzwilliam smirked at the humour in the rebuttal, even as he recognised Lord Vickers, undersecretary to the Exchequer.

"Droll, Vickers. Very droll." Oswald pulled up his breeches as the woman retreated back to the gambling den. "Now, tell me what is so urgent to have interrupted my pleasure. You are aware I leave in the morning to join Miss Bingley?"

"Another of your questionable choices."

"She serves her purpose without making any demands. Now why are you here?"

Vickers lowered his voice to a conspiratorial whisper. "Blainard's body was found this evening. Fished from the Thames."

"I see," Oswald said.

"Good riddance, I say. Oh, I know he was a favourite but really, he was ever a liability."

Oswald held up his right hand. "Let me think."

"What are we to do? The whole endeavour has sunk. And you know we were warned there would be no second chances."

"No, right you are." Oswald paced the shrub-bound enclosure.

The colonel pulled back until Oswald returned to Vickers' side. Then he leaned closer again.

"He got things done, you said. He will arrange everything, you said. Well? Did he?" Vickers's voice climbed to a new pitch.

"Enough, Vick. We must not panic."

"No?" Vickers stepped in front of Oswald, stopping the man mid-stride. "A reckoning must be made. A great deal of money was spent to make this happen, and now what have we to show for it? You know, if we fail, Whitehall will be the least of our concerns."

"I know," Oswald hissed. "Go to Blainard's residence. See what you can find. Who was his contact? And make bloody well sure our names are nowhere to be found."

Richard smirked, knowing Saunderson would be at Blainard's residence within the hour.

"There is another thing." Vickers stepped closer. "Although there is no official enquiry, there are some questions being asked."

"Of course. Wellington was there. His subordinates were there. Of course the military seeks answers even if the multitudes remain ignorant." He paused. "Who leads the enquiry?"

"Lessing."

"Blast. That man is like a dog with a bone."

"Wellington should be dead," Vickers whinged. "But he lives, and we hear nothing. From Matthews—"

"Will you cease this blubbering?" Oswald surveyed their surroundings. "One never knows who may be lurking about."

"Right."

"Now you listen to me. There is no connexion—"

"That we know of. This M—"

Oswald's glare cut off the earl.

"He may have a list. With our names on it."

"I dare say he is not that foolish. Nor careless. If

such a thing exists, rest assured it would be in a code of some sort. These people know their business."

"I hope you are right."

"Of course I am. Have I ever led you astray? Here is what I recommend. Take yourself off somewhere relaxing. The seaside, perhaps."

"I get ill at the sea."

"Then the country. Anywhere that brings you peace. And stay there for, say, a fortnight or two. Let things calm down."

Oswald—O. Vickers—V, Fitzwilliam thought to himself. *A code? O, V…OVO. Latin for that little egg on the bottom of Simmons's list. Oswald and Vickers are on his list!*

The men on the other side of the shrub continued to speak. "I shall send word from Derbyshire."

"Derbyshire?"

"Yes. Miss Bingley's brother is engaged to Mrs Darcy's sister."

"Blainard was sniffing after Mrs Darcy, no? Prior to her marriage, of course. No one would go after Darcy."

"Every man has his price. As well we both know."

"There you are!" Richard's brother, the viscount, hissed from behind him. "McAlfer is asking for you. Make haste. Let us meet with him, then leave this place."

The colonel shook his head and followed his brother.

CHAPTER TWENTY-THREE

Kent

Lord Vickers's pen scratched against a folio late into the night. Pausing, he brought the page close to his eyes as a roll of thunder caught his attention, and he scrambled to the open balcony door. Movement in the garden paused his attempt to close it, and he stepped further outside. "What is that?" Silence replied, broken by an occasional bat flying overhead. "Nothing." Unsettled, he peered out to the darkened gardens before returning to his chamber. Locking the door, he pulled the curtains together and returned to his desk.

He dipped his quill in the inkwell, writing as he dictated to himself. "Oswald, I, as you know, abhor this skulduggery—missing bodies in the Thames and what have you. These people want me only for my position, and I confess to a growing unease in meeting their demands. I am glad the 'attempt' was not fulfilled, and that M— fled rather than commit such an act. And that is what I shall do."

He paused at the sound of footsteps on the stairs. Laying his quill down, he opened a desk drawer, retrieving a pistol and placing it alongside his letter. Reclaiming his quill, he continued. "Once I resign, their interest in me will cease, and I shall leave England. The Canadas are adjacent to America. I trust there is enough wilderness there to hide and recreate my life. I suggest you consider the same. No matter what you think, Pemberley is not far enough away to ensure your safety."

"Lord Vickers." A man stepped suddenly from the adjoining chamber.

He leapt to his feet. "Who…who are you?"

"My name is Simmons. You may know me as Mr Matthews."

"How—"

"I am well trained for almost every contingency." Simmons stepped closer.

"Stay right there." Vickers reached for his gun, shaking as he lifted his hand. Stepping forward, he stumbled, inadvertently pulling the trigger. The blast rang through the silent building.

"You tried to shoot me!" Simmons shouted, advancing. "Are you daft? You will wake the entire house." He closed the distance and grabbed the gun from Vickers' hand. "Get a hold of yourself." With a castigating look, he examined the pistol, seemingly unaware that it pointed at Vickers.

"Please, please!" Vickers begged. "I…I—" He swept his clammy hand across his beaded brow, struggling to catch his breath. His eyes widened as pain crushed his chest, and he slumped to the ground.

SIMMONS RUSHED TO THE BODY, ROLLING HIM TO HIS back. Pressing his ear to Vickers's chest, he scowled and began to untie the cravat, checking for signs of life. "Nothing." Leaning back, hunched on his heels, he grabbed the pistol. Taking a deep breath, he pocketed the firearm, and returned to the desk and the half-written letter, chuckling darkly. He addressed the cooling corpse. "You know nothing of these people, my lord. There is no escape once you agree to their terms. You fool."

He slipped the letter into his coat pocket. Bending again, he searched Vickers's waistcoat and then the jacket hanging on the back of the desk chair. "And what treasures do you hold?" he asked the small key he pulled from a pocket. He then searched all the common places the wealthy secures their valuables. Ten minutes later he had three hundred pounds in his pocket, along with a small journal that chronicled past transactions—information for payment—from the oligarchs over the last three years.

"You fool. This would have earned you the noose." He shook his head at the corpse. Closing the hidden cabinet, he pushed back the sliding panel and replaced the painting. Looking about the room, he patted his pocket. "And now? To Pemberley."

THE BENNETS AND DARCYS ADJUSTED TO LIFE AT Pemberley with ease. The women giggled and gossiped about fashion and decorating their new chambers. Unaccustomed to the cacophony of so many living in close proximity, Georgiana often accompanied Elizabeth on her morning walks around the estate. It was good to escape to the solace and comfort she found at home.

Elizabeth loved Pemberley, finding it the perfect blend of nature and artifice. Her early mornings were spent on its paths with her beloved new sister or her husband, as he led her to his favourite hideaways.

Darcy pushed back the boughs protecting his favourite spot on the grounds. "I found this as a boy and returned whenever possible, especially after my mother died. Here, I could refashion my world in daydreams. Then, when my father died, this was my refuge, when the duties of being master of Pemberley overwhelmed me. I would come here and let everything go." He smiled and tugged her closer. "I would sit and listen to the wind in the trees, watch the sun on the lake." He jutted his jaw to the opposite direction from where they had come. "Once, I found my mother and father there… loving each other." He pulled one of her curls loose from its restraint.

Turning, Elizabeth walked to the edge of the small clearing. "The lake is so close." Wonder filled her at the beauty of the sun glinting on the water. "It is—"

"Lovely." Darcy closed the distance between them, his arms encircling her waist as he nuzzled her neck.

"Fitzwilliam?"

"Hmm?"

"You are sure this—Ah!" she gasped as his lips trailed her neck.

"Yes, Elizabeth?" he smiled against her skin.

Turning, her eyes held his, and he moved his attention to the buttons of her gown. He slipped it off her shoulders, making quick work of her corset, which he dropped to the side, followed by her chemise. His breathing grew laboured as her clothes gathered at her hips. Sinking to his knees, he pulled them to the ground. Kissing the small of her back, he ran his hands along the tops of her stockings, untying each bow, to drag one then the other down her shapely legs.

Elizabeth turned and smiled. She reached her hands behind her and, one-by-one, the pins in her hair fell away, freeing her curls. His mouth dried as the rich, chocolate brown locks cascaded past her shoulders, bouncing as she tossed her head from side-to-side.

Escaping his reach, she shook out her hair and sauntered to the water. Darcy was undressed before he knew what he was about, diving after her into the dark green water, catching her slender waist when she was in the middle of the pond. Treading water, he pressed her to him. Her lips were upon his, wet, cold, yet hot at the same time.

"How I love you," he whispered, and she kissed him again. When their lungs forced them apart, he drew a breath before placing his kisses on her ear and down her neck to the point where it joined her shoulders. She threw her head back, while remaining in his gentle embrace. His passion took over, and the waves their bodies created sent the reeds rollicking. Their cries of bliss startled the birds, and when they reached their release, they exploded in joy, touched by the earth, air, sun, and the mystery of water. They clung to each other, sated and in love, content and happy to be home.

OSWALD REVIEWED THE EXPRESS DELIVERED FOR HIM AT Pemberley five days later.

> *To Mr Oswald,*
> *Lord Vickers left instructions that should anything happen to him, you be notified. I regret to inform you of his lordship's demise. It was unexpected.*
>
> *Sincerely,*
> *Mr H Neely*
> *Personal Secretary to Lord Vickers*

Oswald struck a match to the express, focusing his troubled mind on the parchment crumbling to flaky ash upon the side table. He extinguished the falling embers dancing on the cherry wood, then leaned against the window frame.

"Unexpected. What does that mean? Vickers was never what I would call a robust individual. No, a nervous bundle of brilliance, but he appeared to be in good health." He sank into a nearby chair, panic assailing him as he saw what he believed was the demise of the entire scheme—and by what it meant for his own future. "'Unexpected'. Murder? Is that possible? Blainard was fished from the Thames, and now Vickers is 'unexpectedly' dead."

He tugged his cravat, feeling it close in on his neck. Jumping to his feet, he paced the spacious sitting room. "Could they be related? And what does that mean for me? We used aliases when dealing with that Matthews." He stopped. "But of course, he knew who *we* were. The oligarchs do not do business with just anyone. They research the man, his character, his standing, and what assistance he can offer. Matthews knows who I am. And where I reside. How long before he learns where I am at present?"

He rubbed his head. He needed an escape. "The Canadas, perhaps? No. India. That is far enough away that by the time word reaches the colonies, and they unravel where I have gone, I could be a new man with a new story. I shall write to Halvert to settle my accounts as expeditiously as he can. If I take a loss, so be it. 'Tis a shame I shall not have time to get my hands on Caroline's twenty-thousand pounds. I have earned at least that much for putting up with her these last few months."

He sat at his desk, a gleam of hope in his eyes, and pulled out a piece of parchment, which he addressed to his solicitor.

The next morning's breakfast was a strained affair. Caroline was both agitated and relentless in her interrogation of Elizabeth, in particular, among the Bennet sisters.

"So, Mrs Darcy, are you still an active horse *trader*?" Her lips glistened maliciously.

Elizabeth hid her amusement behind her coffee cup.

"Caroline!" Mr Bingley glared at his sister. "Mrs

Darcy is renowned throughout the country for the animal she breeds."

"Is it not what I said?" Caroline's enquiry held a caustic turn, raising the hackles of all at the table.

"And you, Miss Bingley?" Catherine rejoined. "What are *you* renowned for?"

Caroline startled at the impudent young woman. Her lips twitched, but her hand trembled at the hostile faces of her companions.

"As it could not be as a fashion leader," Lydia quipped with wide, innocent eyes.

"Nor for her wit," said Mary under her breath. Even Oswald smirked, as Caroline glared at Mary.

"Yet it must be quite something to have one's name and reputation bandied about in such an unrefined manner," Caroline stroked her neck with her right hand, her lips drawn in condescension.

"Caroline!" Louisa Hurst hissed behind her napkin. "What are you about?"

Caroline gave her sister a haughty glance. With a flourish, she dropped her napkin to the table, pushed back her chair and swept out of the room.

Her sister followed, murmuring her apologies. Finding her in a nearby parlour, Louisa closed the door. "Have you taken leave of your senses?"

Caroline turned to face her sister, "It galls me to the core to see these *upstarts* seated at what should be *my* place at *that* table. *We* should be the ones residing in the family wing, not those ... those Bennets!"

"You had best get your emotions under control, Caroline," Bingley barged in. "Or you will find yourself on a hired carriage back to London for the remainder of the summer, suspiciously low on funds to support the outlandish wedding you are in the midst of arranging."

She faltered momentarily.

"You are perilously close to insulting not only my best friend, but most importantly, my future wife and family. Think very carefully on where you next spew your venom, Caroline. Do I make myself clear?"

"Yes, Brother," she spat. "I understand that you are so bewitched as to forget your true family in favour of that country nobody."

"That 'nobody' is feted and welcomed throughout the *ton*. With all your airs of prominence, I would think you, of *all* people, would be seeking her favour rather than censure." He glared at his sister's defiant stance and inhaled deeply before speaking more calmly. "Caroline, I thought you had let this go. Elizabeth or no, Darcy does not, has not ever returned your interest. Never."

Her eyes flashed in anger.

"I warn you. One misstep and you *will* be sent away. Get hold of yourself. Not only is Darcy a married man, but *you* are engaged. Attend to your own happiness and let the Darcys enjoy theirs."

"Never!' she hissed, a vindictive gleam in her eyes. She spread her arms wide. "*This* is mine. *I* am *destined* to be mistress here, and nothing *you* say will make me think otherwise."

Bingley shook his head. "Then I shall know how to act. Take heed, Caroline. A threat to Elizabeth is a threat to Jane's and my happiness. Trespass upon *that* and you will face my wrath."

"As if *that* frightens me," Caroline spat before stomping out of the room.

COLONEL FITZWILLIAM PACED HIS CHAMBER AT MATLOCK House, his jacket discarded, his waistcoat unbuttoned, and his hair a wreck as he ran a hand through it. He leaned onto his desk, looking at his notes.

"O is for Oswald. Darcy said his seal has the Ts as a border. V for Vickers, found dead when Saunderson arrived to watch him. And though it appeared he was working on something, we found nothing. No evidence, other than what I overheard linking him to Oswald and this nasty business. Which leaves O. And all I have to go on is a list of missing gentlemen who could be Wellington's would-be assassin." He grabbed the list. "Bascomb, Hollings, Renwick, Galwaith, Oglethorpe."

His eyes widened. "Jason Oglethorpe of Bude. Said to have sailed for America, but who wound up on a slab in Hertfordshire with a note in his boot linking him to Matthews—who we have very good reason to believe is Simmons. Simmons, who has not been seen since that ball in London. Not even in Beyford. His mother has no idea where he is, and from what Saunderson said, she was certain he would not leave without saying goodbye."

Richard pushed off the desk. "Four conspirators, five if you include Blainard, though he was not on any list. But maybe Oswald brought him in without the knowledge of these Olees. Would that be cause to kill him? But why was Darcy notified with the ring?" He shook his head. "Blainard—dead. Oglethorpe—dead. Vickers—dead, under suspicious circumstances, unconfirmed by a doctor's examination. That leaves Matthews, or Simmons, who remains at large. And Oswald." His fingers curled into a fist, and he savoured the thrill of the hunt. "Who is at Pemberley."

DARCY ENTERED HIS STUDY A FEW MORNINGS LATER, surprised to find Bingley working at his desk. "Bingley!"

"Forgive the intrusion, Darcy, but I needed to complete these letters. In private."

"By all means." Darcy smirked, retrieving his own unopened correspondence.

"I shall be but a moment." Bingley lifted his eyes to his friend. "And then if I may have a moment of your time?"

Darcy saw trouble in his eyes. "Of course. I am at your service."

Bingley nodded, then returned to his work. Finished, he read through it before sanding and sealing it. Plopping himself in the large armchair adjacent to Darcy, he stared at the unlit fire. "You recall that Caroline has held a…fascination for—"

"Pemberley, Bingley. Not for me. Never for me," Darcy spat.

Bingley acknowledged Darcy's remark, and was about to reply.

"No," Darcy said sharply, "if Caroline held any true feelings for me, she would have stood by me when Wickham dragged our name through the mud. Not that there was any hope in that regard," he shuddered. "She was very vocal at the time—she encouraged you to drop our friendship, did she not?"

Bingley winced. "She did. But now, being back here at Pemberley…"

"What? She… Bingley, I am happily *married*."

"I understand. But I fear being here, seeing you relaxed, happy, when she is so very *un*happily engaged, has reignited her…passion."

"For Pemberley."

"Agreed. But, as the means to Pemberley, Caroline is relentless in regaining *your* favour."

"Gaining, as I never favoured her before."

Nodding sadly, Bingley looked away. "Ever since she was a young girl, she always fancied an exalted life, and you were her ideal. I had hoped she had let that dream go, but she has not. She will make things unpleasant for us all. I am thinking of removing her to Scarborough."

"You cannot leave! The ball!"

Bingley chuckled. "Is the taciturn Fitzwilliam Darcy so concerned with a dance? Perhaps I could get Hurst to return her to London."

Darcy went to his sideboard. "One thing I have learned from my marriage is to enlist Elizabeth's counsel in all things. It is less complicated in the long run. I believe we should include the ladies in this decision."

"If I were not present to hear these words from your lips, I should not believe they came from you." Both men smiled, Bingley going further to chuckle. "I agree, it is a very good idea."

CHAPTER TWENTY-FOUR

The next morning, Elizabeth and Miss Bingley were both absent from the breakfast table.

"Please excuse my sister," Mrs Hurst said, entering the room. "She is indisposed this morning and wishes to fully recuperate to be in full health for the coming ball."

Bingley and Darcy exchanged glances, while Jane pondered the absence of both her sister and Miss Bingley. "Mr Darcy? How fares Elizabeth this morning?"

"She is well, but tired. I think marshalling the servants for a ball so soon after arriving at Pemberley wears on her."

"Heaven knows she has had an unprecedented few months," Bingley offered.

Jane's eyes darkened.

"Surely a woman of Mrs Darcy's...*stamina* can handle the fripperies of a ball?" Oswald paused in his repast.

At Jane's silence, Darcy's eyes flew to hers. A pall fell upon the table until Lydia diverted the conversation to exercising the colts.

RICHARD DISEMBARKED FROM THE MATLOCK CARRIAGE, eager to stretch his legs and clear his head. His mother had used the journey to harangue him about his prolonged infatuation with bachelorhood.

"Is it so wrong to want my favourite son to find a good woman, settle down, and grace me with grandchildren?"

He handed down Lady Matlock, shaking his head as she gave him a matriarchal arched brow. "Mother, I beg you, please stop." He waited while she shook out her skirts. His breath caught when he beheld the Bennet sisters, arrayed around Darcy. *Individually they are beautiful, but together…* He swallowed, drawing his mother's notice.

The countess smiled, giving him a sidelong glance. "Miss Mary has the eyes of a dreamer—no, a poet, do you not think? And such pretty curls."

He murmured his agreement.

"She is slight but with enough curves to entice a man."

"Mother!" he hissed. "Please." He tugged her hand on his arm, and they continued up the stairs.

"She has a grace about her, does she not? I believe she would not stand for any nonsense. But that is most likely what you need."

"What about the others? No thoughts for the rest of them?"

"The next eldest, Catherine, is that correct?"

He nodded, but his eyes were back on Mary.

"She has a fuller figure than Elizabeth, and she is taller as well. Lovely, lovely eyes."

"It is good that there is but one more sister, as we are almost there."

"The youngest cannot be out and is not to be noticed by anyone yet," she admonished.

"Yes, Mother." Richard patted her hand and smiled broadly. Catching Mary's eye, his smile widened further at her blush.

JANE WATCHED WITH CONCERN AS HER SISTER PUSHED food around her plate that evening. She leaned back, trying to still her whirling thoughts into a coherent theory regarding Elizabeth's pallor and apparent revulsion towards her food. When Elizabeth rushed from the room, Jane noticed Miss Bingley's malevolent grin, and how she turned from looking at Elizabeth's retreating back to Darcy.

"How absolutely…provincial," Miss Bingley said to him from beneath lowered lashes. "It is almost as if Mrs Darcy is averse to such exalted company."

"Excuse me. I shall see to Elizabeth." Jane left the table.

Miss Bingley smugly sipped her wine. "Now then, what shall we do this evening?"

Upstairs, Jane waited in the mistress's chambers. When Elizabeth entered, she smiled at her sister's presence.

"Elizabeth, are you well?"

"As well as may be expected, having cast up my accounts."

"Come." Jane offered her hand. "Let me help you to bed."

"Thank you, *Mama*. Truly, Jane I am likely only over-taxed, what with the ball."

"Yes, that must be it." Jane watched Elizabeth remove the pins from her hair, occasionally rubbing her stomach, avoiding her gaze. She walked to her sister, turning her around to unbutton her gown. "Have you felt this way often? I mean, the uneasy stomach. Are you anxious? Fatigued?" Jane tried to calm her own unease.

"Jane, you are miserable at concealing your fear, least of all from me." She placed her hands on Jane's. "Tell me plainly what you wish to know. Or say. I would rather hear it directly than guess at what plagues your mind."

Jane studied Elizabeth and nodded. "I have noted, as of late, since shortly after Miss Bingley came to Pember-ley, that you are more fatigued."

"More likely in search of some peace."

Both sisters smiled.

"And you avoid certain foods."

Elizabeth's smile faded, and she pulled them both to sit on the window bench. "I have not wished to say anything yet, but I believe I may be with child."

Jane's eyes widened, then her brow furrowed. "Truly?"

"Well, I am fatigued, and I confess, I am averse to some scents that had not bothered me before."

"And your..." she nodded to the necessary.

"No, this is the first." Elizabeth wrinkled her nose in bemusement. "However, my courses are late."

Her sister leaned back, pulling her lower lip between her teeth. "I see. So it is not certain."

"Jane? You think there is no babe? Then what is it?"

"Your behaviour, in general, has altered, dear heart."

Elizabeth grasped her hands together.

"You take little interest in the stable."

Elizabeth looked away.

"If not for my sisters, the horses would be neglected indeed."

"Even you avoid the stables in summer, Jane."

"I saw you last week when Kitty and Georgiana returned from riding Springer and Psyche. You were positively indifferent."

"What are your thoughts on this, Jane?" Darcy stepped into the room, echoing her concerns, and came to sit near them.

Jane looked to Elizabeth who shook her head slightly. Jane grimaced but continued. "While there may be a number of causes for these changes, the one that remains most prominent in my mind is poison."

"Poison!" both Darcys gasped.

"Impossible!" Elizabeth cried.

"Many things have happened recently that we never imagined possible. There is a great distance between kitchen and table, and it need not take much to induce such a result, at first."

"But who would wish to poison me?"

"Well…" Jane looked between them awkwardly. "I suspect…Miss Bingley. She is acting very strangely, and Charles has mentioned her aspirations towards—"

"Being the mistress of Pemberley," Darcy said darkly.

"He has mentioned the same to me. I shall have her packed and removed by the morning."

"What? No!" Elizabeth turned from her husband to her sister, who was sharing a silent communication with him. "No, I am sure there is another explanation for this."

"Elizabeth, I shall take no chances with your health. There is a threat, which means Caroline must be removed. The sooner the better."

"No." She turned from him to Jane. "Think what this will do to Bingley."

"I am thinking what it will do to *you*, my love." Darcy knelt by her side.

"Please, no. The ball is in two days. After that, they will be gone. Surely, with all our family here, we can keep her apart from me. Please." She took his hand.

"Elizabeth…" His resolve weakened.

"Fitzwilliam." She kissed his knuckles. "We shall speak to Mrs Reynolds. She will see to it my food is not tampered with." Her eyes pleaded with him.

"Very well," he sighed. "But you are not to be alone with her, and I shall have her watched."

"Very well," she acquiesced, her smile widening. "Thank you, my love."

Darcy harrumphed, rising to his feet. "I shall speak to Mrs Reynolds immediately," he declared.

"Thank you." Jane swayed with relief. "It may not be as I fear, but there was something in—"

"Miss Bingley's demeanour," Darcy said as he stroked Elizabeth's hand comfortingly.

"You saw it as well?" Jane's eyes widened.

He nodded.

"We must keep them as separate as possible."

"As you command, Captain Bennet." He smiled, bringing Elizabeth's hand to his lips.

Jane noted Elizabeth's eyes glazing over with fatigue and prepared her for bed. When she had drifted off to sleep, Jane whispered, "I shall speak to my sisters, Mr Darcy. We may appear scattered, but when threatened, we band together, a mighty force to protect our own. They have already come to me with their concerns over Miss Bingley. We shall see to Lizzy's safety."

"And me? What role do I play in all this?"

"You have the lion's share, sir," Jane said, giving him an arch look. "To you, we leave distracting Miss Bingley." She laughed as Darcy's face paled and horror filled his eyes.

THE NEXT MORNING, DARCY AND RICHARD RODE TO THE parsonage in Kympton, whose roof required repair. Darcy wished to set things in motion before the autumn rains. The two left after an early breakfast, riding hard through the morning mist, happy to be free from the growing numbers at Pemberley.

Looking to his cousin, Darcy noticed his furrowed brow. "What is it?"

He dismounted and the two took in their favourite resting spot in the last meadow before Kympton proper. "I am curious as to why, exactly, Oswald is here."

They walked to a stone wall. Securing his horse, Darcy shrugged. "He is betrothed to Bingley's sister."

"But why are they here? I am no expert, but I imagine there are a multitude of details to attend to for a wedding. I would not have thought they had the time to spare."

"That is their concern. Elizabeth and I would not slight them, for Bingley's sake." Darcy nodded, crossing his arms. "The Hursts, and now Caroline and Oswald, follow him like—"

"Vultures?"

Chuckling, Darcy shook his head. "Such a wit with words. I wonder you do not write a novel."

Richard assumed a dramatic sigh, hand clutched over his heart.

"Why the curiosity over Oswald?"

"As I am sure you surmised, the attack on Wellington was planned," he replied. "We have concluded that a group of individuals who call themselves oligarchs, primarily based in the Americas but with tentacles here in England, orchestrated the attack at Longbourn."

"But Oswald's connexion?"

"Darcy, I trust your discretion, but this may not be repeated to anyone."

"Not even Elizabeth?"

He shook his head. "If you must, do stress to her the importance of secrecy."

Darcy nodded.

"Lessing and I believe that Oswald aspires to be a member of this group."

Darcy's lips quirked up. "While I believe Oswald would sell his soul to the devil to prosper, to organise the killing of a war hero seems beyond him."

His cousin nodded. "You are right about that. Another was in charge. Oswald may have been useful in gathering information from his friends and associates in high places. I overheard him converse with Lord Vickers at Lady Praxton's. They knew of Blainard's death."

Darcy's eyebrows arched.

"It distressed them because it diminished their chance of joining these oligarchs." After a pause, he added, "Vickers is dead, Darcy. Murdered, we think. There was evidence of a break in. His valet was drugged."

"Drugged?" Darcy was surprised. "And now Oswald is at Pemberley."

"He is indeed."

"Is he a suspect?" When his cousin shook his head, Darcy added, "Then who is? Why is this traitor not under arrest?"

"Because he has gone to ground. But thanks to Elizabeth, we have an idea who is the agent of the oligarchs."

"Simmons," Darcy said flatly, unsurprised.

"Which gives us the advantage."

"Advantage? How so?"

"You and Elizabeth—and, I suppose, all the Bennet girls—know what he looks like. Hopefully he will make his move before the ball."

"Which is tomorrow."

Darcy met his cousin's steely gaze. "I shall double the guard."

"I have requested a squadron."

"A squadron? Is that not excessive?"

"These men are specialised in covert missions. They will blend in and keep their eyes open. And be fully armed."

"As will I, and I venture Bingley as well."

"Bingley cannot know. Pemberley will be well

guarded. I shall be there, and armed, as will you and my men. We must leave it at that."

Darcy nodded reluctantly.

"We will catch him, Darcy."

"Yes, but before or after he strikes and moves on to Elizabeth?"

THE DAY OF THE BALL BROKE WITH THE GLORIOUS golden glimmer of dawn, the air crisp and clear. Elizabeth woke with great enthusiasm. Rustling beneath the sheets, her husband's hands claimed her waist as they lay entwined. She relaxed, and they delayed leaving her bed for another hour.

Exhausted, they flopped back onto the mattress, spent in their desire. Smiles graced their faces as they lay enwrapped in each other until Elizabeth's mind wandered to the awaiting tasks. She slid to the edge of the bed, knowing she needed to start her day.

"Stay, please?" Darcy whispered, trying to pull her back.

She turned to him, her hands moving across his chest to his neck. Pushing her fingers through his hair, she delighted in the silk of his curls. "Tomorrow, after the ball, we shall lie here together all day."

A knock on the door interrupted them, and both their heads jerked up as Elizabeth's maid bustled in. "Your bath awaits, Mrs Darcy."

With a happy smile and lingering kiss, Elizabeth and Darcy left their bed to face the day.

MIDMORNING, AN UNEXPECTED CARRIAGE ROLLED UP TO Pemberley.

"Mr and Mrs Merriweather," Pemberley's butler announced.

Elizabeth raised her brow to Darcy, who sat across the long table, now filled with family and friends. Richard trained his eye on Oswald who appeared nonplussed by the announcement. In low tones, he enquired of Darcy, "Were they expected?"

"Not at all," Darcy replied.

Moving to greet their relations, he said, "Will Georgiana be well with this?"

"I believe so. She and Elizabeth spoke of it after Anne's marriage. She is happy for our cousin. That at last she has the chance for joy."

The Darcys and Fitzwilliams welcomed the Merriweathers. However, it was Oswald who looked most pleased.

THE DAY OF THE BALL WAS A SEA OF SWEET CONFUSION. The young ladies flitted from room to room, making last minute adjustments to their gowns and coiffures for that evening. All were excited by the joy and joviality infusing Pemberley. Even the staid Lord Matlock was humming a tune and practising his dance steps in the hall. Servants, marshalled under the command of Mrs Reynolds, Pemberley's ever efficient housekeeper, bustled about with flowers and chairs, placing serving dishes and plates for later use.

Late in the afternoon, the London musicians arrived. No one paid any mind to the extra servants bustling about, even if they seemed rather large for footmen and ignored Mrs Reynolds's orders. The women headed upstairs hours prior to prepare, and Colonel Fitzwilliam took a ride to calm his nerves.

I cannot recall ever being this excited about a ball. Could it be seeing Darcy finally so well settled? Or perhaps it is the enigmatic Mary Bennet? Oh, I noticed her back at Longbourn, how calm she was in the face of chaos. She certainly has an alluring form wrapped in those modest gowns.

Before descending to greet their guests, the Darcys gathered with their sisters, the Merriweathers, Bingleys, Hursts, and Matlocks in an upper drawing room for a champagne toast. As the glasses were passed around, Richard diverted his attention between Miss Mary Bennet and Oswald. *What an odd gathering. Who would ever have thought such a motley crew would be assembled at Pemberley!* He smiled. As he did, Mary Bennet looked up at him, and returned his mirth.

The ladies glittered in silks and with jewels in their hair, on their necks and dangling from their ears. Despite the adornment, their true beauty lay in their eyes, and the genuine smiles gracing almost all of their faces. The Bennets and Darcys were resplendent; even Louisa Hurst had roused her husband into top form. Richard could see his men dotted about the room and hoped their talents would not be required this evening.

ELIZABETH BREATHED DEEPLY, ENJOYING THE CALM before the storm. The remainder of her guests trickled in, and soon she and her family would face the crush of curiosity. Leaning into her sister, she whispered,

"Although I am looking forward to the ball with great joy, now that it is upon us, all I truly wish for is the peace and tranquillity of my husband's arms."

Jane hid her giggle behind her champagne glass.

With the toasts complete, Elizabeth sighed. When her husband took her hand to his arm, she marshalled the guests of honour to the receiving line to greet the throngs coming to Pemberley to dance, gossip, flirt and celebrate love.

THE NIGHT WAS CLEAR AND BRILLIANT, A FULL MOON illuminating the gardens of Pemberley. The expanded guest list demanded the opening of all the public rooms on the ground floor. The young ladies glowed as their dance cards filled with charming and eligible men. Although not officially out, Lydia and Kitty were allowed to remain, as this ball was at one sister's home celebrating another sister's engagement. Initially reluctant to mingle, Georgiana soon seemed to catch the Bennets' enthusiasm and anticipated the evening with her newfound friends.

Darcy and Elizabeth took their places on the dance floor with Caroline Bingley and Oswald next in line, followed by Bingley and Jane. The earl and countess of Matlock, the Hursts, and, surprisingly, Anne and her husband followed after them.

Standing beside her niece and new nephew, Lady Matlock remarked to her husband on Mrs Merriweather's good health. "How well she looks! As if she had never been sick a day in her life."

"Aye," replied Lord Matlock. "It would seem marriage agrees with our Annie."

"Uncle," Anne drew near. "It has been years since anyone called me that."

"Perhaps we should have done so more often, my dear." Matlock continued, "I am glad to see you so well, Anne. Truly, I am." He returned her full smile.

"It seems seizing my happiness has benefited more than just me."

Her uncle laughed outright.

"MISS MARY, I BELIEVE THE NEXT IS OURS?" SAID Colonel Fitzwilliam as he bent over the hand of Miss Mary Bennet.

"Indeed, Colonel. It is."

He led her to the floor, thinking her exceptionally pretty that night. Her eyes sparkled like emeralds, reflecting the candlelight from the various candelabras throughout the room. The music began, and they joined hands. Their breath mingled before they circled each other, parting to the next set of dancers. Mary was matched by another young man, and Richard grew concerned as puzzlement overtook her features.

"Miss Mary?" he asked, glancing back at the young man when the dance returned her to him. "What is it?'

"That man…" Her forehead scrunched in concentration. "There is something oddly familiar about him." Her eyes cut back to the semi-stranger whose own eyes searched the bustling ballroom.

"You have met him before, perhaps?"

"I suppose, but I cannot recall where. And yet, I feel as though I should be able to."

He gave her a reassuring smile. Looking about the overcrowded hall, he chuckled. "Well, since it appears more than half of the *ton* is here. The chances are that you *have* met him before. And may I say, I am glad he has not made such a memorable impression."

"But I am mostly at school," she said. "Where would I meet him?"

His spine tingled. *Blast! I had nearly forgotten my true purpose this night.* "Where is he now? Do you see him?"

Miss Mary glanced about the room, but the man was nowhere to be seen. "I do not know." Her eyes held dejection and a hint of unease. As they stepped together, she locked gazes with him and he felt her wrap around his heart, as if she were weaving a gossamer web to entangle him. A notion he found quite pleasing.

When the music ended, they bowed and curtseyed respectively. He led her from the floor, bending towards her ear. "I believe Darcy has planned a waltz for the last set, Miss Mary."

"How scandalous! Do you…are you—"

"And I wonder if you would do me the honour of reserving that particular set for me, if you are not otherwise engaged."

"I am not engaged, and I should be happy to."

"Thank you."

"I feel I am in need of some air," she said breathlessly.

"I should be happy to escort you, madam."

"Thank you, sir."

They headed to the terrace, which was almost as busy as the dance hall, with couples and gatherings of men and women standing in various conversations and flirtations. His eyes took in the splendour and greed. Many he recognised from town, the men's clubs he frequented, and the more unsavoury establishments where his work often led. He saw romance in the eyes of very young women, avarice and lust in the eyes of their elders. So focused was he on the crowd, he missed when Miss Mary, seeing the perplexing man walk toward the balcony, went in pursuit of him.

MARY RAN THROUGH ALL THE YOUNG MEN OF HER acquaintance in her mind. The disconcerting recognition forming in her mind decided her course of action.

"Lizzy." Mary waylaid her sister, grabbing her arm.

"What is it?" Elizabeth asked.

Mary twisted her fingers. "I think I saw a man who reminds me of Jamie. His hair is different, and he has a beard now."

"Are you sure?" Elizabeth grabbed Mary's hands in her own.

"No. It has been some time since he went away to America."

"Where is he?"

"There." Mary nodded and headed toward the gardens.

Elizabeth turned to look for her husband or one of the guards. Unable to locate either, she went after her sister.

"I BELIEVE I SHALL GO AND FIND MY WIFE." Merriweather patted Oswald on the back. "It was good to see you."

"And you, Merry. And you."

Mr Simmons appeared, walking towards the two men.

"This is a private conversation." Oswald glared at the young man.

Taking in the sparsely populated lawn beyond the patio, Simmons turned to the men. "It was, but now I need to speak with you."

"See here!" Oswald puffed out his chest.

Simmons pulled a gun from his pocket, aiming it at Oswald. "Have I your attention now, sir?" He nodded to Merriweather. "Leave us."

Oswald also nodded at his friend, wordlessly telling him to go.

"Tell no one of this," Simmons hissed as Merriweather hastily departed. Then, to Oswald, he said, "You are a hard man to find. You were told to remain in town."

Startled at the reminder, Oswald kept his eyes on the gun and stepped back. "But my betrothed, Miss Bingley, um...she wished to attend. Must keep the ladies happy and all." He forced a weak chuckle.

"What one must do, if one is wise," Simmons took another two steps forward as Oswald stepped back, "is attend to the orders of the oligarchs. You requested membership, and now you have it. You cannot escape either their pleasure or their wrath."

"I...I..."

"No allowances are made for disobedience, Oswald."

"See here——"

Simmons chuckled. "When I read the report on you, I could not *believe* the oligarchs chose you. You who are so clumsy, with so little imagination in how you flaunt your so-called influence." He scoffed. "Oh, I know all about you and your nasty habits, while you remain as you always have been—ignorant. Now, here is what we are going to do——"

"That is enough!" Oswald rushed at Simmons, who, by reflex, pulled the trigger as the larger man fell upon him. Oswald grunted in pain. A second shot rang from the left, piercing Simmons's back. Two women screamed as both men dropped dead to the ground.

Elizabeth and Mary surged towards the fallen men as Darcy and his cousin rushed through the crowd, followed by a contingent of liveried soldiers. Colonel Fitzwilliam kicked the pistol from Simmons's hand before rolling him to his back.

Taking a hard look at the man's face, Darcy paused a moment before tugging his hair, dislodging a wig. "Simmons," he declared.

Richard nodded.

Mary and Elizabeth sobbed as the life left Simmons's eyes. "You knew?" Mary looked to the colonel.

"Suspected." He stepped closer to her.

Elizabeth grasped her sister's arm, looking between the bodies of Simmons and Oswald. Coming to her side, Darcy slipped his arm around her, and she turned to him, giving him a smile. He kissed her brow. "It is over. All of it."

Richard surveyed the gathering crowd. "Saunderson, assign someone to redirect the busybodies." He jutted his chin at the curious. "Then note the layout and remove the deceased. Darcy?"

"The ice house."

"If you will follow me, I shall show you where." The butler stepped into the protective circle of guards.

"Thank you," Darcy nodded.

Elizabeth stepped back, keeping her hand within Darcy's clasp as four of the soldiers removed the two bodies. Shaking her head, she looked at Darcy and attempted to rally her spirits. "Such a night! However shall we top this?"

"By throwing you out with the rubbish," Miss Bingley said as she pushed her way to Darcy. "So Mr Darcy will have a woman worthy of his name, not someone who brings murderers into his home."

"Miss Bingley, you forget yourself once again in disparaging my wife. I am a married man." Fury emboldened Darcy's declaration, attracting the crowd's attention.

"Oswald is dead, so I shall be your mistress." Miss Bingley pulled him back.

"My brother has never, *would* never take a mistress," Georgiana said, stepping forward. "He is too good, too honourable to degrade a woman."

"You silly, simpering girl," Miss Bingley sneered. "It is well known that he has had that French woman as his mistress for years." She turned to Darcy, locking her eyes on his as she ran her hands down her bodice. "You had that French tart, now take me. An English rose. Once you taste my wares, you will know we are meant for each other." She pulled his arm against her chest.

Disgust altered Darcy's every feature as he pulled

away. His deep voice boomed, "I have never had a mistress. Antoinette du Marché is my cousin. She escaped France and the rake who seduced and abused her, as a *child*. She has always been no more, and no less, than that—my cousin, and a lady."

The gathered crowd gasped loudly at this revelation, and whispers began to fill the room. Georgiana looked as shocked as the rest of them, but with a proud look at her brother, she spoke over them all. "And like my father, who offered Mademoi—my *cousin*, a safe haven here in England, my brother also saved *me*, and countless other women, from the likes of George Wickham."

Darcy would have marvelled at his sister's courage, but a sudden movement at his side drew his attention. "Elizabeth!" he bayed, as his wife crumpled to the floor. He scooped her in his arms. "What have you done?" he accused Miss Bingley.

"Nothing," she spat. "This is just another indication that she is unfit to—"

"The only one unfit here is you." He stepped toward her, and she recoiled at his ferocity. "You will leave my house by morning's light." He turned and, sending a panicked look to Richard, rushed to the servants' entrance, where they were quickly ushered up the hidden staircase to their chambers.

CHAPTER TWENTY-FIVE

The day after the ball was a whirl of activity as Pemberley's guests departed, eager to bring word of the shootings back to town. As the stately carriages started off to their own estates, the magistrate arrived, and after conferring with Fitzwilliam, agreed to leave the matter to the military authorities. By dinnertime, the only concern weighing on Darcy's mind was Elizabeth's health. After regaining consciousness, she had made a brave attempt at returning to their guests to finish the ball, but to Darcy's trained eye, she was still weary the next morning. He had requested the family's physician, Mr Abernathy, attend her now that Pemberley was quiet once more.

Caroline Bingley was on her way to relations in Scarborough to stay until the furore of her violently ended betrothal died down. The Hursts, along with Bingley, travelled to see her safely installed at Greenwald Manor for the foreseeable future. Bingley promised to write to both Jane and Darcy, informing them of his anticipated return, but for now, Darcy's mind was firmly lodged in the mistress's chambers. He paced his study, imagining the worst in agonising detail until a knock roused him from his brooding.

"Come." He steeled himself for the prognosis.

Abernathy, a short man with thinning, white hair, looked up as Darcy strode into the chamber. "Mr Darcy?"

"Mr Abernathy, how is she?"

The doctor chuckled. "She rests but wishes to speak to you."

Darcy paused to read the man's casual stance before bolting from the room. He knocked on Elizabeth's door. Lady Matlock opened it, smiling at her nephew's eager face. "Come in, Elizabeth is expecting you."

"Thank you, Aunt."

She smiled, stepping out of the room and calling for Jane to leave with her. Jane smiled at him as she departed.

Darcy barely noticed they were there at all. "Elizabeth? Are you well?"

Her eyelids fluttered open, and Darcy fell to his knees at her side. Taking hold of her hand, he searched her face for signs of her health. "I am well, best beloved."

Darcy released a long-held breath as his heart relaxed. "Then why? What did the physician say? What is the matter with you?"

"Nothing, darling. I am...I carry your—*our* child."

Darcy fell back on his heels, pulling her hand along

with him so that Elizabeth followed, lifting herself from the pillows piled beneath her back.

She giggled, placing both hands on his cheeks. "We are to be parents, Fitzwilliam. By early next spring." At his silence, she pulled back, searching his eyes. "Are you not happy?"

"You are not being poisoned?"

She shook her head.

"This is not due to Caroline?"

"I think not," her eyes danced with mirth.

Shaking off his stupor, Darcy took her in his arms and kissed her. "Happy? I am ecstatic! A child! Elizabeth! Our child." He crushed his body to her, rocking them both in delight. "You are safe from that horrid, horrid woman and my darling, my heart has never felt more alive, or full of love, for you, our child, for the entire world. I could dance a jig on the rooftops and shout out the news."

Elizabeth laughed, and the expectant parents enjoyed a private celebration of their own.

EPILOGUE

Catherine and Lydia soon returned to school, while Mary remained at Pemberley, where she and Georgiana continued their plans for the coming Season in London. They also aided Darcy in keeping an eye on Elizabeth, who suffered through a month of morning sickness and lethargy. Jane eagerly awaited Bingley, who wrote with the news that Caroline was coming to terms with remaining in the North, as rumours of her fiancé's murder would entertain the parlours and ballrooms of London for some time to come.

Mary and Georgiana returned to London in January. Coincidently, Colonel Fitzwilliam was also in the capital, and was more than willing to escort them wherever they wished. Much to the delight of the gossiping ladies of society, the second son of the Earl of Matlock appeared besotted by his young cousin's intriguingly attractive new sister. The trio was rarely at the more fashionable balls, preferring museums, musical concerts, the theatre, and the various salons that catered to the more cerebral members of the *ton*. When one young, well-connected artist requested that Miss Mary Bennet sit for a portrait, Richard had decided he had had enough and proposed, thereby cutting the young blade's interest in the lovely Mary Bennet's calm demeanour and sparkling eyes.

Jane Bennet was more than ready to enter the marital state. The autumn had been torture, due to Bingley's absence. Once he returned in early December, he remained at Pemberley for the holidays. Their close proximity decimated the shards of her self-control. Their kisses intensified, and Jane longed for more. The couple decided to marry at Pemberley. Bingley purchased an estate not thirty miles away. Blissham was well situated, and both he and Jane could envision their future happiness in such a secluded haven.

When the family gathered to celebrate their nuptials, Lord Aubrey, as a Matlock family friend, attended the celebration. Learning of Colonel Fitzwilliam's engagement, he took a pointed interest in Mary. After conferring with her, they cornered Fitzwilliam, who, falling prey to his intended wife's beguiling smile, acquiesced to a new family business. Within the month they would both become agents of Aubrey and his schemes of espionage.

Jane, resplendent in a velvet gown of palest green created by Madame Lestrat, walked down the chapel's aisle on Mr Gardiner's arm. Her beatific smile warmed the hearts of all in attendance, as Bingley beamed through the entire ceremony, leaving none in doubt of his joy.

ELIZABETH'S PREGNANCY PROGRESSED, AS DID THE devotion of her husband. With the assurances of her physicians, they continued exploring the amorous opportunities of a great house such as Pemberley. Darcy had to smile at the amount of work piling on his desk, as he was often distracted from estate management on his wife's request. Her lust wrought havoc on his wardrobe, as her impatience sent the buttons of his breeches, waistcoats and shirts skittering across the floor when he could not divest himself quickly enough for her. Yet for all the effort he expended on satisfying the increasing demands of his wife, the master of Pemberley was rarely, if ever, seen without a smile on his face and a glow in his eyes.

The months dissolved, one into the other, as Elizabeth's confinement approached. Darcy's demeanour darkened as he recalled the difficulties his mother suffered during and after Georgiana's birth. Elizabeth prodded and cajoled him into better spirits in the manner she had learned to be most effective.

The night she finally persuaded Darcy to open his heart to her, she began gently. "My time will be soon."

He caressed their child beneath the skin of her swollen abdomen. She moved her hands to rest on his, gently forcing him to minister to her again. "All will be well, my darling. I promise."

Darcy pushed away, moving to the fireplace. "Do not tempt fate so, Elizabeth." He turned from her to stare into the fire.

"It is not to tempt fate." She wrapped her arms around him from behind. "I am young. I am healthy and strong. And I place my faith in God, and in my love for you. I shall not leave you, Fitzwilliam. Ever."

Within a breath, he turned to her, catching her in his arms, crushing his lips to hers. "I would die without you, Elizabeth. Before you came into my life, I was benumbed, like the walking dead. To have tasted your love, your joy...to lose that... I could not, I would not survive if anything were to happen to you."

Pulling back, she looked him in the eye, her soul opening at the fear she found. "Nothing will happen save that you and I shall welcome our child into this world."

"I am sure my mother felt the same before..."

Elizabeth knew there was more behind her husband's fear. *I know first-time fathers fear for their wives' safe delivery, but Darcy is morose. Obsessive for my welfare.* "Tell me of her. Tell me what frightens you so."

He turned away but looked back to her compassionate eyes. "When I was born, my mother suffered greatly. I am told it was many months before she regained strength enough to leave her chambers." He closed his eyes. "After Georgiana's birth, the bleeding did not stop. Within hours, she was gone."

Elizabeth gasped. No one had mentioned the cause of Lady Anne's demise, and now she understood why. She sighed with sorrow. Images of the young Darcy, confused by the joy of his sister's arrival and the devastating sorrow of losing his beloved mother, flooded her mind. Her heart broke for the boy living in the man, and she clutched him, as would a mother soothing her precious child. As his tears flowed, Elizabeth, overwhelmed at the strength of his grief, held onto him, stroking the back of his head as he made his way through his sea of sorrow.

Darcy dragged them to the couch. Elizabeth adjusted, pulling Darcy's head to her chest. She stroked his head whispering sweet words of love and comfort till he slipped gently into sleep.

AFTER CONFERRING WITH HER PHYSICIAN, HER MIDWIFE, and her sister Jane, Elizabeth felt she was as prepared as she would ever be for the coming birth. She was more than ready to bring her and Darcy's child into the world. Her family gathered; Georgiana, Mary and Colonel Fitzwilliam had arrived three days before, as had the Bingleys. Even the Gardiners made the trip north to await the next generation of Bennet blood. Darcy was grateful for the company, vacillating between hovering about Elizabeth in case she misstepped and losing himself in black moods of impending doom. His sisters and Bingley tried to lighten his mood, but childbirth still being the primary cause of death among women of their age, none could totally discount his fear. The Matlocks arrived, and conversation turned to their upcoming ball, to be held in celebration of their youngest son's engagement to Mary Bennet.

Returning from her daily conference with Mrs Reynolds, Elizabeth had just entered the parlour when her eyes widened in confusion. A gripping pain compressed her belly, and she grasped the nearest chair. She looked about the room, as an unfamiliar panic enveloped her. She stepped forward, until the next wave of pain sent her crashing against the nearest pillar of support, which happened to be her brother, Charles Bingley.

"Oh!" she cried, her free hand moving to support her belly. "My stars!" Her eyes widened wider still, and she cried out again.

The house roared to life. Darcy rushed to Elizabeth as her legs buckled at the latest wave of pain. Jane rang for Mrs Reynolds, and Lady Matlock and Mrs Gardiner hovered about Elizabeth until Darcy swept her up in his arms, heading to the birthing chamber.

"Elizabeth!" Darcy, trembling with nerves, climbed the stairs. "Is it time?"

"I certainly hope so, for if it is not, we are in serious trouble."

Lady Matlock and Mrs Gardiner shared a knowing glance, trying to hide their amusement. Lord Matlock and Mr Gardiner waited helplessly by their chess board. With Elizabeth whisked from the room, they wisely stepped back and resumed their game.

HEEDING THE WOMEN'S THREAT OF BODILY HARM, DARCY retreated to pace the floor of his study, where the men then barricaded him. Bingley, Fitzwilliam, Lord Matlock, and Mr Gardiner, each spread on various chairs and sofas, lay snoring, the result of trying to appease Darcy's anxiety with his finely aged brandy. Darcy kept his solitary vigil, pacing in front of the fire. He was a shambles, his jacket strewn over his chair, his shirt nearly pulled from his breeches, and his hair now a tousled mane.

I shall go insane if I endure one minute more with no news.
He simultaneously rubbed his chin and ran his hand

through his locks until a knock broke the silence. He stopped, eyes locked on Georgiana as she entered.

"Brother?" she smiled.

"Georgie, is she…?"

"Elizabeth is well. She asks for you."

Joy jolting through his heart, Darcy ran to the door, stopping only to take his sister by the arm, searching her for signs of distress. Nodding, she took his hands, and smiled. His eyes brightened, and he kissed her forehead before running, unabashedly, to his wife. Approaching the door, he paused. *My life will change forever once I open this door.* Shaking away any remaining doubts, Darcy placed his hand on the doorknob, opening the new chapter in his life.

The room was empty save for the occupants of the bed. Jane, Mrs Gardiner, the midwife, and Mr Abernathy had retired. The chamber was silent. Darcy could hear the soft rustle of sheets as Elizabeth sought a more comfortable position.

"Elizabeth?" he called, loathe to disturb the quiet peace. On the bed, in a circle of candlelight, lay his incredible wife. She smiled weakly, increasing his concern. He was at her side in a heartbeat. "You are well?"

Looking up, Elizabeth's eyes shone with love. Raising her one free hand, he took it to his lips, then his chest, vowing to never let go.

"I am well," she smiled. "Come, my love, meet your son."

Elizabeth released her husband's hand to gently pull back the blanket surrounding the soft, dark curls. She gazed adoringly at the babe suckling at her breast, his tiny, curled fist resting on her bare skin. She caressed his head rhythmically, until her hand was tentatively joined by her husband's, so large it covered the infant's skull. Elizabeth looked up at Darcy, who now sat with one arm around her, the other joining her embrace of their son.

"He is magnificent, Elizabeth. The most amazing sight I have ever beheld!"

"And his name, Fitzwilliam? What have you chosen for our darling, firstborn son?"

He looked her in the eyes, as his shyness bloomed, but she smiled indulgently. He nodded and blushed before turning his gaze to their sleeping child. "Welcome, Bennet Alexander Darcy. Welcome my little one, my dearest, deepest love."

Finis

The favour of your review would be greatly appreciated.

Subscribers to the Quills & Quartos mailing list receive advance notice of new releases and sales, and exclusive bonus content and short stories. To join, visit us at www.QuillsandQuartos.com

ABOUT THE AUTHOR

Mary Anne lives in New Orleans with her husband, David, and two pups, Herbie and Cardie, while her two sons spread their wings at colleges on both coasts. Throughout the pandemic, she's worked to create community even while keeping socially distant.

Ms. Mushatt has been an active part of the Jane Austen universe for over ten years and has published two novels: *Taken* and *Darcy and the Duchess*.

ALSO BY MARY ANNE MUSHATT

Taken

Taken from her home as a young child, Elizabeth Bennet's sense of self is shaken when the mystery behind her true identity is unraveled. Discovering her place as the daughter of a duke, she confronts reclaimed memories of her brutal abduction while making her way in the alien world of Regency England's high society. Facing the *ton* is the least of her concerns as her kidnappers remain determined to keep her from Fitzwilliam Darcy—the man who first professed his love by proposing she become his mistress. Humbled by her refusal, he returns to win her love and respect.

Together with her reunited family, Elizabeth faces her greatest challenges to both her life and her heart—reclaiming herself and finding her happiness.

Darcy and The Duchess

In this 'what-if' retelling of Austen's *Pride and Prejudice*, Elizabeth Bennet enjoys her first love with the ailing Rafael Gainsbridge, the Duke of Deronshire, bringing her into the glittering world of London's high society. When tragedy strikes, Elizabeth must overcome her prejudice against her late husband's dearest friend, Fitzwilliam Darcy, to protect her family. Together they must move beyond their pride to earn a second chance at love.